THE
LAST STAR

ALSO BY RICK YANCEY

The 5th Wave

The Infinite Sea

THE FINAL BOOK OF THE 5TH WAVE

THE LAST STAR

RICK YANCEY

G. P. PUTNAM'S SONS

G. P. PUTNAM'S SONS
an imprint of Penguin Random House LLC
375 Hudson Street, New York, NY 10014

Copyright © 2016 by Rick Yancey.

Penguin supports copyright. Copyright fuels creativity, encourages diverse voices, promotes free speech, and creates a vibrant culture. Thank you for buying an authorized edition of this book and for complying with copyright laws by not reproducing, scanning, or distributing any part of it in any form without permission. You are supporting writers and allowing Penguin to continue to publish books for every reader.

G. P. Putnam's Sons is a registered trademark of Penguin Random House LLC.

Library of Congress Cataloging-in-Publication Data is available upon request.

Printed in the United States of America.

ISBN 978-1-5247-3778-8

1 3 5 7 9 10 8 6 4 2

Design by Ryan Thomann. Text set in Sabon.

Cassiopeia photo copyright © iStockphoto.com/Manfred_Konrad.

For Sandy

"The world ends. The world begins again."

Let no one despair,
even though in the darkest night
the last star of hope may disappear.

—*Christoph Martin Wieland*

—THE GIRL WHO COULD FLY—

MANY YEARS AGO, when he was ten, her father had ridden a big yellow bus to the planetarium.

There the ceiling above him exploded into a million glimmering shards of light. His mouth dropped open. His small fingers clamped down on the edge of the wooden bench upon which he sat. Over his head, pinpricks of white fire spun, pure as the day the Earth emerged as a blackened, pockmarked rock, an average planet orbiting an average star at the edge of an average galaxy in a limitless universe.

The Big Dipper. Orion. Ursa Major. The droning monotone of the astronomer's voice. The children's faces lifted up, open mouths, unblinking eyes. And the boy feeling infinitesimally small beneath the immensity of that artificial sky.

He would not forget that day.

Years later, when his daughter was very young, she would run to him, pudgy toddler legs wobbling, solid little arms lifted up, eyes burning with anticipation and joy, crying, *Daddy, Daddy,* stubby fingers spread wide, reaching for him, reaching for the sky.

And she would leap, a fearless launch into empty space, because he wasn't just her father—he was *Daddy.* He would catch her; he would not let her fall.

Crying: *Fly, Daddy, fly!*

And up she would go, rocketing toward the immensity of the unbounded sky, arms open to embrace the infinite, her head thrown back, rushing to that place where terror and wonder meet, her squeals the distilled hilarity of being weightless and free, of being safe in his arms, of being alive.

Cassiopeia.

From that day at the planetarium, when her life lay fifteen years in the future, there was no doubt what name he would give her.

1

"I WILL SIT WITH YOU"

THIS IS MY BODY.

In the cave's lowermost chamber, the priest raises the last wafer—his supply has been exhausted—toward the formations that remind him of a dragon's mouth frozen in mid-roar, the growths like teeth glistening red and yellow in the lamplight.

The catastrophe of the divine sacrifice by his hands.

Take this, all of you, and eat of it . . .

Then the chalice containing the final drops of wine.

Take this, all of you, and drink from it . . .

Midnight in late November. In the caves below, the small band of survivors will remain warm and hidden with enough supplies to last until spring. No one has died of the plague in months. The worst appears to be over. They are safe here, perfectly safe.

With faith in your love and mercy, I eat your body and drink your blood . . .

His whispers echo in the deep. They clamber up the slick walls, skitter along the narrow passage toward the upper chambers, where his fellow refugees have fallen into a restless sleep.

Let it not bring me condemnation, but health in mind and body.

There is no more bread, no more wine. This is his final Communion.

May the body of Christ bring me to everlasting life.

The stale fragment of bread that softens on his tongue.

May the blood of Christ bring me to everlasting life.

The drops of soured wine that burn his throat.

God in his mouth. God in his empty stomach.

The priest weeps.

He pours a few drops of water into the chalice. His hand shakes. He drinks the precious blood commingled with water, then wipes clean the chalice with the purificator.

It is finished. The everlasting sacrifice is over. He dabs his cheeks on the same cloth he used to clean the chalice. The tears of man and the blood of God inseparable. Nothing new in that.

He wipes clean the paten with the cloth, then stuffs the purificator into the chalice and sets it aside. He pulls the green stole from his neck, folds it carefully, kisses it. He loved everything about being a priest. Loved the Mass most of all.

His collar is damp with sweat and tears and loose about his neck: He's lost fifteen pounds since the plague struck, and abandoned his parish to make the hundred-mile journey to the caverns north of Urbana. Along the way he gained many followers—over fifty in all, though thirty-two died from the infection before reaching safety. As their deaths approached, he spoke the rite, Catholic, Protestant, or Jew, it didn't matter: *May the Lord in his love and mercy help you . . .* Tracing a cross on their hot foreheads with his thumb. *May the Lord who frees you from sin save you . . .*

The blood that seeped from their eyes mixed with the oil he rubbed on their lids. And smoke rolled across open fields and hunkered in woods and capped over roads like ice over languid rivers in deep winter. Fires in Columbus. Fires in Springfield and Dayton. In Huber Heights and London and Fairborn. In Franklin and Middletown and Xenia. In the evenings the light from a thousand fires turned the smoke a dusky orange, and the sky sank to an inch above their heads. The priest shuffled through the smoldering landscape with one hand outstretched, pressing a rag over his nose and mouth with the other while tears of protest streamed down his face. Blood crusted beneath his broken nails, blood caked in the lines of his hands and in the soles of his shoes. *Not much farther*, he encouraged his companions. *Keep moving.* Along the way, someone nicknamed him Father Moses, for he was leading his people out of the obscurity of smoke and fire to the Promised Land of "Ohio's Most Colorful Caverns!"

People were there, of course, to greet them when they arrived. The priest expected it. A cave does not burn. It is impervious to weather. Best of all, it's easy to defend. After military bases and government buildings, caves were the most popular destinations in the aftermath of the Arrival.

Supplies had been gathered, water and nonperishables, blankets and bandages and medicines. And weapons, naturally, rifles and pistols and shotguns and many knives. The sick were quarantined in the welcome center aboveground, lying in cots arranged between the display shelves of the gift shop, and every day the priest visited them, spoke with them, prayed with them, heard their confessions, delivered Communion, whispered the things they wanted to hear: *Per sacrosancta humanae reparationis mysteria . . . By the sacred mysteries of man's redemption . . .*

Hundreds would die before the dying was over. They dug a pit ten feet wide and thirty feet deep to the south of the welcome center to burn them. The fire smoldered day and night, and the smell of burning flesh had become so commonplace, they hardly noticed.

Now it's November, and in the lowermost chamber the priest

3

rises. He is not tall; still, he must stoop to avoid smacking his head into the ceiling or against the stone teeth that bristle from the roof of the dragon's mouth.

The Mass is ended, go in peace.

He leaves behind the chalice and the purificator, the paten and his stole. They are relics now, artifacts from an age receding into the past at the speed of light. *We began as cave dwellers,* the priest thinks as he makes his way toward the surface, *and to caves we have returned.*

Even the longest journey is a circle, and history will always cycle back to the place where it began. From the missal: "Remember you are dust and unto dust you shall return."

And the priest rises like a diver kicking toward the dome of the sky sparkling above the water.

Along the narrow passageway that winds gently upward between walls of weeping stone, the floor is as smooth as the lanes of a bowling alley. Only a few months before, schoolchildren on field trips marched in single file, trailing their fingers along the rock face, their eyes searching for monsters in the shadows that pooled in the crevices. They were still young enough to believe in monsters.

And the priest rising like a leviathan from the lightless deep.

The trail to the surface runs past the Caveman's Couch and the Crystal King, into the Big Room, the main living area for the refugees, and finally into the Palace of the Gods, his favorite part of the caverns, where crystalline formations shine like frozen shards of moonlight and the ceiling sensually undulates like waves rolling in to shore. Here, close to the surface, the air thins, becomes drier, tinged with the smoke of the fires that still feed upon the world they left behind.

Lord, bless these ashes by which we show that we are dust.

Snatches of prayer run through his mind. Fragments of song. Litanies and blessings and the words of absolution, *May God give you pardon and peace, and I absolve you from your sins* . . . And from the Bible: "I went down to the roots of the mountains; to the land whose bars closed behind me forever."

Incense burning in the censer. Soft spring sunlight shattered by stained glass. The creaking of the pews on Sunday like the hull of an ancient vessel far at sea. The stately measure of the seasons, the calendar that governed his life from the time he was an infant, Advent, Christmas, Lent, Easter. He knows he loved the wrong things, the rituals and traditions, the pomp and foppery for which outsiders faulted the Church. He adored the form, not the substance; the bread, not the body.

It didn't make him a bad priest. He was quiet and humble and faithful to his calling. He enjoyed helping people. These weeks in the cave had been some of the most fulfilling of his life. Suffering brings God to his natural home, the manger of terror and confusion, pain and loss, where he was born. *Turn over the currency of suffering,* the priest thinks, *and you will see his face.*

A watchman sits just inside the opening above the Palace of the Gods, his burly frame silhouetted against the spray of stars beyond him. The sky has been scrubbed clean by a stiff north wind auguring winter. The man wears a baseball cap pulled low over his forehead, and a worn leather jacket. He's holding a pair of binoculars. A rifle rests in his lap.

The man nods a hello to the priest. "Where's your coat, Father? It's a cold one tonight."

The priest smiles wanly. "I lent it to Agatha, I'm afraid."

The man grunts his understanding. Agatha is the complainer

of the group. Always cold. Always hungry. Always *something*. He lifts the binoculars to his eyes and scans the sky.

"Have you seen any more of them?" the priest asks. They spotted the first grayish-silver, cigar-shaped object a week before, hanging motionlessly above the caverns for several minutes before silently shooting straight up, dwindling to a pinprick scar in the vast blue. Another—or the same one—appeared two days later, gliding soundlessly over them until it dropped beneath the horizon. There was no question about the origin of these strange craft—the cave dwellers knew they weren't terrestrial—it was the mystery of their purpose that frightened them.

The man lowers the binoculars and rubs his eyes. "What's the matter, Father? Can't sleep?"

"Oh, I don't sleep much these days," the priest says. Then he adds, "So much to do." He doesn't want the man to think he's complaining.

"No atheists in foxholes." The cliché hangs in the air like a rancid smell.

"Or in caves," the priest says. Since they met, he has strained to know this man better, but he is a closed room, the door securely dead-bolted by anger and grief and the hopeless dread of the doomed living on borrowed time. For months there's been no turning from it or hiding from it. For some, death is the midwife to faith. For others, it is faith's executioner.

The man pulls a pack of gum from his breast pocket, carefully unwraps a piece, and folds it into his mouth. He counts the remaining sticks before slipping the pack back into his pocket. He does not offer any to the priest.

"My last pack," the man says in explanation. He shifts his weight on the cold stone.

"I understand," the priest says.

"Do you?" The man's jaw moves with a hypnotic rhythm as he chews. "Do you really?"

The dry bread, the soured wine: The taste lingers on his tongue. The bread could have been broken; the wine could have been divided. He did not have to celebrate the Mass alone. "I believe that I do," the little priest answers.

"I don't," the man says slowly and deliberately. "I don't believe in a goddamned thing."

The priest blushes. His soft, embarrassed laughter is like the patter of children's feet up a long staircase. He touches his collar nervously.

"When the power died, I believed it would come back on," the man with the rifle says. "Everybody did. The power goes out—the power comes back on. That's faith, right?" He gnawed the gum, left side, right side, pushing the green knob back and forth with his tongue. "Then the news trickles in from the coasts that there are no coasts anymore. Now Reno is prime oceanfront property. Big deal; so what? There've been earthquakes before. There've been tsunamis. Who needs New York? What's so special about California? We'll bounce back. We always bounce back. I believed that."

The watchman is nodding, staring at the night sky, at the cold, blazing stars. Eyes high, voice low. "Then people got sick. Antibiotics. Quarantines. Disinfectants. We put on masks and washed our hands until our skin peeled off. Most of us died anyway."

And the man with the rifle watches the stars as if waiting for them to shake loose from the black and tumble to the Earth. Why shouldn't they?

"My neighbors. My friends. My wife and kids. I knew that *all* of them wouldn't die. How could *all* of them die? Some people

7

will get sick, but most people won't, and the rest will get better, right? That's faith. That's what we believed."

The man pulls a large hunting knife from his boot and begins to clean the dirt from beneath his nails with its tip.

"This is faith: You grow up; you go to school. Find a job. Get married. Start a family." Finishing the job on one hand, a nail for each rite of passage, then beginning on the other. "Your kids grow up. They go to school. They find a job. They get married. They start a family." *Scrape, scrape. Scrape, scrape, scrape.* He pushes his hat back with the heel of the hand that wields the knife. "I was never what you'd call a religious person. Haven't seen the inside of a church in twenty years. But I know what faith is, Father. I know what it is to believe in something. The lights go out, they come back on. The floodwaters roll in, they roll out again. Folks get sick, they get better. Life goes on. That's true faith, isn't it? Your mumbo-jumbo about heaven and hell, sin and salvation, throw it all out and you're still left with that. Even your biggest church-bashing atheist has faith in that. Life will go on."

"Yes," the priest says. "Life will go on."

The watchman bares his teeth. He jabs the knife toward the priest's chest and snarls, "You haven't heard a damn word I've said. See, this is why I can't stand your kind. You light your candles and mumble your Latin spells and pray to a god who isn't there, doesn't care, or is just plain crazy or cruel or both. The world burns and you praise the asshole who either set it or let it."

The little priest has raised his hands, the same hands that consecrated the bread and wine, as if to show the man that they are empty, that he means no harm.

"I don't pretend to know the mind of God," the priest begins, lowering his hands. Eyeing the knife, he quotes from the book of

Job: "Therefore I have declared that which I did not understand, things too wonderful for me, which I did not know.'"

The man stares at him for a very long, very uncomfortable moment, absolutely still except for his jaw working the already tasteless knob of gum.

"I'm going to be honest with you, Father," he says matter-of-factly. "I feel like killing you right now."

The priest nods somberly. "I'm afraid that may happen. When the truth hits home."

He eases the knife from the man's shaking hand. The priest touches the man's shoulder.

The man flinches but doesn't pull away. "What is the truth?" the man whispers.

"This," the little priest answers, and drives the knife deep into the man's chest.

The blade is very sharp—it slides through the man's shirt easily, gliding between the ribs before sinking three inches into the heart.

The priest pulls the man to his chest and kisses the top of his head. *May God give you pardon and peace.*

It is over quickly. The gum drops from the man's slackened lips, and the priest picks it up and tosses it through the cave's mouth. He eases the man onto the cold stone floor and stands up. The wet knife glimmers in his hand. *The blood of the new and everlasting covenant . . .*

The priest studies the dead man's face, and his heart burns with rage and revulsion. The human face is hideous, unendurably grotesque. No need to hide his disgust anymore.

The little priest returns to the Big Room, following a well-worn path into the main chamber, where the others twitch and turn in restless sleep. All except Agatha, who leans against the back wall of the chamber, a small woman lost in the fur-lined jacket the little priest had lent her, her frizz of unwashed hair a cyclone of gray and black. Grime nestles in the deep crevices of her withered face, around a mouth bereft of dentures long since lost and eyes buried in folds of sagging skin.

This is humanity, the priest thinks. *This is its face.*

"Father, is that you?" Her voice is barely audible, a mouse's squeak, a rat's high-pitched cry.

And this, humanity's voice.

"Yes, Agatha. It's me."

She squints into the human mask he has worn since infancy, obscured in shadow. "I can't sleep, Father. Will you sit with me awhile?"

"Yes, Agatha. I will sit with you."

2

HE CARRIES THE REMAINS of his victims to the surface two at a time, one under each arm, and throws them into the pit, dropping them down without ceremony before descending for another load. After Agatha, he killed the rest as they slept. No one woke. The priest worked quietly, quickly, with sure, steady hands, and the only noise was the whisper of cloth tearing as the blade sank home into the hearts of all forty-six, until his was the only heart left beating.

At dawn it begins to snow. He stands outside for a moment and lifts his face to a sky that is blank and gray. Snow settles on his pale cheeks. His last winter for a very long time: At the equinox, the pod will descend to return him to the mothership, where he'll wait out the final cleansing of the human infestation by the ones they have trained for the task. Once on board the vessel, from the serenity of the void, he will watch as they launch the bombs that will obliterate every city on Earth, wiping clean the vestiges of human civilization. The apocalypse dreamed of by humankind since the dawn of its consciousness will finally be delivered—not by an angry god, but indifferently, as cold as the little priest when he plunged the knife into his victims' hearts.

The snow melts on his upturned face. Four months until winter's end. One hundred and twenty days until the bombs fall, then the unleashing of the 5th Wave, the human pawns they have conditioned to kill their own kind. Until then, the priest will remain to slaughter any survivors who wander into his territory.

Almost over. Almost there.

The little priest descends into the Palace of the Gods and breaks his fast.

RINGER

BESIDE ME, Razor whispered, "Run."

His sidearm exploded beside my ear. His target was the smallest thing that is the sum of all things, his bullet the sword that severed the chain that bound me to her.

Teacup.

As Razor died, he lifted his soft, soulful eyes to mine and whispered, "*You're free. Run.*"

I ran.

4

I SMASH THROUGH the watchtower window, the ground rushing up to meet me.

When I land on the tarmac, not a single bone will break. I will feel no pain. I have been enhanced by the enemy to withstand greater falls than this. My last fall began at five thousand feet. This one is cake.

I land, roll to my feet, and sprint around the tower, then down the runway toward the concrete barrier and the fence topped in razor wire. The wind screams in my ears. I am faster now than the fastest animal on Earth. The cheetah is a tortoise compared to me.

The sentries on the perimeter must see me, and the man in the watchtower, too, but no shots are fired, no order is given to take me down. I barrel toward the end of the runway like a bullet singing down the muzzle of a gun.

They can't catch you. How can they ever catch you?

The processor embedded in my brain made the calculations before I even hit the ground, and has already relayed the information to the thousands of microscopic drones assigned to my muscular system; I don't have to think about speed or timing or point of attack. The hub does it for me.

12

End of the runway: I leap. The ball of my foot lands on top of the concrete barrier for an instant, then pushes off to launch me toward the fence. The razor wire rushes toward my face. My fingers slip into the two-inch-wide gap between the coils and the top bar to execute a backward roll over the top. I fly over it feetfirst, back arched, arms outstretched.

I stick the landing and accelerate again to full speed, covering the hundred yards of open ground between the fence and the woods in less than four seconds. No bullets chase me. No chopper revs to life to follow me. The trees close behind me like a curtain being drawn, and my footing is sure on the slick, uneven ground. I reach the river, its water swift and black. My feet seem to barely break the surface as I cross.

On the other side, the woods give way to open tundra, unmarred miles stretching toward the northern horizon, a boundless wilderness in which I'll be lost, undetected, unmolested.

Free.

I run for hours. The 12th System sustains me. It reinforces my joints and bones. It bolsters my muscles, gives me strength, endurance, nullifies my pain. All I have to do is surrender. All I have to do is trust, and I will endure.

VQP. By the light of a hundred bodies burning, Razor carved those three letters into his arm. VQP. *He conquers who endures.*

Some things, he told me the night before he died, *down to the smallest of things, are worth the sum of all things.*

Razor understood that I would never leave Teacup to suffer while I escaped. I should have known he was going to save me by betraying me: He'd been doing it from the beginning. He killed Teacup so I could live.

The featureless landscape extends in every direction. The sun falls toward the edge of the cloudless sky. In the bitter wind biting my face, my tears freeze as they fall. The 12th System can protect you from the pain that afflicts your body, but it's helpless against the pain that crushes your soul.

Hours later, I'm still running as the last light leeches from the sky and the first stars appear. And there is the mothership hovering on the horizon, like a lidless green eye staring down. No running from it. No hiding. It is unreachable, unassailable. Long after the last human being crumbles to a handful of dust, it will be there, implacable, impenetrable, unknowable: God has been dethroned.

And I run on. Through a primordial landscape unscarred by any human thing, the world as it was before trust and cooperation unleashed the beast of progress. The world is circling back now to what it was before we knew it. Paradise lost. Paradise returned. I remember Vosch's smile, sad and bitter. *A savior. Is that what I am?*

Running toward nothing, running away from nothing, running across an empty landscape of flawless white beneath the immensity of the indifferent sky, I see it now. I think I understand.

Reduce the human population to a sustainable number, then crush the humanity out of it, since trust and cooperation are the real threats to the delicate balance of nature, the unacceptable sins that drove the world to the edge of a cliff. The Others concluded that the only way to save the world was to annihilate civilization. Not from without, but from within. The only way to annihilate human civilization was to change human nature.

5

I CONTINUED RUNNING into the wilderness. There was still no pursuit. As the days passed, I worried less about choppers swooping in and strike teams dropping down and more about staying warm and finding the fresh water and protein I needed to sustain the fragile host of the 12th System. I dug holes to hide in, built lean-tos to sleep under. I honed tree branches into spears and hunted rabbit and moose and ate their meat raw. I didn't dare make a fire, even though I knew how; at Camp Haven the enemy had taught me. The enemy had taught me everything I needed to know about survival in the wilderness, then gave me alien technology that helped my body adapt to it. He taught me how to kill and how to avoid being killed. He taught me what human beings had forgotten after ten centuries of cooperation and trust. He taught me about fear.

Life is a circle bound by fear. The fear of the predator. The fear of the prey. Without fear, life would not exist. I tried to explain that to Zombie once, but I don't think he understood.

I lasted forty days in the wilderness. And, no, the symbolism wasn't lost on me.

I could have lasted longer. The 12th System would have sustained me well past a hundred years. Queen Marika, the lone, ancient huntress, a soulless husk gnawing on the dried bones of dead animals, uncontested sovereign of a meaningless domain, until the system finally collapsed and her body fell apart or was devoured by scavengers, her bones scattered like unread runes in an abandoned landscape.

I went back. By that point, I realized why they weren't coming. Vosch was two moves ahead of me; he always had been. Teacup was dead now, but I was still bound to a promise I never made to a person who was probably dead, too. But probability had become meaningless.

He knew I couldn't abandon Zombie, not when there was a chance I could save him.

And there was only one way to save him; Vosch knew that, too.

I had to kill Evan Walker.

I

THE FIRST DAY

6

CASSIE

I'M GOING TO KILL Evan Walker.

The brooding, enigmatic, self-involved, secretive bastard. I'm going to put his poor, tortured, human-alien hybrid soul out of its misery. *You're the mayfly. You're the thing worth dying for. I woke up when I saw myself in you.* Oh, puke.

Last night I gave Sams a bath—the first in three weeks—and he damn near broke my nose, or I should say *re*broke my nose, since Evan's old girlfriend (or friend with benefits or whatever she was) broke it first by slamming my face into a door behind which was my little brother, the little shit I was trying to save and the same little shit who nearly broke it again. See the irony there? There's probably some symbolism, too, but it's late and I haven't slept in, like, three days, so forget it.

Back to Evan and the reason I'm going to kill him.

Basically, it boils down to the alphabet.

After Sam hit me on the nose, I burst out of the bathroom, soaking wet, whereupon I smacked into Ben Parish's chest. Ben was lurking in the hallway as if every little thing that has to do with Sam is his responsibility, the aforesaid little shit screaming obscenities at my back, the only dry part of my body after trying to wash his, and Ben Parish, the living reminder of my father's favorite saying that it's better to be lucky than smart, gave me that

21

ridiculous *what's up?* look, so stupidly cute that I was tempted to break *his* nose, thereby making him not so damn Ben Parish-y looking.

"You should be dead," I said to him. I know I just wrote that I was going to kill Evan, but you need to understand—oh, screw it. No one is ever going to read this. By the time I'm gone, there won't be anyone who can read. So this isn't being written for you, future reader who won't exist. It's for me.

"Probably," Ben said.

"What are the odds that someone I knew from *before* would still be here *now?*"

He thought about it. Or pretended to think about it: He's a guy. "About seven billion to one?"

"I think that would be seven billion to two, Ben," I said. "Or three point five billion to one."

"Wow. That much?" He jerked his head toward the bathroom door. "What's up with Nugget?"

"Sam. His name is Sam. Call him Nugget again and I'll knee you in yours."

He smiled. Then he either pretended to get what I said a beat later or he immediately understood what I said, but anyway, the smile morphed into a tight-lipped look of wounded pride. "They're slightly larger than nuggets. Slightly." Then *click!* the smile flashed back on. "Want me to talk to him?"

I told him I didn't give a shit what he did; I had better things to do, like killing Evan Walker.

I stormed down the hallway, into the living room, still close enough—or not far enough away—to hear Sam yell, "I don't care, Zombie. I don't care, I don't care. *I hate her*," past Dumbo and Megan sitting on the sofa working on a jigsaw puzzle somebody

22

found in the kids' room, a scene from a Disney cartoon or something, and their eyes cut away as I barreled past, like *Don't mind us, we won't stop you, you're good, nobody saw nothin'*.

Outside on the porch it's cold as hell because spring refuses to come. Spring is never coming because extinction events piss it off. Or the Others have engineered another Ice Age just because they can, because why settle for doomed humans when you can have cold, starving, and miserable doomed humans? So much more satisfying that way.

He was leaning on the railing to take the weight off his bad ankle, the rifle nestled in the crook of his arm, wearing his uniform of a wrinkled plaid shirt and skinny jeans. His face lit up when he saw me banging open the screen door. His eyes drank me in. Oh, the Evanness of it all, how he gulps down my presence like a guy stumbling upon an oasis in the desert.

I slapped him.

"Why did you just hit me?" he asked, after racking ten thousand years' worth of alien wisdom for the answer.

"Do you know why I'm wet?" I asked.

He shook his head. "Why are you wet?"

"I was giving my baby brother a bath. Why was I giving him a bath?"

"Because he was dirty?"

"For the same reason I spent a week cleaning up this dump after we moved in." She may have been a supercharged, technologically enhanced alien-human hybrid with the looks of a Norwegian ice princess and the heart to match, but Grace was a terrible housekeeper. Dust piled in every corner like snowdrifts, mold growing on top of mold, a kitchen that would make a hoarder blush. "Because that's what human beings *do*, Evan. We don't live in filth.

We bathe. We wash our hair and we brush our teeth and we shave off unwanted hair—"

"Sam needs to shave?" Trying to be funny.

Dumb idea.

"Shut up! I'm talking. When I talk, you don't talk. When you talk, I don't talk. That's another thing humans do. They treat each other with respect. Respect, Evan."

He nodded somberly. "Respect," he echoed—which made me even angrier. He was *handling* me.

"It's all about respect. Being clean and not stinking like a pig is about respect."

"Pigs don't stink."

"Shut. Up."

"Well, I grew up on a farm, that's all."

I shook my head. "Oh no, that isn't all. That isn't half of all. The part of you I slapped didn't grow up on any goddamned farm."

He left his rifle leaning against the railing and limped over to the swing. He sat. He gazed off into the middle distance. "It isn't my fault Sam needed a bath."

"Of course it's your fault. All of this is your fault."

He looked at me, and his tone was controlled. "Cassie, I think you should go back inside now."

"What, before you lose your temper? Oh, please lose it for once. I would love to see what that looks like."

"You're cold."

"No, I'm not." As I realized how badly I was shaking, standing in front of him in my wet clothes. Icy water dripped down the back of my neck and traced a path down my spine. I folded my arms over my chest and willed my (freshly brushed, very clean) teeth to stop chattering.

"Sam's forgotten his ABCs," I informed him.

He stared at me for a long four seconds. "I'm sorry, what?"

"His ABCs. You know, the alphabet, you intergalactic swineherd."

"Well." His eyes wandered from my face to the empty road across from the empty yard that stretched toward empty horizons over which there were more empty roads and woods and fields and towns and cities, the world one big hollowed-out gourd, a slop bucket of emptiness. Emptied by things like him, the whatever-he-was before he inserted himself into a human body like a hand up a puppet's ass.

He leaned forward and shrugged out of his jacket, the same stupid bowling jacket he showed up in at the old hotel (*The Urbana Pinheads*), and held it out.

"Please?"

Maybe I shouldn't have taken it. I mean, the pattern kept repeating itself: I'm cold, he warms me. I'm hurt, he heals me. I'm hungry, he feeds me. I'm down, he picks me up. I'm like the hole at the beach that keeps filling up with water.

I'm not a big person; the jacket engulfed me. And the warmth from his body, that, too. It steadied me—not necessarily the fact that the warmth came from his body, just the warmth itself.

"Another thing human beings do is learn their alphabets," I said. "So they can read. So they can learn things. Things like history and math and science and practically everything else you can name, including the really important things like art and culture and faith and why things happen and why other things don't and why anything even exists in the first place."

My voice broke. Uninvited, there's that image again, of my father pulling a red wagon loaded with books after the 3rd Wave and his lecture about preserving knowledge and rebuilding civilization

25

once that pesky little alien problem was disposed of. God, how sad, how pitiful: a balding, bent-shouldered man shuffling down deserted streets with a wagonload of scavenged library books behind him. While others looted canned goods and weapons and hardware to fortify their homes against marauders, my father decided the wisest course of action was to hoard reading material.

"He can learn them again," Evan tried. "You can teach him."

It took everything in me not to give him another smack. There was a time when I thought I was the last living person on Earth, which made me all of humanity, Evan isn't the only one who owes an unpayable debt. I'm humanity, he's *them*, and after what they've done to us, humanity should break every bone in their bodies.

"That's not the point," I told him. "The point is, I don't understand why you did it this way. You could have killed us all without being so goddamn *cruel* about it. You know what I found out tonight, besides the fact that my little brother hates my guts? It's not just the ABCs he's forgotten. He doesn't remember what our mom looked like. He doesn't remember his own mother's *face.*"

Then I lost it. I wrapped myself tight in that stupid Pinhead jacket and bawled, because I didn't care anymore if Evan saw me lose it, because if anyone should have seen, it's him, the sniper murdering from a distance, comfy in his farmhouse while, two hundred miles over his head, the mothership unleashed three escalating waves of devastation. Five hundred thousand in the first attack, millions in the second, billions in the third. And while the world burned, Evan Walker was smoking deer brisket and taking leisurely walks in the woods and lounging by a cozy fire, buffing his perfect nails.

He should see the face of human suffering up close. Too long he's been like the mothership, hovering above the horror, untouchable and remote; he needs to see it, touch it, press it against his perfectly shaped, wholly unbroken nose and smell it.

The way Sammy has. I felt like running inside and yanking him out of the tub and dragging him naked onto the porch, where Evan Walker could count his bony ribs and feel his tiny wrists and trace the hollowed-out temples and examine the scars and sores of the little boy he's tortured, the child whose mind he's emptied of memories and whose heart he's filled with hate and hopelessness and useless rage.

Evan started to stand—to pull me into his arms, no doubt, to stroke my hair and dry my tears and murmur that everything was going to be all right, because that's his MO—but then he thought better of it. He sat back down.

"I told you, Cassie," he said softly. "I didn't want it to happen this way. I fought against it."

"Until you went along with it." Still working to get a grip. Along came out a three-syllable word. "And what do you mean, you didn't want it to happen 'this way'?"

He shifted his weight. The swing creaked. His eyes strayed back to the empty road. "We could have lived among you indefinitely. Hidden, undetectable. We could have inserted ourselves into leading roles in your society. We could have shared our knowledge, exponentially expanding your potential, speeding your evolution. It's conceivable we could have given you the one thing you've always wanted and never had."

"What?" I snuffled the snot back into my nose; I didn't have a tissue and didn't even care that it was gross. The Arrival had altered the whole definition of *gross*.

"Peace," he answered.

"Could have. *Could* have."

He nodded. "When that option was rejected, I argued for something . . . quicker."

"Quicker?"

"An asteroid. You didn't have the technology to stop it or the time even if you did. It was a simple solution, but it wasn't a clean one. The world wouldn't have been habitable for a thousand years."

"And that matters because why? You're pure consciousness, immortal like gods. What's a thousand years to you?"

Apparently that question had a very complicated answer. Or one he didn't want to share with me.

Then he said: "For ten thousand years we had the thing that you only dreamed of for ten thousand years." He gave a short, humorless laugh. "An existence without pain, without hunger, without any physical needs at all. But immortality has a price. Without bodies, we lost the things that come with them. Things like autonomy and benevolence. Compassion." He opened his hands as if to show me they were empty. "Sam isn't the only one who's forgotten his ABCs."

"I hate you," I said.

He shook his head. "No, you don't."

"I want to hate you."

"I hope you fail."

"Don't lie to yourself, Evan. You don't love me—you love the *idea* of me. You've messed it all up in your head. You love what I represent."

He cocked his head, and his brown eyes were sparkling brighter than the stars. "What do you represent, Cassie?"

"What you thought you lost. What you thought you could never have. I'm not that; I'm just me."

"And what are you?"

I knew what he meant. And, of course, I had no clue what he meant. This was it, the thing between us, the thing neither of us could put our fingers on, the unbreakable bond between love and fear. Evan's the love. I am the fear.

7

BEN WAS WAITING to pounce the minute I went back inside. I knew he was waiting to pounce because the minute I went back inside, he pounced.

"Everything okay?" he asked.

I scrubbed the tears from my cheeks and laughed. *Sure, Parish, aside from this whole annoying alien apocalypse thing, everything's great.*

"The more he explains, the less I understand," I said.

"I told you something's not right with that dude," he said, being very careful not to say *I told you so.* Okay, not really. He was basically saying it.

"What would you do if you didn't have a body for ten thousand years and then all of a sudden you did?" I asked.

He cocked his head and fought back a smile. "Probably go to the bathroom."

Dumbo and Megan had cleared out. We were alone. Ben was standing by the fireplace and golden light danced over his face, which had filled out some in the six weeks we had been holed up in Grace's safe house. Plenty of rest, food, fresh water, and antibiotics, and Ben was almost back to his pre-invasion self. He'd never get all the way back. There was still a haunted look in his eyes, a wariness to him, like a rabbit in a hawk-patrolled meadow.

He wasn't the only one. After we reached the safe house, it took two weeks for me to work up the courage to look in the mirror. The experience was like running into someone you hadn't seen since middle school—you recognize them, but what you really notice is the ways they've changed. They don't match your memory of how they should look and for a second you're thrown off, because your memory of them is *them*. So when I looked in the mirror, I saw a self that didn't match the memory of myself, particularly the nose, which now veered slightly to the right, thanks to Grace, but I've let that go, there's no hard feelings. My nose may be crooked now, but hers has been vaporized—along with the rest of her.

"How's Sam?" I asked.

Ben jerked his head toward the back of the house. "Hanging with Megan and Dumbo. He's okay."

"He hates my guts."

"He doesn't hate your guts."

"He told me he hates my guts."

"Kids say things they don't mean."

"Not just kids."

He nodded. He looked over my shoulder toward the front door. "Ringer was right, Cassie. This doesn't make a lot of sense. He kidnaps a human body so he can murder all the unkidnapped human bodies. Then one day he decides he'd rather murder his own kind so he can save all the unkidnapped human bodies. And not just murder one or two of his kind here or there. *All of them*.

He wants to destroy his entire civilization, and for what? For a girl. A girl!"

Wrong thing to say. He knew it, too. But just in case there was any question, I said, very slowly, "You know, Parish, it may be a little more complicated than that. There is a human part of him, too." *Oh, Jesus, Cass, what's the matter with you? One minute you're furious at him, the next you're defending him.*

His expression hardened. "I'm not worried about the human part. I know you weren't crazy about her, but Ringer's pretty damn smart and she made a good point: If they don't need bodies, they don't need a planet. And if they don't need a planet, why did they come for ours?"

"I don't know," I snapped. "Why don't you ask Ringer, since she's so damn smart?"

He took a breath, and then he said, "I'm going to."

It took a second for me to understand what he meant. Then another to get that he was serious. A third second to do something about the first two seconds, which was to sit down.

"I've thought a lot about this," he began. Then he stopped. "Like he had to mince words—with *me* of all people! Like I had a temper or something. "And I think I know what you're going to say, but before you say it, you need to hear me out. Just hear me out, okay? If Walker's telling the truth, we've got four days until the pod arrives and he leaves to do his thing. That's more than enough time for me to get there and back."

"To get where and back, Ben?"

"I won't go alone. I'll take Dumbo with me."

"Okaaaay. With you *where*?" Then I got it. "The caverns."

He nodded quickly, relieved that I understood. "It's killing

31

me, Cassie, I can't stop thinking about them. Maybe Cup caught up with Ringer and—well, maybe she didn't. She might be dead. Ringer might be dead. Oh, hell, they probably *are* dead—or maybe they're not. Maybe they made it to the caverns and Ringer came back to the hotel to get us, only there was no *us* there to get because there was no *there* to come back to. Anyway, alive or dead, they're out there. And if they're alive, they have no clue what's coming. They'll die unless someone goes back for them."

He took a huge, shuddering breath, the first since he blasted off the verbal launching pad.

"Go back for them," I said. "Like you went back for Sam. Like you *didn't* go back for—"

"Yes. No. Oh, shit." His face was red and it wasn't from standing too close to the fire. He knew what I was saying. "This has nothing to do with my sister . . ."

"You ran away and you've been trying to go back ever since."

He stepped toward me. Away from the firelight, his face plunged into shadow. "You don't know a damn thing. I know that really bothers you, because Cassie Sullivan knows everything, right?"

"What do you want from me, Ben? I'm not your mother or commanding officer or whatever. Do what you want."

I stood up. Then I sat back down. There was nowhere to go. Well, I could go to the kitchen and make a sandwich, except there was no bread or deli meat or cheese. I don't know the particulars, but I'm pretty sure there's a Subway on every corner in heaven. Also Godiva stores. On our second day here, I found Grace's stash of forty-six boxes of Godiva chocolates. Not that I counted them.

"I'm having a bad day," I told him. My little brother hated me, my human-alien personal security guard confessed he doesn't know compassion from compost, and now my old high school

32

crush informs me he's embarking on a suicide mission to rescue two missing and probably dead people. *Plus* I wanted a sandwich that I could never have. Since the Arrival, I've been beset by more cravings than a woman pregnant with triplets, and always for things I'll never taste again. Chocolate ice cream cones. Frozen pizza. Whipped cream in a can. Those cinnamon rolls Mom made every Saturday morning. McDonald's french fries. Bacon. No, bacon was still a possibility. I would just have to find a hog, slaughter it, butcher it, cure the meat, then fry it up. Thinking about the bacon—the *potential* of bacon—gives me hope. Not all is lost if bacon isn't.

Seriously.

"I'm sorry," Ben said. "I shouldn't have gone off like that."

He came over and sat down about two inches too close. I used to fantasize about Ben Parish sitting with me on the sofa at my house while we shared a blanket and watched old horror movies until one A.M., holding a big bowl of popcorn in his lap. It was a Saturday night and he was missing about six killer parties populated by people way cooler than me, but he wouldn't be anywhere else; the pleasure of my company was enough.

Now here he was, only there were no killer parties, no TV, no blanket, and no damn popcorn. The world used to contain two Bens—the real Ben, who didn't know I existed, and the imaginary Ben, who fed me popcorn with buttery fingers. Now there were three. The first two and the one who was sitting two inches too close, wearing a tight black sweater and sporting stubble that made him look like an indie rocker taking a break in the green room between sets. That's a lot of Bens to hold in your head at once. I should give them different names to keep them straight: Ben, Has-Ben, and What-Might-Have-Ben.

33

"I get it," I said. "But why do you have to go now? Why can't you wait? If Evan can pull this off . . ."

He was shaking his head. "Whether or not he pulls it off won't make a difference. The danger isn't the aliens up there. The danger is the humans down here. I need to find Ringer and Cup before the 5th Wave does."

He pulled my hand into his, and a little voice rose up from deep inside: *Ben*. That little voice belonged to the frizzy-haired middle-schooler who refused to die, the freckly-nosed, introverted know-it-all, self-conscious and awkward despite dance lessons and karate lessons and pep talks from her parents, toting around a bulging bag of secrets, the silly, mundane, melodramatic secrets of adolescence that would shock the popular, pretty kids, *if only they knew.*

What was up with her? Why wouldn't she just go away already? Not only was I carrying around too many Bens, there were also too many Cassies. Three Bens, two Cassies, a couple of Sams, and, of course, the literal duality of Evan Walker. Nobody was integrated anymore. Our true selves shimmered like a desert mirage forever receding into the distance.

Ben touched my face, fingertips brushing my cheek, feather-light. And that little voice in my head, that fading cry: *Ben.*

Then my voice: "You're going to die."

"You bet I am," he said with a smile. "And it's gonna happen the way it should. Not *their* way. My way."

The front door creaked on its rusty hinges and a voice said, "She's right, Ben. You should wait."

Ben pulled away from me. Evan was leaning in the doorway.

"Nobody asked you," Ben said.

"The ship is central to the next phase," Evan said slowly and distinctly, like he was talking to a crazy person or a moron. "Blowing it up is the only way we can end this."

"I don't care what you blow up," Ben said. He turned away like he couldn't stand to look at Evan. "I don't even give a shit about ending it. Maybe it's hard for somebody with a savior complex to understand, but I don't want to save the world. Just two people."

He stood up, stepped over my legs, and walked toward the hallway. Evan called after him, and what he said stopped Ben cold.

"The spring equinox is in four days. If I don't get to that ship and blow it up, every city on Earth will be destroyed."

Holy shit. I looked at Ben, he looked back at me, and then we both looked at Evan.

"When you say 'destroyed' . . . ?" I started.

"Blown up," Evan said. "It's the last step before the launch of the 5th Wave."

Ben was slowly shaking his head at him, horrified, disgusted, enraged. "Why?"

"To make it easier to finish the cleansing. And to wipe out anything human that remains."

"But why now?" Ben asked.

"The Silencers will be back on board the ship—it's safe. For us, I mean. Safe for us."

I looked away. I was going to be sick. I should know better by now. Just when I thought it couldn't get any worse, it gets worse.

8

ZOMBIE

I MOTION DUMBO out of the room. Let Sullivan say what she wants—he'll always be Nugget to me. The kid starts to follow me and Dumbo into the hall and I order him to fall back. I close the door and turn to Dumbo. "Grab your gear. We're moving out."

Dumbo's eyes go wide. "When?"

"Right now."

He swallows hard and glances down the hallway toward the family room. "Just me and you, Sarge?"

I know what he's worried about. "I'm good, Bo." Touching the spot where Ringer placed the bullet. "Not 100 percent, more like 86.5, but good enough."

Pain knifes into my side when I reached up to pull my rucksack from the closet shelf. Okay, take off a point and a half, make it 85, still closer to 100 than to zero. Anyway, who's 100 percent this late in the game? Even the good evil alien broke his ankle.

I rummage through the sack, though there's not a hell of a lot to rummage through. I'll need to grab some fresh water and rations from the kitchen, and a knife might come in handy. I dig into the outer pocket. Empty. What the hell? I know I put it there. What happened to it?

I'm kneeling on the bedroom floor, tearing through my stuff for the third time, when Dumbo comes in.

"Sarge?"

"It was here. It was *right here*." I look up at him and something

36

about my expression makes him flinch. "Somebody must have taken it. Jesus Christ, who the hell would have taken it, Dumbo?"

"Taken what?"

I rock back onto my heels and pat my pockets. Shit. There it is, right where I put it. My sister's necklace, the one that tore off in my hand on the night I left her to die.

"Okay, we're good." I push myself to my feet, grab the rucksack from the floor and the rifle from the bed. Dumbo's watching me carefully, but I hardly notice. The kid's been mother-henning me for months now.

"I thought we were leaving tomorrow night," he says.

"If they aren't between here and the hotel, or where the hotel used to be, we'll have to cut through Urbana—twice," I tell him. "And I don't want to be anywhere near Urbana when the bastards go all Dubuque on it."

"Dubuque?" The color drains out of his face. *Oh God, Dubuque again!*

I drop the rucksack over one shoulder and the rifle over the other. "Buzz Lightyear just told us they're blowing up the cities."

That takes a second to sink in. "Which cities?"

"All of them."

His jaw drops. He trails me into the hallway, then around the corner and into the kitchen. Bottled water, some unopened packages of beef jerky, crackers, a handful of protein bars. I divide the supplies between us. Got to be quick before Nugget's radar goes off and he barrels out of that room to Velcro himself onto my leg.

"All of them?" Dumbo asks. He frowns. "But Ringer said they *weren't* going to blow up the cities."

"Well, she was wrong. Or Walker's lying. Some bullshit about having to wait until the Silencers were extracted. You know what

37

I've decided, Private? I'm not wasting any more time worrying about all the things I don't know."

He shakes his head. He still can't wrap his mind around it.

"Every city on Earth?"

"Down to the last shitty one-traffic-light town."

"How?"

"The mothership. In four days, one big swing around the planet, dropping the bombs as she goes. Unless Walker can blow up the ship before it happens, and I don't put a lot of faith in that."

"Why?"

"Because I don't put a lot of faith in Walker."

"I still don't get it, Zombie. Why'd they wait till now to start dropping bombs?"

Every part of him is shaking, including his voice. He's losing it. I put my hands on his shoulders and force him to look at me. "I told you. They're pulling out the Silencers. Sending down pods for every last infested one of them, except for handlers like Vosch. Once they've been evac'ed and the cities are gone, there's no place for survivors to hide, making it a turkey shoot for the poor bastards they brainwashed into finishing the job: the 5th Wave. Get it?"

He wags his head from side to side. "It don't matter. I go where you go, Sarge."

A shadow moves behind him. A damned Nugget-shaped shadow. I took too long.

"Zombie?"

"Okay," I sigh. "Dumbo, give us a second."

He leaves the kitchen with a single, muttered word: *Dubuque!*

Then there's just me and Nugget. I didn't want this, but you can't

38

run from anything, not really. It's all a circle; Ringer tried to tell me that. No matter how far or fast you run, sooner or later you're back where you started. I got mad when Sullivan threw my sister up in my face, but we both knew she was right. Sissy was dead; Sissy would never die. I'm forever reaching for her. She's forever falling away, the silver chain breaking off in my hand.

"Where are Privates Teacup and Ringer?" I ask him.

His freshly scrubbed face is lifted up to mine. He pooches out his lower lip. "I don't know."

"Neither do I. So me and Dumbo are gonna find out."

"I'm coming with you."

"That's a negative, Private. I need you to watch your sister."

"She doesn't need me. She has *him*."

I don't try to argue with that. He's too sharp for me to win.

"Well, I'm putting you in charge of Megan."

"You said we weren't splitting up. You said no matter what."

I take a knee in front of him. His eyes shine with tears, but he isn't crying. He's a tough little son of a bitch, way older than his years.

"I'll only be gone a couple of days." *Déjà vu*: practically the same thing Ringer said before she left.

"Promise?"

And that was practically what I said back to her. Ringer didn't promise; she knew better. Me, I'm not that smart. "Have I broken one yet?" I take his hand, peel back his fingers, and press Sissy's locket into his palm. "Hold on to this," I order him.

"What is it?" Staring at the metal glittering in his hand.

"Part of the chain."

"What chain?"

"The chain that holds it all together."

He shakes his head, mystified.

He isn't the only one. I have no clue what just came out of my mouth, what it means, or why I said it. That cheap piece of costume jewelry—I thought I kept it out of guilt and shame, to remind myself of my failure, of all the things that had been ripped away, but maybe there's another reason, a reason I can't put into words because I don't have the words for it. Maybe there aren't any.

9

HE TRAILS AFTER me into the family room.

"Ben, you haven't thought this through," Walker says. He's where I left him, standing by the front door.

I ignore him. "They're either at the caverns or they're not," I tell Sullivan, who's hugging herself beside the fireplace. "If they are, we'll bring them back. If they aren't, we won't."

"We've been holed up here for six weeks," Walker points out.

"Under any other circumstance, we'd be dead. The only reason we aren't dead is because we neutralized the agent who patrolled this sector."

"Grace," Cassie translates for me. "To get to the caverns, you'll have to cross through three—"

"Two," Walker corrects her.

She rolls her eyes. Whatever. "Two territories patrolled by

Silencers just like him." She glances at Walker. "Or not *just* like him. Not *good* Silencers. Really bad Silencers who are really good at silencing."

"You might get lucky and slip past one," Walker says. "Not two."

"But if you wait, there won't be any Silencers to slip past." Cassie is beside me now, touching my arm, pleading. "All of them will be back on the mothership. Then Evan does his thing and then you can . . ." Her voice trails off. She's run out of the breath necessary to blow smoke up my ass.

I'm not looking at her. I'm looking at Walker. I know what he's going to say next. I know because I'd say the same thing: If there's no way Dumbo and I can make it to the caverns, there's no way Ringer and Teacup could, either. "You don't know Ringer," I tell him. "If anybody could have made it, she could."

Walker nods. But he's agreeing with the first statement, not the second. "After our awakening, we were enhanced with a technology that makes us nearly indestructible. We turned ourselves into killing machines, Ben." And then he takes a deep breath and finally spits it out, the obtuse bastard. "There's no way they could have survived this long, not against us. Your friends are dead."

I left anyway. Fuck it. Fuck everything. I've sat around long enough waiting for the world to end.

Ringer hasn't kept her promise, so I'm keeping it for her.

10

RINGER

SENTRIES ARE WAITING for me at the gates. I'm escorted immediately to the watchtower overlooking the landing field, another circle completed, where Vosch waits for me—as if he hasn't moved from the spot in the last forty days.

"Zombie is alive," I said. I looked down and saw I was standing on the bloodstain that marked where Razor fell. A few feet away, beside the console, that's where Razor's bullet cut Teacup down. *Teacup.*

Vosch shrugged. "Unknown."

"Okay, maybe not Zombie, but someone who knows me is still alive." He didn't answer. *It's probably Sullivan,* I thought. *That would be just my luck.* "You know I can't get close to Walker without someone he trusts to vouch for me."

He folded his long, powerful arms across his chest and peered down his nose at me, bright birdlike eyes glittering. "You never answered my question," he said. "Am I human?"

I didn't hesitate. "Yes."

He smiled. "And do you still believe that means there is no hope?" He didn't wait for an answer. "I am the hope of the world. The fate of humankind rests upon me."

"What a terrible burden that must be," I said.

"You are being facetious."

"They needed people like you. Organizers and managers who knew why they came and what they wanted."

He was nodding. His face glowed. He was pleased with me—and pleased with himself for choosing me. "They had no choice, Marika. Which means, of course, that *we* had no choice. Under every likely scenario, we were doomed to destroy ourselves and our home. The only solution was radical intervention. Destroy the human village in order to save it."

"And it wasn't enough to kill seven billion of us," I said.

"Of course not. Otherwise, they would have thrown the big rock. No, the best solution is the child in the wheat."

My stomach rolled at the memory. The toddler bursting through the dead grain. The little band of survivors taking him in. The last remnant of trust blown apart in a flash of hellish green light.

On the day I met him, I got the speech. Every recruit did. *The last battle of Earth will not happen on any plain or desert or mountaintop . . .* I touched my chest. "This is the battlefield."

"Yes. Otherwise the cycle would merely repeat itself."

"And that's why Walker's important."

"The program embedded in him has fundamentally failed. We must understand why, for reasons that should be obvious to you. And there is only one way to accomplish that."

He pressed a button on the console next to him. Behind me, a door opened and a middle-aged woman wearing lieutenant's bars on her collar stepped into the room. She was smiling. Her teeth were perfectly even and very large. Her eyes were gray. Her hair was sandy blond and pulled back into a tight bun. I immediately disliked her. It was a visceral response.

"Lieutenant, escort Private Ringer to the infirmary for her pre-deployment checkup. I will see you in Briefing Room Bravo at oh four hundred."

He turned away. He was done with me—for now.

In the elevator, the sandy-haired woman asked, "How are you feeling?"

"Fuck off."

Her smile persisted as if I'd answered, *Fine, and you?* "My name's Lieutenant Pierce. But call me Constance."

The bell dinged. The doors slid open. She slammed her fist into my neck. My vision went black; my knees buckled.

"That's for Claire," she said. "You remember her."

I came up, driving the heel of my hand into her chin. The back of her head hit the wall with a satisfying *crack*. Then I punched her in the gut with all the force my enhanced muscles could muster. She collapsed at my feet.

"That's for the seven billion. You remember them."

11

IN THE INFIRMARY I was given a thorough physical. Diagnostics were run on the 12th System to ensure it was fully operational. Then an orderly brought in a tray groaning with food. I tore into it. I hadn't had a decent meal in over a month. When the plate was empty, the orderly came back carrying another. I knocked that off, too.

They brought my old uniform. I stripped. I washed up the best I could in the sink. I could smell the stench of forty unwashed days hovering around me, and for some reason I felt embarrassed. There was no toothbrush, so I rubbed my finger over my teeth.

I wondered if the 12th System protected my enamel. I pulled on the clothes, laced the boots tight. I felt better. More like the old Ringer, the blissfully ignorant, naïve, unenhanced Ringer who left Zombie that night with the unspoken promise: *I will come back. If I can, I will.*

The door swung open. Constance. She'd changed out of her lieutenant's uniform and into a pair of mom jeans and a tattered hoodie.

"I feel like we started off on the wrong foot," she said.

"Fuck off."

"We're partners now," she said sweetly. "Buddies. We should get along."

I followed her down three flights of stairs into the underground bunker, a snarl of gray-walled passageways pocked with unmarked doors, under fluorescent lights that bled a constant, sterile glow, reminding me of the hours with Razor while my body fought its losing battle against the 12th System. Playing chaseball and creating secret codes and plotting the phony escape that would lead me back beneath this ghastly light, another circle bound by uncertainty and fear.

Constance was a half step in front of me. Our footfalls echoed in the empty space. I could hear her breathe. *It would be so easy to kill you right now,* I thought idly, then pushed the thought away. That time would come, I hoped, but it wasn't now.

She pushed open a door identical to the fifty or so other unmarked doors we'd passed, and I followed her into the conference room. A projection screen against one wall. A long table in front of the screen. A small metal box on the center of the table.

Vosch was sitting behind the table. He stood up as we came in. The lights dimmed and the screen lit up with an aerial shot

45

looking straight down at a two-lane road that cut through empty, rolling fields. In the center of the frame, the rectangular rooftop of a house. A solitary, shimmering dot on the left edge of the rect-angle—the heat signature of someone on the watch. A cluster of glowing smudges inside the house. I counted them first, then gave them names: Dumbo, Poundcake, Sullivan, Nugget, Walker, and one more makes Zombie.

Hello, Zombie.

"From a reconnaissance flight six weeks ago," Vosch said. "Ap-proximately fifteen miles southeast of Urbana." The video feed went black for an instant, then popped back on: same thin black ribbon of the road, same dark rectangle of the house, but fewer glowing smudges inside it. Two were missing.

"This is from last night."

The camera zoomed out. Woods, fields, more clusters of black rectangles, dark blotches against gray landscape, the world emp-tied, abandoned, lifeless. The thin black ribbon of road slid out of the shot. Then I saw them: two glowing dots far to the northwest. Someone was on the move.

"Where are they going?" I asked, but I was pretty sure I knew the answer already.

Vosch shrugged. "Impossible to know for certain, but the most likely destination is here." The image froze. He pointed to a spot at the top of the screen and gave me a knowing look.

I closed my eyes. I saw Zombie wearing that ugly yellow hoodie, leaning against the counter in the lobby of the old hotel, that stupid brochure clutched in his hands, and me saying, *I'll scope it out and be back in a couple of days.*

"They're going to the caverns," I said. "To look for me."

"Yes, I think so," Vosch agreed. "And that's exactly who they'll find." The lights came up. "You'll be dropped in tonight, well ahead of their arrival. Lieutenant Pierce is tasked with target acquisition. Your only responsibility is getting her within striking distance. At the completion of the mission, Lieutenant Pierce and Walker will be extracted and returned to base."

"Then what?" I asked.

He blinked slowly. He expected me to know. "And then you and your companions are free to go."

"Go where?"

A small smile. "Wherever the wind might take you. But I suggest you keep to open country. Urban areas won't be safe."

He nodded to Constance, who brushed past me on her way to the door. "Take it, cupcake. You'll want it."

I watched her leave. Take it? Take what?

"Marika." Vosch crooked his finger at me. Come here.

I didn't move. "Why are you sending her with me?" Then I answered my own question: "You're not letting us go. Once you have Walker, you're going to kill us."

His eyebrow rose toward his crew cut. "Why would I kill you? The world would be a much less interesting place without you in it." He looked away quickly, biting his lower lip, as if he'd said too much.

He gestured toward the box sitting on the table. "We will not see each other again," he said gruffly. "I thought this was appropriate."

"What?"

"A parting gift."

"I don't want anything from you." Not my first thought. My first thought was Stick it up your ass.

He slid the box toward me. He was smiling.

I lifted the lid. I wasn't sure what to expect. Maybe a travel-sized chess set—a reminder of all the good times we had together. Inside the box, nestled in a foam cushion, was a green capsule encased in clear plastic.

"The world is a clock," he said softly. "And the time is coming when the choice between life and death will not be a difficult one, Marika."

"What is it?"

"The child in the wheat carried a modified version of this inside his throat, except this model is six times as powerful—everything within a five-mile radius is instantaneously vaporized. Place the capsule in your mouth, bite down to break the seal, and all you have to do is breathe."

I shook my head. "I don't want it."

He nodded. His eyes sparkled. He'd expected me to refuse. "In four days, our benefactors will release bombs from the mothership that will destroy every remaining city on Earth. Do you understand, Marika? The human footprint is about to be wiped clean. What we built over ten millennia will be gone in a day. Then the soldiers of the 5th Wave will be unleashed upon the survivors, and the war will begin. The last war, Marika. The endless war. The war that will go on and on until the final bullet is spent, and then it will be fought with sticks and rocks."

My puzzled expression must have tried his patience; his voice went hard. "What is the lesson of the child in the wheat?"

"No outsider can be trusted," I answered, staring at the green capsule in its bed of foam. "Not even a child."

"And what happens when no one can be trusted? What becomes of us when every stranger could be an 'other'?"

"Without trust there's no cooperation. And without cooperation there's no progress. History stops."

"Yes!" He beamed with pride. "I knew you would understand. The answer to the human problem is the death of what makes us human."

His arm came up, his hand toward me, as if he was going to touch me, and then he stopped himself. For the first time since I met him, he seemed troubled by something. If I hadn't known better, I'd have guessed he was afraid.

But that would be ridiculous.

He dropped his hand to his side and turned away.

12

THE SKIN OF THE C-160 glistened in the light of the setting sun. It was freezing on the airstrip, but the sunlight flirted on my cheeks. Four days until the spring equinox. Four days until the mothership drops her payload. Four days until the end.

Beside me, Constance was running through one last check of her gear while the ground crew ran through one last check of the plane's. I had my sidearm and rifle and knife, the clothes on my back, and the small green pill in my pocket.

I'd accepted his final gift.

I understood why he wanted me to have it. And I knew what the offer meant: He's going to keep his promise. Once Constance snatches Walker, we're free.

What risk did we pose, really? There's nowhere to hide. Months may pass before we face the ultimate choice between death on their terms or death on ours. And when we're cornered or captured, out of all options except those two, I will have his gift. I will have that choice.

I looked down at Constance fussing with her rucksack. The back of her exposed neck glowed golden in the failing light. I imagined taking my knife and plunging it to the hilt into the soft skin. Hate was not the answer; I knew that. She was as much a victim as me, as the seven billion dead, as the child running through the sea of wheat. In fact, she and Walker and the thousands infected with the Silencer program were the saddest, most pitiful victims of all.

At least when I die, I'll do it with my eyes wide-open. I'll die knowing the truth.

She looked up at me. I wasn't sure, but I thought she was waiting for me to tell her to fuck off again.

I didn't. "Do you know him?" I asked. "Evan Walker. You must all know each other, right? You spent ten millennia together up there,"—with a tilt of my head toward the green smudge in the sky, "Did you have any idea he'd go rogue?"

Constance bared her big teeth and didn't answer.

"Okay, that's bullshit," I said. "Everything you think is the truth is bullshit. Who you think you are, your memories, all of it. Before you were born, they embedded a program in your brain that booted up when you hit puberty. Probably a chemical reaction kick-started by the hormones."

She nodded, still all teeth. "I'm sure that's a comforting thought."

"You've been infected with a viral program that literally rewired your brain to 'remember' things that didn't happen. You aren't an alien consciousness here to wipe out humanity and colonize the Earth. You're human. Like me. Like Vosch. Like everyone else."

She said, "I'm not anything like you."

"You probably believe that at some point you'll return to the mothership and let the 5th Wave finish the human genocide, but you won't, because they aren't going to do it. You'll end up fighting the very army you've created until there are no bullets left and history stops. Trust leads to cooperation leads to progress, and there'll be no more progress. Not a new Stone Age, a *perpetual Stone Age*."

Shouldering her rucksack, Constance rose from the tarmac. "That's a fascinating theory. I like it."

I sighed. There was no breaking through. I didn't blame her, though. If she told me, *Your father wasn't an artist and a drunk; he was a teetotaling Baptist minister,* I wouldn't believe her. *Cogito ergo sum.* More than the sum of our experiences, our memories are the ultimate proof of reality.

The plane's engines roared to life. I flinched at the sound. I spent forty days in the wilderness without any reminders of the mechanized world. The smell of the exhaust rushing over me and the air vibrating against my skin brought on the ache of nostalgia in my heart, because this, too, will end. The final battle hadn't started, but the war was already over.

As if with a weary sigh, the sun dipped beneath the horizon. The green eye brightened against the darkening sky. Constance and I jogged up the platform into the plane and strapped in side by side.

The door locked into place with a loud hiss. A second later we were taxiing toward the runway. I looked over at Constance: her grin frozen in place and her dark eyes expressionless as a shark's.

My hand shot out and grabbed her forearm, and I felt the hate boiling through the fabric of her heavy parka. The hate and rage and disgust cascaded from her into me, and I *knew*: Regardless of her orders and all of Vosch's promises, once she acquired the target and our usefulness was over, she would kill me and Zombie and everyone else. There was too much risk in letting us live.

Which meant I had to kill her.

The plane lurched forward. My stomach protested; a wave of nausea rolled over me. Weird. I'd never had motion sickness before.

I leaned my back against the bulkhead and closed my eyes. The hub, answering my desire, shut down my hearing and tactile senses. In the gift of the numb silence that enfolded me, I worked through the options.

Constance had to die, but killing Constance compounded the Evan problem. Vosch might dispatch a second operative, but he'll have lost all tactical advantage. If I kill Constance, he might decide to take us all out with a Hellfire missile.

Unless he didn't need to kill Walker.

Unless Walker was already dead.

There was a sour taste in my mouth. I swallowed, fighting the urge to throw up.

Vosch had to run Walker through Wonderland. It was the only way to know why Evan rebelled against his programming—if the flaw lay in Walker or in the program or in some toxic combination of the two. A fundamental flaw in the program would create an unsustainable paradigm.

But if Walker was dead, Vosch couldn't identify the flaw in the system, and the whole operation could collapse: You can't have a war, especially of the endless variety, if everyone's on the same side. Whatever went "wrong" in Walker could go wrong in the other Silencers. He had to know *why* Evan's programming failed.

I can't let it happen. I can't risk giving Vosch what he wants.

Denying him what he wanted might be the only hope we had left. And there was only one way to do that.

Evan Walker had to die.

13

SAM

ZOMBIE ON THE ROAD, shrinking.

Zombie and Dumbo walking down the empty road awash in starlight, fading.

Sam pulls the silver chain from his pocket and holds it tightly in his hand.

Promise?

Have I broken one yet?

And the dark closing around Zombie like a monster's mouth until there is no Zombie, only the monster, only the dark.

He presses his other hand against the cold glass. On the day the bus took him to Camp Haven, he watched Cassie on the brown road, holding Bear, shrinking away to nothing, swallowed by the dust like Zombie was swallowed by the dark.

Behind him, Cassie says to Evan Walker in her angry voice, "Why didn't you stop him?"

"I tried," Evan Walker answers.

"Not very hard."

"Short of breaking his legs, I don't know what I could have done."

When Sam takes his hand away, the glass holds the memory of it like the bus window once did, a misty imprint of where his hand had been.

"After you lost Sam, could anyone have stopped you from finding him?" Evan Walker asks. Then he goes outside.

Sam can see his sister's face reflected in the glass. Like everything else since they came, Cassie's changed. She's not the same Cassie shrinking on the dusty road. Her nose is kind of crooked, like the nose of someone pressing her face against a windowpane.

"Sam," she says. "It's late. What do you say—wanna sleep in my room tonight?"

He shakes his head. "I have to watch Megan. Zombie's orders." She starts to say something. Then she stops. Then she says, "Okay. I'll be there in a minute to say your prayers with you."

"I'm not going to pray."

"Sam, you have to pray."

"I prayed for Mommy and she died. I prayed for Daddy and he died, too. When you pray for people, they die."

"That isn't why they died, Sam."

She reaches for him. He pulls away. "I'm not going to pray for anybody anymore," he tells her.

"Zombie left," Sam tells her.

"Where'd he go?" she whispers. A whisper is as loud as her voice goes. Cassie and Evan Walker hurt something in her throat when they pulled out the pill-bomb.

"He's going on recon to find Ringer and Teacup."

In the bedroom, Megan sits on the bed, holding Bear.

Megan shakes her head. She doesn't know who Ringer and Teacup are. Her hand squeezes Bear's head and Bear's mouth puckers like he wants a kiss.

"Be careful," Sam says. "Don't hurt his head."

The window in this bedroom is boarded up. You can't see outside. At night, after you turn off the lamp, the dark is so heavy, you can feel it pressing against your skin all over. Dangling from the ceiling are loose wires and a couple of balls that Zombie said were supposed to be Jupiter and Neptune. This is the room where Evan Walker tried to kill the evil Grace lady with wire from the mobile. There're bloodstains on the carpet and splatters of blood on the walls. It's like his mother's bedroom after she got the Red Death and her nose wouldn't stop bleeding. She bled from her nose and her mouth, and near the end, blood came out of her eyes and even her ears. Sam remembers her blood; he can't remember her face.

"I thought we were all staying here until Evan blew up the ship," Megan whispers, squeezing Bear.

Sam opens the closet door. Besides clothes and shoes that smell faintly of the plague, there are board games and action figures and a big Hot Wheels collection. One day Cassie came into the room and saw him on the floor playing with the dead kids' stuff. She watched him sitting on the big bloodstain in the middle of the floor. He'd made a camp, and there was his old squad, Squad 53, and they had a Jeep and a plane and they were on a mission to infiltrate an infested stronghold. Only, the infesteds saw them coming and their drones dropped bombs and everybody was hurt except Sam, and Zombie told him, *It's up to you now, Private. You're the only one who can save us.* His sister watched him play for a few minutes and then she started to cry for no reason, and that made him mad. He didn't know she was watching. He didn't understand why she was crying. He felt embarrassed. He was a soldier now, not a baby who played with toys. He stopped playing after that.

He hesitates before stepping into the closet. Megan is watching him from the bed. She doesn't know about his secret. Nobody does. But Zombie gave him an order and he has to follow it. Zombie is his commanding officer.

"If he blows up the ship, how does he keep from blowing himself up, too?" she asks.

Sam looks over his shoulder at her before stepping into the closet. "I hope he does," he says.

Zombie said he didn't trust Evan Walker. He was an infested and it didn't matter that he had been helping them. The enemy was the enemy, and you can't trust traitors, Zombie said. Cassie said Evan Walker wasn't her boyfriend, but Sam saw the way she looked at him and heard the way she talked to him, and he didn't believe her when she said they could trust him or that he would make everything okay. He had trusted the soldiers at Camp Haven, too, and they turned out to be the enemy.

Inside the closet, he kneels beside the heap of clothes piled against one wall. Nobody knows what he hid there, not even Zombie.

When they first got to the house, they checked out every room until only the basement was left, and Zombie wouldn't let him go down there. Zombie went down with Dumbo and Evan Walker, and when they came up again, they were carrying weapons. Rifles and pistols and explosives *and* a very big tube-shaped gun with a shoulder mount that Zombie called an FIM Stinger. You could blow up helicopters and planes with it, Zombie explained, blow 'em right out of the sky. Then he told Sam the basement was unauthorized; Sam wasn't allowed to go down there or touch any of the weapons. Even though he was a soldier just like Dumbo and just like Zombie. It wasn't fair.

Sam reaches beneath the mound of clothes and pulls out the gun. An M9 Beretta. So *cool*.

"What are you doing in there?" Megan asks, plucking at Bear's ear. She shouldn't do that. He told her not to a thousand times. Dumbo's had to sew up Bear's ear twice since they came to the house. He let Megan keep Bear even though Bear has always been his for as long as he can remember, even though she squishes his head and plucks at his ears and calls him a different name. They got in a fight about it.

"His name is Bear," Sam told her that day.

"That's not a name. A bear is what he *is*. I named him Captain."

"You can't do that."

She shrugged. "I did."

"He's mine."

"Then take him back," she said. "I don't care."

He shook his head. He didn't want Bear back. He wasn't a baby anymore. He was a soldier. All he wanted was for her to call Bear by his right name.

"You used to be Sam and now you have a different name," Megan said.

"That's not the same. Bear's not part of the squad."

She didn't stop. Once she found out he hated the name, she called Bear Captain all the time, just to bug him.

Keeping his back to Megan, he jams the gun into his waistband and pulls the big red sweatshirt over his stomach to hide the bulge.

"Sam? Captain wants to know what you're doing in there."

He asked Zombie that night if he could have one of the guns.

57

There were dozens of them, *a freakin' armory down there*, Zombie said, but he also said no. Cassie was standing there, so Sam waited until she was out of the room and asked Zombie again if he could have a gun. It wasn't right that everybody carried one except him and Megan, but she didn't count. She was a civilian. She hadn't been trained like he had.

They had taken her from the bus and hidden her until it was time to plant the pill-bomb in her throat. She wasn't alone, she said. There were a lot of kids they pulled from the buses. Hundreds of children, and Evan Walker said each of them was used to trick survivors. The children were airlifted or driven to places where the enemy knew people were hiding. The people brought in the children to save them. Then the people died.

And Cassie said they had to trust Evan Walker!

The gun under his shirt is cold against his bare skin. It's a nice feeling, better than a hug. He isn't afraid of the gun. He isn't afraid of anything. His orders are to watch Megan, but Zombie left nobody in charge of watching Evan Walker. So Sam will do that, too.

At Camp Haven, the soldiers in charge said they would protect him. They told him he was perfectly safe. They told him everything was going to be all right. And they lied. They lied about everything because everybody is a liar. They make promises they don't keep. Even his mommy and daddy lied. When the mothership came, they said they would never leave him, and they did. They promised everything would be all right, and it wasn't.

He crawls into the bed opposite Megan's and stares at the bare wires and the two dusty metal balls hanging from the ceiling. Megan is watching him, pulling Bear tight against her chest, and her mouth hangs open a little, like the air is running out.

He turns his head toward the wall. He doesn't want Megan to see him cry.

He isn't a baby. He's a soldier.

There's no way you can tell who's human anymore. Evan Walker looked human but he wasn't, not inside, not where it matters. Even people like Megan, who are human—*maybe*—couldn't be trusted, because you can't know what the enemy has done to them. Zombie, Cassie, Dumbo . . . you can't really trust them, either. They could be just like Evan Walker.

In the pressing dark beneath the broken mobile, Sam's heart speeds up. Maybe they're *all* tricking him. Even Zombie. Even Cassie.

His breath catches in his throat. It's hard to breathe. *You have to pray,* Cassie said. He used to pray every night, all the time, and the only answer God ever gave was no. *Let Mommy live, God.* No. *Let Daddy come back, God.* No. You can't trust God, either. Even God is a liar. He put rainbows in the sky as a promise he'd never kill everyone again, and then he let the Others come and do it. All the people who died must have prayed, too, and God said, *No, no, no,* seven billion times, seven billion nos, God said *no, no, no.*

The cool metal of the gun against his bare skin. The cold like a hand against his forehead, pressing. Megan breathing through her mouth, reminding him of bombs triggered by human breath.

They won't stop, he thinks. *They'll never stop until everyone is dead. God let it happen because God wants it to happen. And nobody can win against God. He's God.*

Megan's breathing fades away. Sam's tears dry. He floats in a vast, empty space. There's nothing and no one, just empty space that goes on and on and on.

Maybe that's it, he thinks. *Maybe there's already nobody human left. Maybe they're all infested.*

Which means he's the last one. He's the last human on Earth.

Sam presses his hands against the pistol. Touching the gun comforts him. Megan has Bear. He has the gun.

If it is a trick, if they're all aliens in disguise, he won't let them win. He'll kill them all if he has to. Then *he'll* ride the rescue pod up to the mothership and blow it up. They'll lose—the last human will die—but at least the Others won't win.

God said no. He can, too.

II

THE SECOND DAY

14

ZOMBIE

IT TAKES LESS than an hour to reach the city limits sign. Urbana, dead ahead. Literally. I pull Dumbo off the road before we go in. I've been debating with myself whether to tell him, but there's really no choice. He needs to know.

"You know what Walker is," I whisper.

He nods. His eyes dart left, right, then back to my face. "He's a freaking alien."

"That's right, it was downloaded into Walker's body when he was a kid. You've got some, like Vosch, running the camps, and then you've got others, like Walker, lone operatives who patrol assigned territories, picking off survivors."

Dumbo's eyes leave my face to confront the dark again. "Snipers?"

"We're gonna be passing through two of those territories. One that runs between Urbana and the caverns. And one that begins on the other side of this sign."

He wipes the back of his hand across his mouth. He tugs on an earlobe. "Okay."

"And they're loaded for bear. I don't know, some kind of technology that jacks them up. Gives them super strength, speed, senses, that kind of thing. We go quick and we go quiet." I lean toward him. Important he understands. "If something happens to me, you abort this mission. Get back to the safe house."

He's shaking his head. "I won't leave you, Sarge."

"Yes, you will. And that's an order, Private, in case you're wondering."

"Would you leave me?"

"You bet your ass I would." I pat him on the shoulder. He watches silently as I dig the eyepiece out of my rucksack and slip it on. His head lights up through the lens, a bright ball of green fire. I survey our surroundings for any other telltale green blobs while he puts on his own eyepiece.

"One last thing, Bo," I whisper. "There are no friendlies."

"Sarge?"

I swallow. My mouth is dry. I wish there were another way. It makes me sick, but I didn't invent this game. I'm just trying to stay alive long enough to play.

"*Unclean glows green.* Anything that lights up, we take out. No hesitation. No exceptions. Understand?"

"That won't work, Zombie. What if it's Ringer or Teacup?"

Damn. Hadn't thought of that. I also hadn't thought through Ringer's options, which were identical to mine. Shoot first and ask questions later? Or fire only if fired upon? I think I know which she'd choose. She's Ringer.

A little voice in my head whispers: *Two of you double the risk. Send Dumbo back.* The cool, quiet voice of reason, which has sounded a lot like Ringer's ever since I met her. Points you just can't argue with, like somebody telling you that granite is hard and water is wet.

Dumbo is shaking his head. We've been through the shit together; he knows me. "Two sets of eyes are better than one, Sarge.

We go like you said, quick and quiet, and hopefully we see them before they see us."

He gives me what I guess is supposed to be a reassuring smile. I return what I hope passes for a confident nod. Then we go.

Double-timing straight up Main into the burned-out, debris-strewn, rat-infested, boarded-up, graffiti-decorated, sewage-stained guts of Urbana. Overturned cars and downed power lines and trash piled against foundations by wind and water, trash blanketing yards and parking lots, trash hanging from the winter-bare tree limbs. Plastic bags and newspapers, clothing, shoes, toys, broken chairs and mattresses, TVs. It's like a cosmic giant grabbed the planet with both hands and shook it as hard as he could. Maybe if I were some evil alien overlord, I'd blow up all the cities, too, just to get rid of the mess.

We probably should have swung around this hellscape, used the back roads and open country—I'm certain Ringer would have—but if she and Cup are gonna be anywhere, it's the caverns, and this is the shortest route.

Quick and quiet, I'm thinking as we trot down the sidewalk, our eyes cutting left to right and back again, *quick and quiet.*

Four blocks in, we come to a six-foot-high barricade blocking off the street, a jumble of cars and tree branches and smashed furniture festooned in faded American flags, I'm guessing thrown together as the 2nd Wave bled into the 3rd, when it dawned on people that our fellow humans were a bigger threat than the alien spaceship that soared two hundred miles overhead. It blows your mind, how quickly we slid into anarchy after they pulled the plug. How easy it was to sow confusion and fear and distrust. And how goddamned *fast* we fell. You'd think a common enemy would have forced us to set aside our differences and band together against the escalating threat. Instead, we built barricades. We hoarded food and supplies and weapons. We turned away the stranger, the outsider, the unrecognized face. Two weeks into the invasion and civilization had already cracked at its foundation. Two months, and it collapsed like an imploded building, falling down as the bodies piled up.

We've seen a few of those, too, on our way into Urbana. From piles of blackened bones to corpses wrapped head to toe in tattered sheets and old blankets, just lying there in the open like they'd dropped from the sky, alone or in groups of ten or more. So many bodies that they faded into the background, just another part of the mess, another piece of the urban vomit.

Dumbo's eyes swing back and forth restlessly, searching the dark for green fireballs. "Messed up," he breathes. Despite the cold, sweat shines on his forehead. He shivers as if gripped by a fever. On the other side of the barricade, I call a break. Water. A power bar. I've developed this thing about power bars. Found a whole case of them in the safe house and now I can't get enough of them. We find a small gap in the makeshift wall and nestle inside, facing north down Main Street. There's no wind. The sky is clear, stuffed with stars. You can feel it deep in your bones because it's older than your senses: the end of winter, the Earth sliding toward spring. Before I became Zombie, that meant prom and cramming for finals and the nervous chatter in the hallways between classes because graduation was coming, a different kind of apocalyptic event after which nothing would ever be the same.

"You ever been to Urbana, Dumbo?" I ask.

He shakes his head. "I'm from Pittsburgh."

"Really?" I'd never asked. It was the unwritten rule in camp:

Talking about our past was like handling hot coals. "Well. Go, Steelers."

"Naw." He bites off a hunk of power bar and chews slowly. "I was a Packers fan."

"I played some, you know."

"Quarterback?"

"Wide receiver."

"My brother played baseball. Shortstop."

"Not you?"

"I quit Little League when I was ten."

"How come?"

"I sucked. But I kill at e-sports."

"E-sports?"

"You know, like *COD*."

"Competitive fishing?"

He shakes his head with a smile. "No. *Call of Duty*, Zombie."

"Oh! You're a gamer."

"I was borderline MLG."

"Oh, MLG, right." I don't have the first clue what he's talking about.

"Max Level, Prestige Twelve."

"Wow, really?" I shake my head, thoroughly impressed. Except I'm totally lost.

"You have no idea what I'm talking about." He crumples the wrapper in his fist. He glances around at the garbage littering every square inch of Urbana, then slips the wrapper into his pocket.

"There's something that's been bugging me, Sarge."

He turns to me. His exposed eye is wide with anxiety. "So, way before their ship showed up, they downloaded themselves into babies and didn't 'wake up' inside them until they were teenagers."

I nod. "That's what Walker said."

"My birthday was last week. I'm thirteen."

"For real? Damn it, Dumbo, why didn't you tell me? I would've baked you a cake."

He doesn't smile. "What if I got one inside me, Sarge? What if one of *them* is about to wake up in my brain and take over?"

"You're not serious, right? Come on, Private, that's crazy talk."

"How do you know? I mean, how *do* you know, Zombie? And then it happens and I waste you and I go back to the house and waste all of them . . ."

He's losing it. I grab his arm and make him look at me.

"Listen to me, you big-eared son of a bitch, you go Dorothy on me now and I'm gonna kick your ass from here to Dubuque."

"Please," he whines. "Please stop bringing up Dubuque."

"There's no alien asleep inside you, Dumbo."

"Okay, but if you're wrong, you'll take care of it, right?"

I know what he means, but I go, "Huh?"

"Take care of it, Zombie." Pleading with me. "Kill the motherfucker."

Well, happy frigging birthday, Dumbo. This conversation has given me the heebie-jeebies.

"It's a deal," I tell him. "An alien wakes up inside you, I'll blow your brains out."

Relieved, he sighs. "Thanks, Sarge."

I stand up, hold out my hand, and help him to his feet. His arm swings around and shoves me to one side. His rifle comes up. He's aiming at the car dealership half a block down. I lift my weapon, close my right eye, and squint through the eyepiece. Nothing. Dumbo shakes his head. "Thought I saw something," he whispers. "Guess not."

We hold for a minute. It's so damn quiet. You'd think the town would be overrun with packs of wild dogs barking and feral cats howling or even a damn owl hooting, but there's nothing. Is it all in my head, this feeling of being watched? That there's something out there I can't see but can sure as hell see me? I glance at Dumbo, who's clearly just as spooked.

We move out, not on the quick now but sidestepping to the opposite side of the street, where we slide along the wall of the consignment store facing the dealership (SPRING INTO SAVINGS THIS MEMORIAL DAY!). We don't stop until we reach the next intersection. Check right, check left, then straight ahead toward downtown, three blocks away, the buildings' big boxy shadows silhouetted against the starry sky.

We trot across the intersection, then stop again on the other side, pressing our backs against the wall and waiting—for what, I'm not sure. We scoot past busted-out doors and shattered windows, the sound of glass crunching under our boots louder than sonic booms, another block, then repeating the drill, left around the corner, right across Main, then zipping to the relative safety of the next building on the opposite corner.

We make it another fifty yards and then Dumbo tugs on my sleeve, leading me through a broken glass door and into the near dark of a shop. Brown pebbles crunch underfoot. No, not pebbles. The smell is faint, barely discernible beneath the familiar rot of sewage and the spoiled-milk odor of plague, but we both pick it up, and there's a little ache of nostalgia when we do. Coffee.

Dumbo eases down in front of the counter, facing the doorway, and I give him a look: *What's up?*

"I loved Starbucks," he sighs. Like that makes everything perfectly clear.

I sit beside him. I don't know, maybe he needs a break. We don't talk. The minutes drag out. Finally, I say, "We gotta be the hell out of this town by sunrise."

Dumbo nods. He doesn't move. "There's someone out there," he says.

"You saw them?"

He shakes his head. "But I *feel* them. You know? I feel them." I think about it. Paranoia. Has to be. "We could try to draw their fire," I suggest, humoring him.

"Or distract them," he says, glancing around the store. "Blow something up."

He rummages through his sack and pulls out a grenade.

"No, Dumbo. Not a good idea." I ease the grenade from his hand. His fingers are colder than the metal.

"They're gonna slide in behind us," he argues. "We won't even see it coming."

"Well, I'd rather *not* see it coming." I smile at him. He doesn't smile back. Dumbo's always been the coolest player on the team, probably why they picked him to be the medic. Nothing fazed the kid. At least, nothing till now.

"Sarge, I got an idea," he says, leaning so close, I can smell the chocolate from the power bar on his breath. "You stay here. I go on ahead—but in a different direction. Once I draw them off, you can haul ass due north and—"

I stop him. "That's a terrible idea, Private. A really, really terrible idea."

He isn't listening. "That way, at least one of us makes it."

"Stow that shit. We're both gonna make it."

Shaking his head. His voice breaks. "I don't think so, Sarge."

He rips off his eyepiece and stares at me for one very long, very

72

uncomfortable moment. He looks startled, as if he's seen a ghost. Then Dumbo lunges at me, rising to his feet and coming straight at me with hands outstretched like he's going to grab me by the throat and choke the life out of me.

I raise my own hands instinctively to block the attack. *Oh Christ, oh Christ, the big-eared sonofabitch was right, it woke up,* the thing woke up in him.

My fingers catch hold of his jacket. Dumbo's head snaps back. His body stiffens, then goes limp.

I hear the report of the sniper rifle a second later, the kind of rifle with a laser-guided scope, which fired the bullet that a second before was coming straight at my head.

The bullet that Dumbo took for me, accepted without hesitation, because I'm the man, the CO, the thick-headed moron that the enemy in all his infinite wisdom put in charge of keeping our asses alive.

15

I GRAB HIM by the shoulders and drag him behind the counter. Out of the line of fire but also cornered; I don't have much time. I put him on his stomach, yank up the jacket and the two shirts underneath to expose the wound. A quarter-sized hole right in the middle of his back. The bullet has to be inside him—otherwise I'd be hit, too. His chest moves. He's breathing. I lean down and whisper in his ear, "Tell me what to do, Dumbo. Tell me." He doesn't say anything. Probably needs all his energy just to breathe.

Zombie, you can't stay here. That calm, Ringerish voice again. Cut him loose.

Sure. Cut him loose. That's my thing. That's how I roll. I cut my sister loose, I cut Poundcake loose. They go down and I keep going.

Fuck that.

I crawl around to the front of the counter, grab Dumbo's bag, and go back to him. He's curled into a ball, knees pressed against his chest, and his eyelids flutter like someone having a bad dream. I tear through his med kit, looking for the gauze. I have to pack the wound. I remember that much from my one and only course in battlefield injuries at Camp Haven. If I don't pack it and pack it fast, he could bleed out in less than three minutes.

The other thing I remember from that course: It hurts like hell. Hurts so goddamned bad, the first thing you're supposed to do is take away the patient's weapons.

So I pull his sidearm from the holster and tuck it behind my back.

There should be a thin metal rod in the kit—you use it to push the gauze into the wound—but I can't find it.

Bug out, Zombie. You're outta time.

I push the gauze into the hole in his back with my finger. Dumbo bows up. He screams. Then he instinctively tries to escape, clawing at the base of the counter for a handhold, and I wrap the fingers of my free hand around his neck to keep him still.

"It's good, Bo. It's all good . . ." Whispering in his ear as my finger sinks inside him, pushing the wad of gauze ahead of it. *More gauze. Gotta pack it tight. If that bullet sliced an artery . . .*

I pull my finger out. He lets loose another banshee howl, and I cup his chin, forcing his mouth closed. I don't move slow. I don't go gentle. I ram another wad into the wound. Dumbo is jerking

74

against me, sobbing helplessly. I lie on my side behind him and throw my leg over his waist to keep him still. "One more time, Bo," I whisper. "Almost there . . ."

Then it's done. The gauze pokes out of the wound; I can't push any more inside. I tear open a bandage with my teeth and slap it over my handiwork. I roll onto my back, pulling hard for air. Probably too little, too late. Beside me, Dumbo continues to cry, the sobs dwindling to whimpers. His body shudders against mine; he's going into shock.

Back to the bag to find something for the pain. He's on his way out, he's dying, I'm pretty sure of that, but at least I can help him go easy. I tear open a morphine syrette and jab the needle into his exposed hip. The effect is almost immediate. His muscles relax, his mouth goes slack, his breathing slows.

"See? Not so bad," I tell him, like I'm settling an argument.

"I'm coming back for you, Bo. I'm finding the bastard and then I'm coming back."

Oh boy, Zombie, you've done it now. The promise feels like a death sentence, a cell door slamming shut, a stone around my neck that's destined to carry me down.

16

BACK AROUND THE COUNTER to fetch my rifle. Rifle, side-arm, knife, a couple of flash grenades. And one more thing, the most essential weapon in my arsenal: a heart full of rage. I'm blowing the bastard who shot him back to Dumbo's favorite town.

Scooting on my hands and knees down the hallway to the emergency exit door (WARNING! ALARM WILL SOUND!). Onto the side street, beneath the cold starlight. I'm alone for the first time since my family's murder—not running away this time, though. No more of that.

I head east. At the next block, I turn north again, paralleling Main Street. I'll cut back after a couple more blocks, cross Main to the next street, then come at the shooter from the rear. Assuming he hasn't already crossed the street to finish the job.

Might not be the Silencer. Could be a civilian who's learned the first lesson of the last war.

Not that it makes any difference.

Back at the safe house, Cassie told me about finding a soldier inside a convenience store while she was foraging for supplies. She killed him. Thought he was pulling a weapon that turned out to be a crucifix. It tore her up. She couldn't get it out of her head. He must have thought he was the luckiest son of a bitch on Earth. Separated from his unit, badly wounded, unable to do anything but wait for a rescue that would probably never come, and then out of nowhere this random girl shows up; he was saved. Then the random girl opened up with her rifle and turned his body into a pincushion.

"Not your fault, Sullivan," I told her. "You didn't have a choice."

"Bullshit," she snapped at me. She tended to snap at me a lot. Well, not just me. The girl's a snapper. "That's the lie they want us to believe, Parish."

Back on Main. Easing up to the corner, I peek around the edge of the building toward the coffee shop. Directly across from it is a three-story, windows boarded up on the bottom floor, fractured on the top two. Nothing glows in the windows or on the roof; no green balls of light through the eyepiece. I hold for a few seconds, watching the front. I know the drill. That building has to be cleared. We practiced it a thousand times in camp, only we had seven guys to do it. Flint, Oompa, Ringer, Teacup, Poundcake, Dumbo—down to just one now. Down to me.

Hunched over, I trot across Main Street, every inch of my body tingling, expecting the punch of the sniper's bullet. Whose bright idea was it to cut straight through Urbana? Who put *that* guy in charge?

Keep moving, stay focused, check those windows up there, those doors over there. The street is choked with trash and broken glass, slick with the residue from ruptured sewer lines and water mains, puddles of oily water glimmering in the starlight. One block over, then cutting back south. The building is straight ahead at the end of the block, and I force myself to slow down. You're taught to stay in the moment, but the moment I'm in is the one that happens after I've neutralized the shooter. Do I abort the mission to find Ringer and Teacup? Get Dumbo back to the safe house? Or leave him here and pick him up later on my way back from the caverns?

I've reached the end of the block. Time to make the call. Once I penetrate the building, I'm all in, there's no going back.

I step through a broken plate-glass window and into the lobby of a bank. A carpet of paper covers the floor: deposit slips and brochures and old magazines and the remnants of a banner (OUR LOWEST RATES EVER!) and bills in every denomination—I can see hundreds among the fives and tens.

The damp, rotting carpet squishes beneath my boots. I sweep the room in less than thirty seconds. *Clear.*

I find the stairway door opposite the elevator and ease it open. I'm down to zero visibility, but I'm not risking light; I might as well scream out my name or yell *Hey, bud, here I am!* In the stairwell, the door clicks shut behind me, sealing me inside absolute darkness. One step up, pause, straining my ears, another step, pause. Faintly, the building groans around me like an old house settling. The harsh winter, the broken pipes within the walls, water worming its way into the mortar, freezing, expanding, breaking apart the bones and sinews that hold the structure together. If the Others weren't dropping the bombs in four days, Urbana would crumble on its own. In a thousand years, you could hold the entirety of the city in the palm of your hand.

First landing, second floor. I keep moving up, one hand on the metal railing, step, pause, step. I'll start on the roof and work my way down. I don't think he's nesting up there; Dumbo and I were hunkered by the back counter, and the trajectory from the rooftop into the coffee shop is too sharp. More likely the sniper's set up on the second floor, but I'm going to be methodical about this. Think through every move before I make it.

I smell it halfway to the second floor, on the landing where the stairs turn: the unmistakable stink of death. I step on something small and soft. Probably a dead rat. In the tight, closed-in space, the stench is overwhelming. My eyes pour water, my stomach rises into my throat. Another good reason to blow up the cities: It's the fastest way to get rid of the smell.

Above me, a razor-thin bar of golden light shines beneath the door. Holy crap and WTF, he's a brazen bastard.

78

I press my ear against the door. Silence. Though it might seem obvious, I'm not sure what to do. The door could be booby-trapped. Or the light could be a ruse—bait to lure me into an ambush. At the very least, the door's gotta be rigged to make a sound if it's opened. You don't have to be a Silencer to take that precaution.

I drop my hand onto the cold metal door handle. I fiddle with the eyepiece, stalling. *You don't ease in, Parish—you bust through.*

The worst part isn't the busting through, though. The worst part is the second before you do.

I throw open the door, whip sharply to my left, then step into the hall and turn back hard to the right. No bell jingled, no stack of empty cans clattered to the floor. The door swings closed silently behind me on well-oiled hinges. My finger twitches on the trigger as a shadow races across the wall, a shadow that's attached to a small, orange, furry creature with a striped tail.

A cat.

The animal darts through an open doorway halfway down the corridor, out of which pours the golden light that I saw in the stairwell. As I ease toward the light, the smell of decay is overcome by two very different smells: hot soup, maybe beef stew, warring with the unmistakable odor of a dirty litter box. I can hear a high-pitched voice warbling softly:

When through the woods and forest glades I wander
And hear the birds sing sweetly in the trees . . .

I've heard this song before. Many times. I even remember the refrain:

Then sings my soul, my Savior God, to thee:
How great thou art! How great thou art!

Her voice reminds me of another, thin and scratchy from age, slightly out of tune, singing with fierce determination and the self-assurance that comes with unshakable faith. How many Sundays did I stand beside my grandmother while she sang this hymn? Bored out of my adolescent mind, silently bitching about my itchy collar and uncomfortable shoes, daydreaming about my latest crush and sacrilegiously changing (in my head) the last line to *How great thy ass! How great thy ass!*

Hearing that song opens a floodgate through which the memories pour, unstoppable. Grandma's perfume. Her thick legs encased in white stockings and her square-toed black shoes. The way the powder caked in the deep crevices of her face, at the corners of her mouth and her dark, kind eyes. The knobbiness of her arthritic knuckles and how she held the steering wheel of that ancient Mercury like a desperate swimmer clutching a lifesaver. Chocolate chip cookies fresh from the oven and apple pies cooling on racks and her voice in the other room rising in excitement as the latest bombshells were delivered by a lady in her prayer circle.

Stopping just short of the doorway, I pull out one of the stun grenades. I slip my finger into the pin. My hands are shaking. A dribble of sweat courses down the middle of my back. This is how they get you, this is how they crush the spirit right out of you. Out of the blue the past is rammed down your throat, a gut punch of memories of all the things you took for granted, the things that you lost in the blink of an eye, the stupid, trivial, forgettable things you didn't know could crush you, things like an old woman's quivery voice, high-pitched and far away, calling you inside for a plate of warm cookies and a glass of ice-cold milk.

Then sings my soul, my Savior God, to thee!

I pull the pin and toss the grenade through the open door. A blinding flash, the terrified chorus of cats screeching, and a human being crying out in pain.

I swing into the doorway, sighting the crumpled figure in the far corner of the room, her face hidden behind the swirl of green fire created by my eyepiece. *Take her, Zombie. One shot and done.*

But I don't pull the trigger. I'm not sure what stops me. Maybe it's the cats, dozens of them leaping and diving over and under furniture. Maybe it's her singing, how she reminded me of my grandmother and all the uncountable lost things. Maybe it's Sullivan's story, her Crucifix Soldier cowering in a corner, defenseless and doomed. Or maybe it's the simple fact that the light from kerosene lamps placed around the room show me that she isn't armed. Instead of a sniper's rifle, she's clutching a wooden spoon.

"Please, God, don't kill me!" the old lady shrieks, curling herself into a tight little ball and throwing her hands over her face. I sweep the room quickly. Corners clear, no way in or out except the way I just came. The window facing Main Street is hidden behind heavy black drapes. I step over to it and push the material aside with the muzzle of my rifle. The window's been boarded up. No wonder I didn't see the light from the street. The barrier also tells me this isn't any sniper's nest.

"Please don't," she whimpers. "Please don't hurt me."

The green fire surrounding her head is bugging me; I yank off the eyepiece. Next to the window is a small table on which a pot of stew burbles over a can of Sterno. There's a Bible next to it, open to the Twenty-Third Psalm. There's a sofa piled with blankets and pillows. A couple of chairs. A desk. A potted plastic tree. Listing towers of magazines and newspapers. It's not the sniper kind, but it's definitely a nest.

She's probably been holed up here since the 3rd Wave rolled through town. And that raises an important question: How'd she make it this long without the resident Silencer finding her?

"Where is he?" I ask. My voice sounds weak and too young to my own ears, like I've fallen backward through time. "Where's the shooter?"

"Shooter?" she echoes. Her gray hair is stuffed into a knit cap, but a few wispy strands have escaped and fall on either side of her pale face. She's wearing black sweatpants, her upper half encased in several layers of sweaters. I step toward her, and she shrinks farther into the corner, clutching the spoon to her chest. Cat hair flits and dances in the smoky, golden light, and I sneeze.

"Bless you," she says automatically.

"You had to hear it," I tell her, meaning the shot that took down Dumbo. "You have to know he's here."

"There's no one here," she squeaks. "Just me and my babies. Please don't hurt my babies!"

It takes me a second to understand she's talking about the cats. I move around the room, along the narrow paths that wind through the stacks of old magazines, one eye on her, the other looking for weapons. There're a hundred places to hide a gun in this clutter. I poke through the mound of blankets on the sofa. I check under the desk, pulling open a couple of drawers, then behind the plastic plant. A cat dashes between my legs, hissing. I weave my way over to her corner and order her to stand up.

"Are you going to kill me?" she whispers.

I should. I know I should. The risk is in letting her live. The shot that Dumbo took for me came from somewhere in this building. I sling the rifle over my shoulder, draw my sidearm, and order her up again. It's a struggle for both of us—her physical battle to get her legs beneath her, my psychological one to resist the instinct to help her. Upright, she sways, hands to her chest, worrying with that damn spoon.

"Drop the spoon."

"You want me to drop my spoon?"

"Drop it."

"It's just a spoon . . ."

"Drop the damn spoon!"

She drops the damn spoon. I tell her to face the wall and put her hands on top of her head. She swallows back a sob. I step up behind her, place one hand on top of hers—they're cold as a corpse's—and pat her down. *Okay, Zombie, she's clean. Now what? Time to fish or cut bait.*

Maybe she didn't hear the shot. Her hearing may be bad. She is an old lady, after all. Maybe the shooter knows she's here but doesn't bother with her because, after all, she's an old cat lady, what threat can she really pose?

"Who else is here?" I say to the back of her head.

"No one, no one, I swear, no one. I haven't seen a living soul in months. Just me and my babies. Just me and my babies . . . !"

"Turn around. Keep your hands on top of your head."

She executes a one-eighty, and now I'm looking down into a pair of bright green eyes nearly lost in folds of withered skin. The mounds of clothes hide how thin she is, but you can see the signs of slow starvation in her face, the cheekbones poking out, the hollows at her temples, the eyes sunken and ringed in black. Her mouth hangs open a little—she has no teeth.

Oh Christ. The last human generation has been forged into killing machines by false hope and lies, and come spring, the 5th Wave will roll across the world, slaughtering everyone in its path, including the wounded boys who hide in coolers holding their crucifixes and old cat ladies clutching their wooden spoons.

Pull the trigger, Zombie. Everybody's luck runs out. If you don't kill her, someone else will.

I raise my pistol to the level of her eyes.

17

SHE FALLS TO her knees at my feet, and she raises her empty hands toward me, and she doesn't say anything because there isn't anything to say: She's sure she's going to die.

They trained me to do this, prepared me for it, emptied me and filled me up again with hate, but I've never shot anyone—not in all this time. Cassie Sullivan's hands are bloodier than mine.

The first time's the hardest, she told me. By the time I shot that last soldier at Camp Haven, I felt nothing. I can't even remember what he looked like.

"My friend's been shot." My voice breaks. "Either you shot him or someone you know did. Play straight with me."

"I don't leave this room. I haven't in weeks. It isn't safe out there," she whispers back. "I stay in here with my babies and wait . . ."

"Wait? Wait for what?"

She's stalling. And I'm stalling, too. I don't want to be wrong—

84

or right. I don't want to step over that line and be the person the Others have made me. I don't want to kill another human being—innocent or not.

"The Lamb of God," she answers. "He's coming, you know. Any day now, and the wheat shall be separated from the chaff, the goats from the sheep, and he will come in his glory to judge the living and the dead."

"Oh, sure," I choke out. "Everybody knows that."

She senses it before I do: I'm not pulling the trigger. I can't. A sweet, childlike smile spreads across the furrowed landscape of her face like the morning sun breaking over the horizon.

I shuffle backward, knocking into the little table by the window. The stew sloshes over the rim of the pot, and the small can of fire beneath it hisses angrily.

"My soup!" she cries, struggling to her feet, and I back farther away, keeping the gun on her, but it's a hollow threat; we both know it. The old lady scoops the spoon from the floor and hobbles over to the bubbling pot. The sound of the wood knocking against the metal sides of the pot draws a dozen cats from their hiding places. My stomach tightens. I have eaten nothing but a power bar in over twelve hours.

Grandma gives me a sideways look that borders on sly, and asks if I'd like a taste.

"I don't have time," I tell her. "I have to get back to my friend."

Her eyes fill with tears. "Five minutes, please? I've been so lonely." She stirs the soup. "Ran out of the cans a month ago, but one makes do." Glancing over again. A shy smile. "You could bring your friend here. I have medicines and we can pray for him. The Lord heals all who ask with a pure heart."

My lips are dry, though my mouth is watering. The blood pounds in my ears. A cat rubs against my calf, having decided I'm not such a bad guy after all.

"That wouldn't be a good idea," I tell her, "It isn't safe here."

She gives me a startled look. "And there's a place that is?"

I almost laugh. She's old, but sharp. And tough. And fearless. And full of faith. She'd have to be to survive this long. Whoever's left now will have her kind of spirit—what did Cassie call them? The bent but unbroken ones. For a desperate instant I consider taking her up on the offer, leaving Dumbo with her while I race to the caverns to find Cup and Ringer. It might be his best chance—no, his *only* chance.

I clear my throat. "You ran out of cans? So what's in the soup?"

She raises the spoon to her lips, closes her eyes, sips the brownish broth. The cat at my feet lifts its mangy head and stares up at me with huge yellow eyes.

I know what she's going to say a microsecond before she says it.

"Cat."

In one fluid motion, she hurls the scalding liquid toward my face. I stumble backward, knock against a stack of magazines, and lose my balance. She's on me before I hit the floor, her fingers locking around a fistful of my jacket, which she uses to hurl me across the room as easily as a kid throws a stuffed animal. The rifle falls from my shoulder when I hit the far wall. Lying on my side, I point my sidearm at the shimmering blob hurtling toward me.

She's too fast or I'm too slow—she knocks the gun out of my hand. Her fingers lock around my throat. She yanks me upright, shoves my head against the wall and brings her face close to mine, her deep green eyes sparking with infinite malice.

"You shouldn't be here," she hisses. "It's too soon."

Her face swims into and out of focus. *Too soon?* Then I

understand: She saw the eyepiece. She thinks I'm part of the 5th Wave, which won't be launched for another week, *after* she returns to the mothership, *after* Urbana and every other city on Earth is gone.

I've found the Urbana Silencer.

18

"CHANGE OF PLANS," I gasp. She's allowing me just enough air. The grip of her icy fingers is so hard, the strength behind it so obvious, I'm sure she could snap my neck with a flick of her bony wrist. That would be bad. Bad for Dumbo, bad for Ringer and Teacup, and especially bad for me. The only thing that's kept me alive is her surprise that I'm here, miles from the nearest base and in a place that won't exist at week's end.

Your fault, Zombie. You had the chance to neutralize her and you blew it.

Well. She reminded me of my grandmother.

Grandma Silencer cocks her head at my response, like a curious bird spying a tasty morsel. "Change of plans? That isn't possible."

"Air support's already been called in," I gasp, desperate to buy time. "Didn't you hear the plane?" Each second I keep her off balance is another second of life. On the other hand, telling her that bombers are on their way may be the shortest path to the quickest death.

"I don't believe that," she tells me. "I think you're a filthy little liar."

My rifle lies a couple of feet away. Very close. Too far. Again she reminds me of a bird, the way she cocks her head when she looks at me, her head tilted to one side like a damned green-eyed crow, and then I feel it—the violent thrust of an invading consciousness, *her* consciousness, ripping into me like a drill into soft wood. I feel hidden from her, nothing safe or sacred. It's like the Wonderland program, only it's not my memories she's mining, it's *me*.

"So much pain," she murmurs. "So much loss." Her fingers tighten on my throat. "Who are you looking for?"

When I refuse to answer, she cuts off my air. Black stars begin to bloom within my sight. Out of the darkness, my sister calls my name. And I think, *Christ, Sullivan, you were right*. This she-witch wouldn't have me in a chokehold if I hadn't answered that call. My sister brought me here—not Teacup, not Ringer.

My fingertips brush the stock of the rifle. The old cat-eating Silencer is laughing in my face, sour-breathed and tooth-deprived, buzz-sawing into my soul, chewing up my life as she chokes it out of me.

I can still hear my sister, but now I see Dumbo curled up behind the counter in the coffee shop, crying out for me with his eyes because he has no strength left to speak.

I go where you go, Sarge.

I left him, left him like I left my sister, alone and defenseless.

Jesus, I even took his gun.

Holy crap. The gun.

88

19

FIRST SHOT IS at point-blank range, right into her saggy, cat-filled gut.

The bullet doesn't break her hold. Unbelievably, she hangs on to my throat, squeezing. I answer with a squeeze of my own: A second shot that lands in the vicinity of her heart. Her rheumy eyes widen slightly, and I'm able to worm my arm between our bodies and push her away. Her crabby fingers around my neck loosen, and I suck in a lungful of the sweetest sour-smelling dander-infested air I've ever breathed. Grandma Silencer isn't down, though. She's just catching her second wind.

She lunges at me. I roll hard to my right. Her head smacks the wall. I fire again. The round smashes through her rib cage, but still she pushes herself from the wall and crawls toward me, hacking up wads of bright red, oxygen-rich blood. What drives that ancient body is ten thousand years old and contains more hate than the oceans hold water. Plus she's been augmented by technology that strengthens and sustains her—*psh! What's a bullet or two? Come here, sonny!* Still, I don't think it's the technology that drives her.

It's the hate.

I back up. She comes on. My heel knocks against a stack of paper and I drop to the floor with a bone-jarring thump. Her ragged claws scratch at my boot. I hold the gun with hands that are bloody at last.

Her back bows like a cat stretching on a windowsill. Her mouth opens but no sound comes out, a lot of blood, but no sound. She makes one last lunge. Her forehead knocks against the muzzle just as I squeeze the trigger.

20

I SCOOP UP my rifle—screw the pistol—and bolt from the room. Hall, stairs, bank lobby, street. Finally, back at the coffee shop, I crawl behind the counter. *You better be alive, you big-eared son of a bitch.*

He is. Fluttery pulse, shallow breath, ashy skin, but he's alive.

So now what?

Go back to the safe house? The safest option, the option of minimal risk. The one Ringer would recommend, and she's the expert on risk. Don't know what I'll find at the caverns, even if we manage to reach them: There's another Silencer out there. The odds are that Ringer and Cup are already dead, which means that I'm not only marching to my own execution, but bringing Dumbo to his.

Unless I leave him here and pick him up on my way back, assuming I make it back. Better for him, better for me. He's a burden now, a liability.

So I'll leave him behind after all. *Hey, Dumbo, I know you took a bullet for me and everything, but you're on your own, pal. I'm outta here. Isn't that how Ben Parish rolls?*

Damn it, Zombie, decide already. Dumbo knew the risk and he came anyway. Taking that bullet for you was his call. Going back means he took the bullet for nothing. If he's gonna die, at least give his death meaning.

I check the dressing for fresh bleeding. I gently lift his head and slide his rucksack beneath it for a pillow. I take the last syrette of morphine from the med kit and jab it into his forearm.

I lean down and whisper, "See, Bo, I came back." Smoothing his hair with my hand. "I got her. The infested bitch who shot you. Popped her right between the eyes." His forehead is blazing hot beneath my hand. "I can't stay here right now, Bo. But I'm coming back for you. I'm coming back or I'll die trying. Probably die, so don't get your hopes up."

I look away from him. But there's nothing else to look at. I'm all jacked up, about to lose it. I'm bouncing from one brutal death to another. Eventually, something very important inside is going to crack.

I pull his hand into mine. "Now, listen to me, you elephant-eared motherfucker. I'm gonna find Teacup and Ringer, and then we're picking you up on our way back and we're all going home together, and everything's gonna be *fine*. Because I'm the sarge and that's how I say it's gonna be. You got that? Are you listening to me, soldier? You are not allowed to die. Understand? That's a direct order. *You are not allowed to die.*"

His eyes jitter behind the lids; maybe he's dreaming. Maybe he's sitting in his room, playing *Call of Duty;* I hope so.

Then I leave him lying in coffee grounds and wads of paper napkins and scattered coins.

Dumbo's alone now and so am I, plunging into the black, dead heart of Urbana. Squad 53 is gone, broken apart, dead or missing or dying or running.

RIP, Squad 53.

21

CASSIE

I HAVE TO get this straight. Now. Like, right now. *This* being my head.

Four A.M. Jazzed up on too much chocolate (thanks, Grace) and too much Evan Walker. Or not enough Evan Walker. That's an inside joke, if you can make inside jokes in a private journal. I'll get to the private parts later. Ha! Another joke. You know you've reached a very sad place when the only person who can make you laugh is yourself.

The house is quiet, not even a whisper of wind against the boarded-up window, the silence of the void, as if the world stopped breathing and I'm the last person on Earth. *Again.* Damn, I wish there was someone I could talk to.

Ben and Dumbo are gone. All I have left are Sam, Megan, and Evan. Two are asleep in their room. The other (*Other*, ha! it's really pitiful) is awake and on watch and is someone with whom the more I talk, the more crooked my head gets. For over a month now he's been fading away. Here and then not here. Talking, then saying nothing. Mr. Spaceman staring off into space. *Damn it, Evan, where have you gone?* I think I know, but knowing why doesn't help my feelings of Evanlessness.

And somehow neither does the smell of his aftershave lingering in the room. After Ben left, Evan shaved. He washed his hair and scrubbed a week's worth of grime from his body. He even

92

trimmed his nails and addressed his neglected cuticles. When he came into this room, he looked like the old Evan, the first Evan, the Evan I believed to be a fully human Evan.

I miss that Evan, the one who pulled me frozen from the ice pack and thawed me out and made me hamburgers and pretended to be something he wasn't and hid the thing he was.

The calm, quiet, steady, reliable, strong Evan. Not this Other-Evan, the tortured, haunted, conflicted Evan who clips off his sentences as if he's afraid he'll say too much, the Evan who's already gone, already *up there*, two hundred miles up with no way back down. Not *their* Evan. *My* Evan. The imperfectly perfect guy.

Why do we always get the Evan we deserve instead of the Evan we want?

22

I DON'T KNOW why I bother writing this. No one will ever read it—and if you do, Evan, *I will murder you.*

I suppose I could turn to Bear. It was always easy to talk to him. We had hours of conversation, *good* conversation, during those weeks when it was just me and him hiding in the woods. Bear's an excellent listener. He never yawns or interrupts or walks away. Never disagrees, never plays games, never lies. *I go where you go, always,* that's Bear's jam.

Bear proves that true love doesn't have to be complicated—or even reciprocated.

93

Evan, in case you're reading this: I'm dumping you for a teddy bear.

Not that you and I were ever a couple.

I was never one of those girls who daydreamed about her wedding day or meeting the perfect guy or raising 3.2 kids in the 'burbs. When I thought about the future, it usually involved a big city and a career or living in a cabin somewhere leafy, like Vermont, writing books and taking long walks with a dog I'd name Pericles or some other random Greek name to show people how educated and cultured I was. Or maybe I'd be a doctor treating sick kids in Africa. Something meaningful. Something worthwhile that maybe somebody someday would notice and then give me a plaque or an award or name a street after me. *Sullivan Avenue. Cassiopeia Way.* Guys didn't enter into my daydreams much.

In college, I was going to have sex. Not drunken sex or sex with the first guy who asked or sex just to say *Hey, I had sex* the way people try exotic food, like, *Hey, I had fried grasshopper.* It would be with someone I cared about. Love wasn't necessary, but mutual respect and curiosity and tenderness would be nice. And he would also be someone I found attractive. Too much sex is wasted on people who aren't. Why would you sleep with someone who didn't turn you on? But people do. Or they used to. No, they probably still do.

Why am I thinking about sex?

Okay, that's insincere. That's a lie. Dear God, Cass, if you can't be honest in your own private journal, where can you be? Instead of saying what's true, you make inside jokes and sly references like one day a million years from now somebody will read this and embarrass the hell out of you.

94

Seriously.

At least when he showed up tonight, he knocked first. Evan always had an issue with boundaries. He rapped on the door, then entered in stages: head, shoulders, torso, legs. Stood there in the doorway for a minute: *Is it okay?* I noticed the change immediately: newly shaven, hair still wet, wearing a fresh pair of jeans and an Ohio State T-shirt. I can't remember the last time—or really the first time—I saw Evan exercise his Second Amendment right to bare arms.

Evan Walker has biceps. It's not important to mention this fact, as biceps are muscles most people have. I just thought I'd mention it.

I was kind of hoping for an *aw-shucks* look—I'd seen it often enough in the old farmhouse back in the day, when that was his go-to expression. Instead, I got the furrowed brow and the slightly downturned mouth and the dark, troubled eyes of a poet contemplating the void, which I guess he was—not a poet but a contemplator of the void.

I made a space for him on the bed. There was nowhere else to sit. Though we'd never done the deed, it felt like we were old lovers forced into an awkward post-split negotiation over who gets the silverware and how the souvenirs from all their trips together are going to be divvied up.

Then I smelled the Ralph Lauren aftershave.

I don't know why Grace kept a stash of men's grooming products. Maybe they belonged to the former owners of the house and she never bothered to get rid of them. Or maybe she had sex with her victims before chopping off their heads or ripping out their hearts or eating them alive like a black widow spider.

He'd nicked his chin shaving; there was a dab of white styptic stuff on the cut, a tiny mar in his otherwise otherworldly beautiful face. Which was a relief. Flawlessly beautiful people annoy the hell out of me.

"I checked on the kids," he said, as if I'd asked if he'd checked on the kids.

"And?"

"They're okay. Sleeping."

"Who's on the watch?"

He stared at me for a couple of uncomfortable seconds. Then he looked down at his hands. I looked, too. He was so perfectly put together when we met that I thought I'd lucked into the most narcissistic person left on the planet. *It makes me feel more human*, he told me, meaning grooming. Later, when I found out he wasn't quite human, I thought I understood what he was getting at. Even later—and by *even later* I mean *now*—I realized cleanliness isn't necessarily next to godliness, but it is damn near indistinguishable from humanness.

"It'll be okay," he said softly.

"No, it won't," I shot back. "Ben and Dumbo are going to die. *You're* going to die."

"I'm not going to die." Leaving out Ben and Dumbo.

"How are you getting out of the mothership once you set the bombs?"

"The same way I got in."

"The last time you took a ride in one of your little pods, you broke several bones and nearly died."

"It's a hobby," he said with a crooked smile. "Nearly dying." I looked away from his hands. The hands that lifted me when

I fell, held me when I was cold, fed me when I was hungry, healed me when I was hurt, washed me when I was covered in forest filth and blood. *You're going to destroy your entire civilization, and for what? For a girl.* You would think a sacrifice like that would make me feel just a little bit special. It didn't. It felt *weird*. Like one of us was batshit crazy and that person wasn't me.

I couldn't see a single romantic element in genocide, but maybe that's just my lack of insight into the nature of love, having never been in love. Would I wipe out humanity to save Evan? Not likely.

Of course, there's more than one kind of love. Would I kill everyone in the world to save Sam? That's not an easy question to answer.

"Those times you nearly died, you were sort of protected, though, right?" I asked. "The technology that made you superhuman—which you said crashed on the way to the hotel. You won't have that this time."

He shrugged. *There's the aw-shucks thing I thought I missed.* Seeing it again reminded me how far we'd traveled from the farmhouse, and I fought the urge to slap it off his face.

"What you're going to do—it isn't for me, or . . . it isn't *just* for me, you get that, right?"

"There's no other way to stop it, Cassie," he said. Slingshotting back to his tormented-poet look.

"What about the way you mentioned right before the last time you almost died? Remember? Rigging Megan's throat-bomb to blow it up."

"Hard to do without the bomb," he said.

"Grace didn't have a stash hidden in the house somewhere?"

Instead, she kept the place well-stocked with men's aftershave. Postapocalyptic priorities.

"Grace's assignment wasn't to blow things up. It was to kill people."

"And have sex with them." I didn't mean for that to come out—but I don't mean to say about 80 percent of what I say.

Really, though, who cares if they had sex? It's a silly thing to worry about when the fate of the planet hangs in the balance. Trivial. Unimportant. The hands that held me holding Grace. The body that warmed me warming hers. The lips that touched mine touching hers. It doesn't matter, I don't care, Grace is dead. I plucked at the sheets and wished I hadn't said it.

"Grace lied. We never—"

"I don't care, Evan," I told him. "It's not important. Anyway, Grace was a fantastically good-looking homicidal killing machine. Who could say no?"

He placed a hand over mine to still my plucking fingers. "I would tell you if we had."

What a liar. I could fill the Grand Canyon with all the things he's refused to tell me. I pulled my hand away and looked right into those chocolate-fondue-fountain eyes. "You're a liar," I said. He surprised me by nodding. "I am. But not about that."

I am? "What have you lied about?"

He shook his head. *Silly human girl!* "About who I really was."

"And who is that exactly? You've told me *what* you were, but you've never said *who* you are. Who are you, Evan Walker? Where do you come from? What did you look like before you looked like nothing? What was your planet like? Did it look like ours? Were there plants and trees and rocks and did you live in cities and what did you do for fun and was there music? Music is universal like mathematics. Can you sing me a song? Sing me an alien song, Evan. Tell me what it was like growing up. Did you go to school or was knowledge just downloaded into your brain? What were your parents like? Did they have jobs like human parents? Brothers and sisters? Sports. Start anywhere."

"We had sports." With a tiny, indulgent smile.

"I don't like sports. Start with music."

"We had music, too."

"I'm listening." I folded my arms over my chest and waited.

His mouth opened. His mouth closed. I couldn't tell if he was about to laugh or cry. "It isn't that simple, Cassie."

"I'm not expecting performance quality. I can't carry a tune, either, but that never kept me from lighting up a little Beyoncé."

"Who?"

"Oh, come on. You gotta know who she was."

He shook his head. Maybe he didn't grow up on a farm but under a rock. Then I thought it would be a little odd for a ten-thousand-year-old superbeing to have his finger on the pulse of pop culture. Still, we're talking about Beyoncé!

He's even weirder than I thought.

"Everything is different. Structurally, I mean." He pointed at his mouth, stuck out his tongue. "I can't even pronounce my own name." For a moment, the pathos was so thick, it almost snuffed out the lamp.

"Then hum something. Or whistle. Could you whistle or didn't you have lips?"

"None of that matters anymore, Cassie."

"You're wrong. It matters a lot. Your past is what you are, Evan."

Tears welled in his eyes. It was like watching chocolate melt.

"God, Cassie, I hope not." He lifted his freshly scrubbed hands, with their trimmed and buffed nails, toward me. The hands that held the gun that slaughtered innocent people before he almost murdered me. "If the past is what we are . . ."

I might have pointed out that we've all done things we aren't proud of, but that was too flippant. Even for me.

Damn it, Cassie. Why were you forcing him to think about that? I was so obsessed with the past I didn't know about that I forgot the one I did: To save the ones he had come to destroy, Evan Walker the Silencer was planning to silence an entire civilization—*his* civilization—forever.

No, Ben Parish, I thought. *Not for a girl. For the past he can't escape. For the seven billion. Your little sister, too.*

Before I knew what was happening or even how it happened, I was holding him with hands that had never comforted him, never lifted him up, never found him when he was lost. I was the taker, the recipient, always; from the moment he pulled me from that snowbank, I have been his charge, his mission, his cross. Cassie's pain, Cassie's fear, Cassie's anger, Cassie's despair. These have been the nails that impaled him.

I stroked his damp hair. I rubbed his arched back. I pressed his smooth, sweet-smelling face into my neck, and his tears were warm against my skin. He whispered something that sounded like *Mayfly.*

Heartless bitch would have been more accurate.

"I'm sorry, Evan," I whispered. "I'm so sorry."

I bowed my head; he raised his. I kissed his wet cheek. *Your pain, your fear, your anger, your despair. Give them to me, Evan. I'll carry them for a while.*

100

He reached up and ran his fingertips lightly over my lips, moist with his tears.

"'The last person on Earth,'" he murmured. "Do you remember when you wrote that?"

I nodded. "Stupid."

He shook his head. "I think that's what did it. When I read that. 'The last person on Earth'—because I felt the same way."

My hands were mauling that old OSU shirt. It was very maulable. That's a good word, *maulable*. It applies to so many things.

"You're not coming back," I said, because he couldn't say it.

His fingers combed through my hair. I shivered. *Don't do that, you bastard. Don't touch me like you'll never touch me again. Don't look at me like you'll never see me again.* I shut my eyes. Our lips touched.

The last person on Earth. With my eyes closed, I could see her walking down a wooded path in Vermont, a place she has never been and will never go, and the leaves that embrace the trail sing arias of bright red and gold. And there is a big dog named Pericles running ahead of her in that self-important way of dogs, and she has everything she ever wanted, this girl—no, this woman—nothing left behind, nothing left undone. She traveled the world and wrote books and took lovers and broke hearts. She didn't allow life just to happen to her. She punched and pummeled and beat the living shit out of it. She *mauled* it.

His breath hot in my ear. I'm clawing at his chest, digging my nails into his skin, the hungry lioness with her catch. *Resistance is futile, Walker.* I'll never take that path in the golden woods or own a dog named Pericles or travel the world. There'll be no recognition of a life well-lived, no street named after me, no difference in the world because I once occupied it. My life is a catalog of the undone and the never-will-be-done. The Others stole all of my unmade memories, but I won't let them steal this one.

My hands roamed his body, an undiscovered country, which henceforth I shall call Evanland. Hills and valleys, desert plains and forest glens, the landscape pockmarked with the scars of battle, crisscrossed by fault lines and unexpected vistas. And I am Cassie the Conquistador: The more territory I conquer, the more I want.

His chest heaved: a subterranean quake that rose to the surface like a tsunami wave. His eyes were wide and wet and filled with something that closely resembled fear.

"Cassie . . ."

"Shut up." My mouth surveying the valley beneath his rolling chest.

His fingers entangled now in my hair, "We shouldn't."

I almost laughed. *Well, the shouldn't list is awfully long, Evan.* I scored my teeth across his stomach. The land beneath my tongue quivered, shock and aftershock.

Shouldn't. No, we probably shouldn't. Some cravings can never be satisfied. Some discoveries demean the quest.

"Not the time . . . ," he gasped.

I rested my cheek on his tummy and tugged the hair from my eyes. "When is the time, Evan?"

His hands captured my roving ones and held them still.

"You said you loved me," I whispered. *Damn you, Evan Walker, why did you ever say such a ridiculous, crazy, imbecilic thing?*

No one tells you how close rage is to lust. I mean, the space between molecules is thicker. "You're a liar," I told him. "You're the worst kind of liar, the kind who lies to themselves. You're not in love with *me*. You're in love with an *idea*."

His eyes cut away. That's how I knew I nailed him. "What idea?" he asked.

"Liar, you know what idea." I got up. I pulled off my shirt. I stared him down, daring him to look at me. *Look at me, Evan. Look at me. Not the last person on Earth, the stand-in for all the people you shot on the highway. I'm not the mayfly; I'm Cassie, an ordinary girl from an ordinary place who was dumb enough or unlucky enough to live long enough for you to find. I am not your charge, your mission, or your cross.*

I am not humanity.

He turned his face toward the wall, hands beside his head as if in surrender. Well. I'd gone this far. I tugged the jeans over my hips and kicked them away. I couldn't remember a time when I was this angry—or this sad—or this . . . I wanted to punch him, caress him, kick him, hold him. I wanted him to die. I wanted *me* to die. I wasn't self-conscious, not at all, and it wasn't because he'd seen me naked before—he had.

That time I didn't have a choice. Then I'd been unconscious, close to death. Now I was awake and very much alive.

I wished there were a hundred lamps to light me up. I wanted a spotlight and a magnifying glass so he could examine every im- perfectly perfect human inch of me.

"It's not about the time, Evan," I reminded him, "but what we do with it."

23

RINGER

AT THIRTY-FIVE THOUSAND FEET, it's hard to tell which seems smaller: the Earth below or the person above it, looking down.

Due north and a couple of miles from the caverns, Constance unbuckles her harness and grabs her chute assembly from the overhead. One last check-through before the jump. We'll be inserted from this altitude to reduce the chance of being spotted from the ground. It's called a HALO insertion. *High Altitude—Low Opening*. Risky as hell, but no more risky than jumping from five thousand feet with no parachute at all.

Constance must know about my jump from the doomed chopper, because she says, "Gonna be a lot easier than last time, huh?"

I tell her to fuck off, and she grins at me. I'm glad. I want to find nothing sympathetic or likable about her. Those things might make killing her hard.

Well, harder, I'm still going to kill her.

"Thirty seconds!" the pilot's voice squawks in our ears. Constance checks my assembly. I check hers. We toss our headsets onto the seats as the rear bay door opens. Sliding our gloved fingers over the guide cable, we shuffle toward the screaming maw, the subzero wind like a fist pummeling our faces. My stomach tightens as the C-160 rocks side to side, buffeted by turbulence. I've been fighting the urge to throw up for nearly the entire flight.

Better to do it now than in freefall. If I position myself correctly, the vomit will land directly in Constance's face.

I wonder why the hub doesn't subdue my digestive system; weird, but I feel let down by a trusted friend.

I follow Constance into the black gullet of a moonless night. We won't deploy the chutes until well after we've reached terminal velocity. I can see her clearly with my enhanced vision, fifty feet farther down and off to my left. Time slows as my speed picks up; I'm not sure if that's the hub's doing or a natural reaction to falling at 120 miles per hour. I don't hear the plane. The world is wind.

Twenty thousand feet. Fifteen. Ten. I can make out a highway, rolling fields, clusters of bare-limbed trees. The closer I get, the faster they seem to rush toward me. Five thousand feet. Four. Minimum distance to ground for a safe deployment is eight hundred feet, but that's pushing the envelope.

Constance pulls her cord at eight-fifty. I'm a little below that, and the ground roars toward me like the face of a runaway locomotive.

I bend my knees on impact and duck my shoulder toward the ground, rolling twice before stopping flat on my back, tangled in cords. Constance is there before I can take my next breath, slicing me free with her combat knife. She yanks me to my feet, gives me a thumbs-up, and then takes off across the field toward a couple of silos that stand next to the ubiquitous red barn and, a stone's throw away, the white farmhouse.

White house, red barn, a narrow country lane: We couldn't have fallen into a more quintessential slice of Americana. The name of the hamlet where the caverns are? West Liberty.

I join her at the base of a silo, where she's busy stripping off her jumpsuit. Beneath it, she's wearing mom jeans and a hoodie. She has no weapon except the knife, which she tucks into a sheath strapped to her leg.

"Half a click south and west of our position," she breathes. The entrance to the caverns. "We're a couple of hours ahead of them." Zombie and whoever was crazy enough to come with him to look for me and Teacup. Poundcake, probably. My gut tightens at the thought of telling Zombie about Teacup. "You hang here and wait for my signal."

I shake my head. "I'm coming with you."

She flashes that goddamned stupid smile. "Honey, you don't want to do that."

"Why?"

"Our cover story won't fly if there's anyone around to contradict it."

The vise around my stomach tightens another turn. *Survivors. Constance is going to kill everyone she finds hiding in those caves, and that's probably a lot of people. Dozens, maybe hundreds.* It will be tough work. They'll be well-armed and wary of strangers—it's hard to imagine that anyone's unaware of the 4th Wave this late in the game. Which means I might not have to kill Constance after all. Maybe they'll do it for me.

It's a pleasant thought. Unrealistic, but pleasant. My next thought is not pleasant at all, so I blurt out the first thing that pops into my head.

"We don't need to take the caverns. We can intercept Zombie before he gets there."

Constance shakes her head. "Not our orders."

"Our orders are to rendezvous with Zombie," I argue. I'm not

106

letting this go. If I let it go, innocent people will die. I'm not to-tally against people dying—I *am* planning to kill her and Evan Walker—but this is avoidable.

"I know it bothers you, Marika," she says kindly. "That's why I'm going in solo."

"It's a stupid risk."

"You've reached a conclusion without knowing all the facts," she scolds me.

That's been a problem from the beginning—as in the beginning of human history.

My hand drops to the butt of my sidearm. She doesn't miss it. Her answering smile lights up the night.

"You know what happens if you do that," she says gently, a kindly aunt, a caring big sister. "Your friends—the ones you've come back for—how many lives are their lives worth? If a hun-dred had to die so they could live, or a thousand, or ten thousand, or ten million . . . When would you say *enough*?"

I know this argument. It's Vosch's. It's *theirs*. What are seven billion lives when existence itself is at stake? My throat burns. I can taste stomach acid in my mouth.

"It's a false choice," I answer. One last try, a plea: "You don't have to kill anyone to get Walker."

She shrugs. Apparently, I'm just not getting it. "If I don't, nei-ther of us is going to live long enough to have that chance." She lifts her chin and turns her face slightly away. "Hit me." Taps her right cheek. "Here."

Why not? The blow rocks her back on her heels. She shakes her head impatiently, turns the other cheek. "Again. Harder this time, Marika. *Hard*."

107

I hit her harder. Hard enough to break bone. Her left eye immediately begins to swell. She feels no pain from the punch. Neither do I.

"Thanks," she says brightly.

"No problem. Anything else you need busted, let me know."

She laughs softly. If I didn't know better, I'd swear she likes me, finds me charming. Then she's gone so quickly that only enhanced vision like mine could follow her, zipping across the field to the road that leads to the caverns, then cutting into the woods on the northwest side.

As soon as she's out of sight, I sink to the ground, shaky, lightheaded, my gut churning. I'm beginning to wonder if something is wrong with the 12th System. I feel like shit.

I lean against the cold metal of the silo and close my eyes. The darkness behind my lids spins around an invisible center, the singularity before the universe was born. Teacup is there, falling away from me; the blast from Razor's weapon resounds in timeless space. She falls away, but she will always be mine.

Razor is there, too, in the absolute center of absolute nothing, the blood still fresh on his arm from the self-inflicted wound, *VQP*, and he *knew* the cost of sacrificing Teacup would be his own life. I'm certain by the time we spent the night together, he'd already decided to kill her—because killing her was the only way to set me free.

Free me to do what, Razor? Endure so I can conquer what?

With my eyes still closed, I pull the combat knife from the sheath strapped to my calf. I can imagine Razor lingering in the doorway to the warehouse; the golden light from the pyre outside washing over his lean features; his eyes lost in shadow as he rolls up his sleeve. The knife in his hand then. The knife in my hand now. He probably winced when the tip broke the skin. I do not.

I feel nothing. I am cocooned in nothingness, the answer, after all, to Vosch's riddle of *why?* I can smell Razor's blood. I can't smell mine, because none breaks the surface of the wound; thousands of microscopic drones stanch the flow.

V: How do you conquer the unconquerable?

Q: Who can win when no one can endure?

P: What endures when all hope is gone?

Out of the singularity, a voice cries out. "My dear child, why do you cry?"

I open my eyes.

It's a priest.

24

AT LEAST, he's dressed like one.

Black pants. Black shirt. White collar, yellowed by sweat, spotted with rust-colored stains. He's standing just outside my reach, a small guy with a receding hairline and a pudgy, babyish face. He sees the wet knife in my hand and immediately raises his.

"I am not armed." His voice is high-pitched, as childlike as his features.

I drop the knife and draw my sidearm. "Hands on top of your head. Kneel."

He obeys instantly. I glance toward the road. *What happened to Constance?*

"I didn't mean to startle you," the little guy says, "It's just that I haven't seen another person in months. You're with the military, yes?"

"Shut up," I tell him. "Don't talk."

"Of course! I—sorry." His mouth clamps shut. His cheeks are flushed with fear or maybe embarrassment. I step behind him. He remains very still while I run my free hand over his torso.

"Where did you come from?" I ask.

"Pennsylvania—"

"No. Where did you come from just now?"

"I've been living in the caves."

"With who?"

"No one! I told you, I haven't seen anyone in months. Since November . . ."

A hard metal object in his right-hand pocket. I fish it out. A crucifix. It's seen better days. The cheap gold finish is chipped; the face of Christ has been worn down to a bald nub. I think of Sullivan's Crucifix Soldier cowering behind the beer coolers.

"Please," he whimpers. "Don't take that."

I toss the crucifix into the tall, dead grass between the silos and the barn. *Where the hell is Constance?* How did this dweeby little guy slip past her? More important, how did *I* let this dweeby little guy sneak up on me?

"Where's your coat?" I ask him.

"Coat?"

I step in front of him and level the gun at his forehead. "It's freezing. Aren't you cold?"

"Oh. Oh!" He hiccups a nervous laugh. His teeth match the rest of him: small and scruffy with grime. "I completely forgot to grab it. I was so excited when I heard that plane—I thought rescue had finally arrived!" The smile dies. "You *are* here to rescue me, aren't you?"

My finger twitches on the trigger. *Sometimes you're in the wrong place at the wrong time and what happens is nobody's fault,* I told Sullivan after hearing the story of the soldier.

"How old are you, may I ask?" he asks. "You seem much too young to be soldier."

"I'm not a soldier," I tell him. And I'm not.

I am the next step in human evolution.

I answer truthfully, "I am a Silencer."

25

HE SPRINGS TOWARD ME, an explosion of pale pink and black. A flash of tiny teeth, and the gun flies from my hand. The blow breaks my wrist. The next punch, flying faster than even my enhanced eyes can follow, hurls me six feet straight back into the silo. The metal screeches, folds around my body like a taco. Now Constance's words come home: *You've reached a conclusion without knowing all the facts.*

She wasn't going into those caves to neutralize survivors. She was going in to silence a Silencer.

Thanks, Connie. You might have told me.

The fact that I don't die on impact saves my life. The phony priest pauses, cocking his head at me in a weird, birdlike way. I

111

should be dead or at least unconscious. How is it that I'm still standing?

"My! This is . . . curious."

Neither of us moves for several seconds. I've thrown off his game. *Stall, Ringer. Wait for Constance to come back.*

If Constance comes back.

Constance may be dead.

"I'm not one of you," I say, pulling free of the metal nook. "Vosch gave me the 12th System."

His bemused expression doesn't change, but his shoulders tense. It is the only explanation that makes sense, yet it makes no sense.

"Curiouser and curiouser!" he murmurs. "Why would the commander enhance a human?"

Time to lie. The enemy taught me that great things can be accomplished by the smallest of lies.

"He's turned on you. He's given the 12th System to all of us."

He shakes his head and smiles. He knows I'm full of shit.

"And we're coming for all of you now," I go on. "*Before the pods can bring you to the ship.*"

My rifle lies on the ground a yard from his foot. I don't know where my sidearm ended up. The knife is very close, lying about halfway between us. He'll expect me to go for the knife.

Okay, so the lie doesn't seem to be working. I'll try the truth, but my hopes aren't high. "I'm probably wasting my breath here, but you should know that you're as human as I am. You're being used, just like they're using everyone else. Everything you think you know about who you are, everything you remember, is a lie. Everything."

He nods, smiling at me the way you smile at a crazy person. *That's your cue, Constance. Jump out of the shadows and plunge your knife into his back.* But Constance misses her entrance.

"I'm really at a loss," he says. "What should I do with you?"

"I don't know," I answer honestly. "What I do know is I'm going to take that knife and bleed you out like a pig."

I don't look at the knife. I know if I look, I won't stand a chance—he'll see through the ruse instantly. By not looking, I force him to look. He glances down only for a second, but a second is longer than I need.

The tip of my steel-toed boot catches him under the chin and his little body flies ten feet before thumping down hard. Before he can get his feet beneath him, the knife leaves my hand and rockets toward his throat; he bats it into the air, then catches the knife on its descent, a move so wickedly graceful, I can't help but admire it. I dive for the rifle. He beats me to it. His fist slams into my temple and I fall. My mouth smacks the ground; my upper lip splits open. *Here it comes.* Now he'll slit my throat. He'll pick up the rifle and blow my brains out. I'm a piker, an amateur, a newbie still adjusting to the augmentation he's lived with since he was thirteen.

He twists a fistful of my hair into his hand and flings me onto my back. Blood filling my mouth, I gag. He towers over me, all five feet three of him, knife in one hand, rifle in the other.

"Who *are* you?"

I spit the blood from my mouth. "My name is Ringer."

"Where are you from?"

"Well, I was born in San Francisco—"

He kicks me in the ribs. Not full force. Full force would have

113

punctured a lung or burst my spleen. He doesn't want to kill me—not yet.

"Why are you here?"

I look into his eyes and answer, "To kill you."

He flings the rifle away. It sails a hundred yards, arching over the road into the field beyond. He seizes me by the throat and hauls me into the air. My toes leave the ground. His head turns: the curious crow, the alert owl.

Against the next attack there is no defense. His consciousness lances into me, a savage thrust that rips into my mind with such force that my autonomic system shuts down. I am plunged into darkness absolute. No sound, no sight, no sensation. His mind chews through mine, and what I feel in him is a hatred wider than the universe, pure rage and utter disgust and, weird as it sounds, *envy*.

"Ahhhh," he sighs. "Who do you seek? Not the ones who were lost. A little girl, a sad, soulful boy. They died that you might live. Yes? Yes. Oh, how lonely you are. How empty!"

I'm holding Teacup against me in the old hotel, fighting to keep her warm. Razor is holding me in the bowels of the base, fighting to keep me alive. *It's a circle, Zombie, bound by fear.*

"But there is another," the priest murmurs. "Hmmm. Do you know? Have you discovered it yet?"

His soft chuckle is cut short. I know why. There's no guessing: We are one. He's dredged up Constance and that stupid, vapid soccer-mom smile.

He flings me away like he flung the rifle—disdainfully, a useless piece of human-made garbage. The hub prepares my body for impact. There's plenty of time for that while I sail through the air.

I smash into the rotten porch railing of the white farmhouse. The wood explodes with a loud wallop as the old boards crack beneath me. I lie still. The world spins.

Worse than the physical beating, though, was the pummeling of my mind. I can't think. Fragmented, disconnected images explode into being, fade, bloom again. Zombie's smile. Razor's eyes. Teacup's scowl. Then Vosch's face, cut from stone, massive as a mountain, and the eyes that pierce to the very bottom, that see everything, that *know* me.

I roll onto my side. My stomach heaves. I throw up on the porch steps until there's nothing left in my stomach, and then I throw up some more.

You have to get up, Ringer. If you don't get up, Zombie's lost.

I try to stand. I fall.

I try to sit up. I keel over.

The Silencer priest felt them inside me—I thought they were gone, I thought I had lost them, but you never lose those who love you, because love is a constant; love endures.

Someone's arms are lifting me up: Razor's.

Someone's hands steady me: Teacup's.

Someone's smile is giving me hope: Zombie's.

I should have told him when I had the chance how much I love the way he smiles.

I rise.

Razor lifting, Teacup steadying, Zombie smiling.

You know what you do when you can't stand up and march, soldier? Vosch asks. *You crawl.*

26

ZOMBIE

NORTH OF URBANA, the old highway cuts through farm country, the fallow fields on either side glowing silver-gray in the brilliant starlight, the burned-out shells of the farmhouses black freckles against the sheen. The caverns lie nine miles as the crow flies to the northeast, but I'm no crow; I'm not leaving this highway and risking getting lost. If I keep up the pace without stopping to rest, I should reach the target before dawn.

That'll be the easy part.

Superhuman assassins who can look like anyone—for example, a sweet, hymn-singing senior citizen. Little kids who wander near encampments and hideouts with bombs embedded in their throats. Doesn't exactly encourage hospitality to strangers.

There'll be sentries, hidden bunkers, snipers' nests, maybe a vicious German shepherd or a Doberman or two, trip wires, booby traps. The enemy has blown apart the fundamental glue that binds us together, turning every outsider into the intolerable *other*. That's funny, the sick type of funny: After the aliens arrived, *we* became aliens.

Which means the odds of them shooting me on sight are pretty high. Like in the 99.9 percent neighborhood.

Oh, well. YOLO, right?

I've looked at the little map printed on the back of the brochure so many times, it's burned into my memory like an after-image. US 68 north to SR 507. SR 507 east to SR 245. Then a half mile north and you're there. Easy-peasy, no problemo. Three to four hours quick-stepping on an empty stomach with no rest or sleep and sunrise coming.

I'll need time to reconnoiter. I have no time. I'll need a game plan of how to approach a hostile sentry. I have no plan. I'll need the right words to convince them I'm one of the good guys. I have no words. All I've got is my winning personality and a killer smile.

At the corner of 507 and 245 there's a waist-high sign with a big rust-colored arrow pointing north: Ohio Caverns. The ground rises; the road arches toward the stars. I adjust my eyepiece and scan the woods on the left for green glow. I drop to my belly shy of the hillcrest and crawl the rest of the way to the top. A paved access road winds through more trees toward a cluster of buildings, tiny black smudges against gray. Fifty yards away are two stone markers with white signs mounted on top of each: OC.

I inch forward the way we were taught in camp, low-crawl-style: face in the dirt, rifle in one hand, the other extended forward. At this pace, I won't reach the caverns until well after my twenty-first birthday, but that's preferable to not being alive to celebrate it. Every few feet I pause to lift my head and scan the terrain. Trees. Grass. A snarl of downed power lines. Trash. A single, tiny tennis shoe lying on its side.

After another hundred yards—and a hundred years later—my outstretched fingers brush metal. I don't lift my head; I drag the object in front of my face.

A crucifix.

A chill goes down my spine. *I didn't have time to think,* Sullivan told me. *I saw the light glinting off the metal. I thought it was a gun. So I killed him. Over a crucifix, I killed him.*

I wish she'd never told me that story. If I didn't know better, I'd

117

consider finding a random crucifix in the dirt to be a good sign. I might even hang on to it for luck. Instead, it feels like a big black cat crossing my path. I leave Jesus lying in the dirt.

Scooch, scooch, pause. Look. *Scooch, scooch,* pause. Look. I can see buildings now, a gift shop and welcome center, the remnants of a stone well. Beyond the buildings, weaving between the tree-shaped gashes in the dark, is a thumbnail-sized, fiery green blob of light headed straight toward me.

I freeze. I'm totally exposed. No place to take cover. The blob grows larger, edging along the front of the welcome center now. I rise to my elbows and sight him through the scope of the M16. He's such a little guy that at first I think he's a kid. Black pants, black shirt, and a collar that in better days was white.

Looks like I've found the owner of the crucifix.

I should probably shoot him before he sees me.

Oh, how stupid. What a dumb idea. Shoot him and you'll have the whole encampment on your ass. Fire only if you're fired upon. You're here to save people, remember?

The man in black with the green blobby head disappears around the corner of the building. I count the seconds. When I reach 120 and he hasn't reappeared, I high-crawl it to the nearest tree, where I brush the dead grass and dirt from my face and try to collect my breath and my thoughts, in that order. I do better on the breath part.

I'm getting now why Vosch passed over Ringer to promote me to squad leader. She was definitely the wiser choice: smarter than me, a better shot, sharper instincts. But I got the nod instead because I had one thing that she didn't: blind loyalty to the cause, and unflinching faith in its leader. Okay, that's actually *two* things. Whatever. My point is that faith trumps smarts every time. Guts beat brains. At least that's true if you want an army of misguided, suicidal buffoons willing to sacrifice their lives so the enemy doesn't have to.

Can't hide here forever. And I didn't leave Dumbo behind so he could die while I hid with my thumb up my ass waiting for an idea to spring forth in this Cro-Magnon brain I've been blessed with.

What I really need, I decide, is a hostage.

Of course, that idea comes five minutes after the perfect candidate disappears.

I peek around the tree toward the welcome center. Nothing. I haul ass to the closest tree, stop, drop, peek. Nothing. Two trees later and about fifty yards closer, I still don't see him. He probably just found a private place to take a leak. Or he's already below, safe and warm and telling Ringer all's clear topside while he gently rocks Teacup to sleep.

I've been having fantasies about these caves since Ringer left, minus the priest, in which she and Teacup stay warm and dry and well-fed throughout this endless goddamned winter. I think about what I'll say when I finally see her. What she'll say to me. How the perfectly dropped phrase might finally make her smile. There's a part of me that's convinced this everlasting war will end when I coax a smile out of that girl.

Okay, I decide, forget the priest. That welcome center has to be manned. I might end up with half a dozen hostages instead of one, but beggars can't be choosers. I need to get into those caves ASAP.

I scan the terrain, plot my route, mentally rehearse the assault. I have one flash grenade left. I have the element of surprise.

119

Surprise is good. I have my rifle and Dumbo's sidearm. Probably will not be enough. I'll be outgunned, which means I will die. Which means Dumbo will die.

There's a single window facing me. I'll smash it with the butt of my rifle, toss the grenade, and then hoof it around the building to the front door. Six seconds, tops. They won't know what hit them.

That'll be my story, anyway, when I tell my grandkids about this day: I was so focused on the window, I forgot to look where I was going.

I wish I had another explanation for how I fell into that damn hole, six feet wide and twice as deep, a hole you couldn't miss, even in the dark, not only because of its size but because of what it contained.

Bodies.

Hundreds of bodies.

Big bodies, little bodies, medium-sized bodies. Clothed bodies, half-clothed bodies, naked bodies. Freshly dead bodies and bodies not-so-freshly dead. Whole bodies and body parts and parts that used to be inside bodies but no longer were.

I went down to my hips into the slimy, reeking mass, and my feet found no bottom—I just kept . . . sinking. Nothing to grab hold of except bodies, which slid down with me. I came face-to-face with a fresh one as I sank—like a *really* fresh one, a woman in her thirties, her blond hair caked in dirt and blood, two black eyes, one cheek swollen to the size of my fist, her skin still pink, her lips plump. She couldn't have been more than a few hours dead.

I twist away. I'd rather face a dozen rotted faces than one that looks that alive.

I'm shoulder-deep by this point and still being sucked under.

I'm going to be suffocated by human remains. I'm going to drown in death. It's so ridiculously metaphorical, I nearly bust out laughing.

That's when the fingers lock around my neck.

Then her definitely-not-corpse-cold lips against my ear: "Don't make a sound, Ben. Play dead."

Ben? I try to turn my head. No way. Her grip is too strong.

"We've got one shot," the voice whispers. "So don't move. It knows where we are now and it's *coming*."

27

A SHADOW RISES at the pit's edge, silhouetted against the blaze of stars overhead, a small figure, its head cocked to one side, listening. I don't even think about it: I hold my breath and go limp, watching him through slitted lids. He's holding a familiar-looking object in his right hand. A KA-BAR combat knife, standard issue to all recruits.

The woman's fingers loosen on my throat. She's gone limp, too. Who do I trust? Her, him, neither?

Thirty seconds pass, a minute, pushing two. I don't move. She doesn't move. He doesn't move. I won't be able to hold my breath—or put off the decision—much longer. I'll have to take either a breath or a shot—at *somebody*. But my arms are entangled with dead ones, and anyway, I lost the rifle when I fell. I don't even know where it landed.

He does, though, the priest who traded his crucifix for a knife.

"I see your rifle, son," he says. "Come on up. There's nothing to fear. They're all dead and I'm completely harmless." He kneels at the edge of the ossuary and holds out his empty hand. "Don't worry, you can have your rifle back. I don't like guns. I never have."

He smiles. Then the not-dead lady's got him by the wrist. Then he's flying into the pit with us and then there's Dumbo's sidearm against his temple and her voice saying, "Then you're gonna hate this," and then the priest's head explodes.

Not sure, but I think that's my cue to get the hell out of that hole.

28

I'VE LOST MY RIFLE. And somehow the not-dead lady ended up with the pistol. I have no idea if she saved my life or just started with the priest and I'm next.

Pushing and clawing your way out of a mass grave wasn't something they covered in camp. Because under normal circumstances, if you find yourself neck-deep in dead people, the odds are you're probably one yourself.

"I'm not going to hurt you," she says. She smiles broadly, and that's gotta hurt with a broken cheek.

"Then drop the gun."

She does, immediately. She holds up her empty hands.

"How do you know my name?" I ask. More of a shout, really.

"Marika told me."

"Who the hell is Marika?" I scoop up the pistol. She makes no move to stop me.

"The girl standing behind you."

I pivot quickly to the left, keeping her in my peripheral vision. There's nobody behind me.

"Look, lady, I'm having a really bad day. Who are you and who was that little guy you just killed and where is Teacup? Where's Ringer?"

"I told you, Zombie." With a trilling little laugh. "She's *behind* you."

I raise the gun to the level of her eyes. I'm not scared or confused anymore. I'm just pissed. I don't know if she's the Silencer of the caverns and I really don't care. I'm killing every stranger in my path until I find somebody who isn't one.

I know what's what. Jesus Christ, of course I know. I knew it before I left the safe house. It's all been for nothing, *nothing*. Dumbo's going to die for nothing, because Ringer is nothing. She's lying in that tangle of bodies, a raven-haired, smile-less nothing, along with Teacup, both of them nothing, like the seven billion other nothings busy breaking down into random molecules of nothing. And I'm going to help. I'm going to do my part. I'm going to murder every dumbass stupid bastard who's unlucky enough to cross my path.

They wanted a mindless, stone-cold killer to let loose on the world. They wanted a zombie. Now they've got one.

I take aim at that silly, smiling, busted-up face and squeeze the trigger.

29

RINGER

I'M PROBABLY going to regret this.

Keeping Constance around is like finding a viper in bed with your kids. Going after it risks hurting the kids more than the snake.

So I almost let Zombie do it. It was tempting. But a millisecond before the bullet exits the barrel, I ram my open palm into his elbow, throwing off the shot. His gun is in my hand by the time the report sounds.

He whirls around, his hand balled into a fist, which is aimed at my head. I catch it.

Zombie's shoulder jerks on impact—as if he's punched a brick wall—and then his mouth drops open and his eyes grow wide with astonishment and disbelief, a reaction so clichéd and predictable, he almost does it: He almost gets me to smile.

Almost.

"Ringer?" he says.

I nod. "Sergeant."

His knees wobble. He falls into me and presses his face against my neck, and over his shoulder I can see Constance smiling at us. I'm not sure who's holding up whom at this point.

Using the 12th System, I pour myself into him. Where there is pain, I give comfort. Where there is fear, hope. Where there is rage, peace.

"It's all right," I tell him, looking at Constance. "She's with me. You're safe now, Zombie. We're all perfectly safe."

My first lie to him. It won't be the last.

30

HE PULLS OUT of my arms. His eyes wander over the starlit fields, the road beyond, the bare, uplifted arms of the trees. He wants to ask but doesn't want to, either. I tense, waiting for the question. Is it cruel to make him say it aloud?

"Teacup?"

I shake my head.

He nods. Lets out the deep breath he's holding. Finding me was a kind of miracle, and when one miracle happens, you expect another.

"The little shit," he mutters. Looking away. Fields, road, trees. "She snuck off on me, Ringer." He gives me a hard look. "How?"

I say the first thing that pops into my head. "One of *them*." I nod toward the pit. The second lie. "We've been dodging them all winter." The third. It's like I've jumped off a cliff—or pushed Zombie off. With each lie, he recedes from me, accelerating as we fall.

"But not Cup." He steps over to the pit and stares into the mass of decomposing remains. "Is she in here?"

Constance jumps into the conversation; I'm not sure why. "No. We gave her a proper burial, Ben."

125

Zombie looks at her. Glowering. "Who. The fuck. Are you?"

Her smile expands. "My name is Constance. Constance Pierce. I'm sorry. I know we've never met, but it feels like I know you. You're practically all Marika talks about."

He stares at her for a second. "Marika," he echoes.

"That would be me," I tell him.

Now staring at me. "You never told me your name was Marika."

"You never asked."

"I never . . . ?" He hiccups a humorless laugh and shakes his head. Then, without another word, he drops into the pit. I rush to the edge, thinking he's lost his mind, gone Dorothy, that Teacup's death was the final, tiny straw that broke his back. Why else would he jump in there? Then I see him grab his rifle, sling it over his shoulder, and crawl back to the edge. We lock our fingers around each other's wrists and I pull him out.

"Where're the others?" he demands.

"Others?" That loaded word.

"Survivors. Are they in the caves?"

I shake my head. "There are no other survivors, Zombie."

"Just Marika and me," Constance chirps. Why does she have to be so goddamned *cheerful*?

Zombie ignores her. "Dumbo's been shot," he informs me. "I left him in Urbana. Let's go."

He brushes past me and strides toward the road without looking back. Constance is watching me.

"My! Isn't he a cutie?"

I tell her to fuck off.

126

31

I FALL IN next to him. Constance trails several yards behind—out of normal human earshot, but Constance isn't a normal human. Zombie walks with shoulders hunched, head thrust forward, eyes darting up, down, side to side. The road stretches before us, cutting across rolling farmland that will never be farmland again.

"What Teacup did was her choice," I say. "Not your fault, Zombie."

A sharp shake of his head, then: "Why didn't you come back?"

Deep breath. Time to lie again. "Too risky."

"Yeah. Well. It's all about the risk, isn't it?" Then: "Poundcake is dead."

"Impossible." *I saw the surveillance tape. I counted the people in the safe house. If Poundcake's dead, who's the extra person?*

"Impossible? Really?" he says. "How do you figure?"

"What happened?"

He waves his hand at me like he's brushing away a gnat. "Had a little trouble after you left. Long story. Short story: Walker found us. Vosch found us. A Silencer found us. Then Cake blew himself up." His eyes close briefly, snap open again. "We rode out the rest of the winter in the dead Silencer's safe house. We have four days left, which is why Bo and I decided to come for you." He swallows. "Why *I* decided."

"Four days left till what?"

He glances at me, and the smile that crawls across his face is frightening. "The end of the world."

32

THEN HE TELLS ME what happened in Urbana.

"How about that, huh?" he asks. "My first kill of the war, and it's some random old cat lady."

"Except she wasn't random and wasn't a cat lady."

"I never saw so many cats."

"Cat ladies don't eat their pets."

"Handy food supply, though. You'd think after a while the cats would get wise."

He sounds like the old Zombie, the one I left behind in that rat-infested hotel wearing a ridiculous yellow hoodie while he flirted with me. The voice is right but the appearance is wrong: restless, sleep-deprived eyes, downturned, grayish mouth, cheeks camouflaged in dried blood. He glances back at Constance, then ducks his head slightly and lowers his voice. "So what's her story?"

"The typical one," I begin. Here comes lie number five. "Rode out the plague in Urbana, then headed north to the caves after her family was gone. She guesses over two hundred people were holed up down there by the first snow of the season. Then the priest showed up. Around Christmas," I add, a nicely ironic detail. You can't have a good story without one or two of those.

"Nobody caught on at first. Someone goes missing one night, well, maybe they panicked and hit the road. One day, they wake up and realize over half the population is gone. You know what happened next, Zombie. Paranoia. People forming factions, alliances. Your basic tribal response. This person is accused. That

128

person. Fingers pointing everywhere, and in the middle of it all, this priest trying to keep the peace."

I rattle on. Adding detail, nuance, a snatch of dialogue here and there. I'm surprised by how effortlessly the bullshit flows from my mouth. Lying is like murder—after the first one, each one that follows is easier.

Eventually, inevitably, the priest is found out for the Silencer he is. Mayhem ensues. By the time the survivors realize they're no match for him, it's too late. Constance barely manages to escape, returning to Urbana and skipping from abandoned house to abandoned house, by dumb luck staying in an area between the cat lady's territory and the priest's—a place that's rarely patrolled by either of them.

"That's where we found each other," I tell him. "She warned me off the caverns, and ever since then we've been—"

"Teacup," he snaps. He doesn't give a shit about The Adventures of Constance and Ringer. "Tell me about Teacup."

"She found me," I say without thinking. The truth. Now for the next lie. Sixth? Seventh? I've lost count. This lie to shift the burden from his hunched shoulders onto the ones to which it belonged. "Just south of Urbana. I didn't know what to do. Didn't want to risk bringing her back. Didn't want to risk taking her with me. Then that choice was taken away."

"Cat lady," he breathed.

I nod, relieved. "Just like Dumbo, only Teacup wasn't so lucky." *See, Zombie, I'm the one who lost her—and you're the one who avenged her.* Not exactly absolution but the nearest I can give him.

"Tell me it was quick."

"It was quick."

"Tell me she didn't suffer."

"She didn't suffer."

He turns his head and spits on the side of the road. A bad taste in his mouth. "A couple of days, you said. 'I'll scope them out and be back in a couple of days.'"

"I don't make the rules, Zombie. The odds—"

"Oh, take the odds and stuff them up your ass. You should have come back. Your place is with us, Ringer. We're all you've got and you left us."

"That's not what happened and you know it."

He stops suddenly. Beneath the rust-colored mask, his face is a deeper red. "You don't run from the people who need you. You fight for them. You fight *beside* them. No matter the cost. No matter the *risk*." He spits out the word. "I thought you understood that. You told me in Dayton that you did. You said you were an expert on what matters, and I guess you are, if what matters is saving yourself while the rest of the world burns."

I don't say anything because he isn't talking to me. I am the mirror.

"You shouldn't have left," he goes on. "We needed you. If you hadn't left, Teacup would still be alive. And if you'd come back, Poundcake might be alive. Instead, you decided to hang out with a total stranger, to hell with us, and now Dumbo's blood is on your hands, too." He jabs a finger at my face. "If he dies, it's *your* fault. Dumbo came looking for *you*."

"Hey, kids, is everything all right?" Constance, her smile withered to a concerned grin.

"Oh, sure," Zombie says. "We were just discussing where we should go for dinner. Chinese sound good to you?"

"Well, it's closer to breakfast," Constance answers brightly. "I could really go for some pancakes."

Zombie looks at me. "She's fun. What a blast you must have had this winter."

Constance's worried grin disappears. Her bottom lip quivers. Then she bursts into tears and flops down on the asphalt, resting her elbows on her knees and burying her broken face in her hands.

Zombie takes in the act for a long, uncomfortable moment.

I know what she's doing: The best hammer to break the bonds of distrust is natural human sympathy. Pity has killed more people than hate.

When the last day comes for Zombie, it won't be another person who betrays him; it will be his heart.

He glances at me. *What's with this woman?*

I shrug. *Who knows?* My apathy fuels his pity, and he gives in to it, squatting beside her.

"Hey, look, I was being an asshole, I'm sorry."

Constance mutters something that sounds like *pancakes*. Zombie touches her shoulder gently. "Hey, Connie . . . It's Connie, right?"

"Con-stan-stan . . ."

"Constance, right. I have a friend, Constance. He's hurt pretty bad and I need to get back to him. Now." Rubbing her shoulder. "Like, right now."

It makes me sick to my stomach. I turn away. Across the eastern horizon a slash of garish pink glows. Another day closer to the end.

"I just—I just don't know—how much more—I can take . . ." Constance is moaning, on her feet now and leaning her whole body into Zombie's, a hand on his shoulder, a not-so-young-and-fair

131

damsel in distress. If I had to give Constance a nom de guerre, I would pick *Cougar*.

Zombie gives me a look: *A little help here?*

"Of course you can take more," I say to her, my stomach still churning. I wish the hub would get a grip on my gut. "And then you're gonna take a little more, then a little more, and after that a little more." I pull her off him, not gently. She snuffles loudly, pouring it on.

Oh dear God.

"Please don't be mean to me, Marika," she whimpers. "You're always so *mean*."

"Here," Zombie says, taking her arm. "She can walk with me. You should be covering the rear anyway, Ringer."

"Oh yes," Constance purrs. "Cover the rear, Marika."

The world spins. The ground heaves. I stumble a couple feet off the road and double over, at which point everything in my stomach comes out in a violent gush.

A hand on my back: Zombie's. "Hey, Ringer—what the hell?"

"I'm okay," I gasp, shrugging off his hand. "Must be the under-cooked rabbit." Another lie and not even a necessary one.

33

MIDMORNING, DOWNTOWN URBANA, under a cloudless sky, the temperature in the midforties. You can feel it coming. *Spring*.

Zombie and Constance rush into the coffee shop while I cover the street. From the doorway, I hear Zombie's startled cry, and then he's skittering back to me across the treacherous coffee-bean-covered floor.

"What?"

He pushes past me and lurches onto the street, whipping right, then left, then back again. Constance comes over and says, "Apparently the kid's gone."

In the middle of Main Street, Zombie throws back his head and howls Dumbo's name. As if in mockery, the echo ricochets back at him.

I trot over to his side. "Screaming probably isn't a good idea, Zombie."

His response is a wide-eyed, uncomprehending stare. Then he turns and races down the street, calling his name over and over, *Dumbo! Dumbo!* and *Dumbo, you dumbass, where are you?* He loops back to us after a couple of blocks, out of breath and shaking with panic.

"Somebody took him."

"How do you know?" I ask.

"You're right, I don't. Thanks for the reality check, Ringer. He probably got up and ran all the way to the safe house, except for the inconvenient fact that he was *shot in the back*."

I ignore the sarcasm. "I don't think anyone took him, Zombie."

He laughs. "That's right. I forgot. You're the one with the answers. Come on, the suspense is killing me. What happened to Dumbo, Ringer?"

"I don't know," I answer. "But I don't think anyone took him because there's nobody left to do the taking. Your cat lady would have seen to that."

I start off down the street. He watches me for a few seconds, then shouts at my back, "Where the hell are you going?"

133

"The safe house, Zombie. Didn't you say it was south on Highway 68?"

"*Unbelievable!*" He erupts in a torrent of curses. I keep walking. Then he shouts: "What the hell happened to you out here, anyway? Where's the Ringer who told me that *everyone* matters?"

"*Mean,*" Constance whispers to him. I hear her clearly. "I told you."

I keep walking.

Five minutes later, I find Dumbo crumpled at the base of a barricade that stretches from sidewalk to sidewalk across Main. That he made it this far—nearly ten blocks from where he was hit—is extraordinary. I kneel beside him and press my fingers against his neck. I whistle loudly. When Zombie comes sprinting to the scene, he's out of breath and ready to collapse. So is Constance, except her exhaustion is an act.

"How the hell did he get here?" Zombie wonders aloud. He looks around wildly.

"The only way he could," I answer. "He crawled."

34

ZOMBIE DOESN'T ASK why Dumbo would drag himself ten blocks in great pain and with a bullet in his back. He doesn't ask because he knows the answer. Dumbo wasn't fleeing danger or looking for help: Dumbo was looking for his sarge.

It's more than Zombie can handle. He falls against the side of the barricade, gulping air, his face lifted up to the sky. Lost, found, dead, alive, the cycle repeats; there's no escape, there's no reprieve. Zombie closes his eyes and waits for his breath to slow, his heart to steady. A small break before it begins again: the next loss, the next death.

It's always been this way, I wanted to tell him. We bear the unbearable. We endure the unendurable. We do what must be done until we ourselves are undone.

I scooch next to Dumbo and lift up his shirt. The bandage is soaked. The packing beneath the bandage is saturated. If he wasn't bleeding out before, he is now. I press my hand onto his ashen cheek. His skin is cool, but I am going deeper than the skin. I am going into *him*. Beside me, Constance watches; she knows what I'm doing.

"Is it too late?" she whispers.

Dumbo feels me inside him. His eyelids flutter, his lips part, and breath roils from his open mouth. In the dwindling twilight of his consciousness, a question, an aching need. *I go where you go.*

"Zombie," I murmur. "Say something to him."

"Tell him he made it, Zombie. Tell him he found you."

To live, Dumbo would need a massive blood transfusion. He won't get one.

But he didn't crawl ten blocks in blistering pain for that. That isn't why he held on.

"Tell him he made it, Zombie. Tell him he found you."

There is a light that glimmers along the darkening edge of an infinite horizon. In that light the heart finds what the heart seeks. In that light, Dumbo goes where his beloved Zombie goes. In that light, a boy named Ben Parish finds his baby sister. In that light,

Marika saves a little girl called Teacup. In that light are promises kept, dreams realized, time redeemed.

And Zombie's voice, speeding Dumbo toward the light: "You made it, Private. You found me."

No darkness slamming down. No endless fall into lightlessness. All was light when I felt Dumbo's soul break the horizon.

Lost, found, and all was light.

III

THE THIRD DAY

35

ZOMBIE

I WON'T LEAVE Dumbo to rot where he fell. I won't leave him for the rats and the crows and the blowflies. I will not burn him, either. I will not abandon his bones to be picked over and scattered by vultures and vermin.

I will dig a grave for him in the cold, stubborn earth. I will bury his med kit with him, but no rifle. Dumbo was not a killer; he was a healer. He saved my life twice. No, three times. I have to count his telling Ringer where to shoot me that night in Dayton.

There are dozens of faded flags stuck throughout the barricade. I will mark his grave with them. The fabric will fade to white. The wooden dowels will fall and slowly decay. Or, if Walker fails to blow up the mothership, the bombs that are coming will leave nothing behind—no flags, no grave, no Dumbo.

Then the earth will settle and grass will grow over my friend, covering him in a blanket of vivid green.

"Zombie, there's no time," Ringer informs me.

"There's time for this."

She doesn't put up another argument. I'm sure there are about twelve she could whip out, but she holds back.

It's past noon by the time I'm finished. Dear Christ, it's turned into a beautiful goddamned day. We sit by the mound of freshly turned dirt and I pull out the rest of my power bars to share. Ringer takes a few tiny bites, then shoves the rest into her jacket pocket.

"The rabbit?" I ask.

She grunts a nonanswer. The woman named Constance gobbles down her bar. Speaking of rabbits: Her eyes dart around like one's, nose twitching as if she's sniffing the air for danger. Dumbo's rifle lies on the ground beside her. She refused to take it at first. Said she had a problem with guns. Like, for real? How'd she live this long?

The other odd thing: Father Silencer had said something very similar about guns—right before Constance blew his head off with mine.

"Anybody want to say something?" I ask.

"I hardly knew him," Ringer answers.

"I didn't know him at all," Constance says. Maybe she thinks that sounded harsh, because she adds, "Poor thing."

"He was from Pittsburgh. He loved the Packers. Video games. He was a gamer." I took a breath. Damn. Didn't seem like much. Nothing, really. "Call of Duty. Borderline MLG."

And Ringer goes, "Irony."

"I'm sure he was a very sweet boy," Constance chimes in.

I shake my head. "I didn't even know his real name." Then to Ringer: "It's just you and me now."

"What do you mean?"

"Squad 53. We're the last." I snap my fingers. "Christ, I forgot Nugget. Three, then. Who would have thought it, huh, back in the day? That it'd be down to the three of us. Well, I would have put my money on you. Not that money means anything anymore. Or my judgment. Nugget, Jesus, that kid's indestructible. But me?

142

Never. Never in a million years. I should have died so many times, I've lost count."

"You're here for a *purpose*." Constance leans toward me and points at my chest. "There's a special place in his plan for you."

"Whose plan? Vosch's?"

"God's!" She looks at Ringer, then back at me. "A place for *all* of us."

I'm looking at the mound of dirt at my feet. "What was *his* place? What purpose did God have for Dumbo? Take the bullet for me so I could get on to my purpose, whatever the hell that is?"

"I think you're right, Zombie," Ringer says. "It doesn't have meaning. It's just luck."

"Right. Luck. His bad. My good. Like stumbling onto Constance hiding in that pit and then you stumbling into both of us."

"Yes. Like that." Blank-faced.

"Talk about beating the odds. You know what it's like, Ringer?"

"What is it like, Zombie?" Her voice, too—blank, without inflection, without emotion.

"One of those *no way* moments in movies. You know what I'm talking about. The thing that makes you shake your head and go *no way*. The good guys showing up in the nick of time. The bad guys suddenly getting a case of the stupids. Ruins it for you. Wrecks it all to shit. The real world doesn't work that way."

"It's the movies, Zombie," Ringer says. Holding herself very still. She knows where this is going. She *knows*. I've never met anyone smarter. Or scarier. Something about this girl scares the living crap out of me. Always has, from the first day I saw her in camp, watching me do knuckle push-ups in the yard until the blood pooled beneath my hands. The way she looks at you, flaying you open like a fish on the cutting block. And *cold*. Not the

143

cold of a walk-in freezer or the cold of this never-ending fucking winter. The cold of dry ice. The cold that burns.

"Oh, the movies!" Constance cries softly. "How I miss the movies!"

I've had enough. I am done. I level my sidearm at Constance's head.

"Touch that rifle and I will kill you. Move one inch and you will die."

36

THE WOMAN'S MOUTH drops open. Her hands fly to her chest. She starts to say something and I hold up my free hand.

"And no talking. Talking will also get you killed." To Ringer, but keeping my eye on Constance: "You can come clean now. Who is this person?"

"I told you, Zombie—"

"You're good at a lot of things, Ringer, but you suck at lying. Something's seriously twisted here. Tell me what it is and I won't waste her."

"I'm being honest. You can trust her."

"The last person I trusted threw cat stew in my face."

"Then don't trust her. Trust *me*."

I look at her. Blank face, dead eyes, and the coldness that burns. "Zombie, I would never lie to you," Ringer says. "Without Constance, I wouldn't have made it through the winter."

"Yeah, tell me how you did that. Tell me how you survived an entire winter in the most obvious hiding place inside a Silencer's territory without freezing to death, starving to death, or getting knifed to death. Tell me."

"Because I know what needs to be done."

"Huh? What the hell does that even mean?"

"I swear to you, Zombie, she's okay. She's one of us."

The gun is shaking. That's because my hand is. I bring up the other to support my wrist.

Constance is giving Ringer a look. "Marika."

"Okay, now that's another thing!" I shout. "You would never tell her your name, not in a million years. Shit, you wouldn't even tell *me*."

Ringer slides into the space between me and Constance. Her eyes are not so dead now, her face not so masklike. I've seen the look once before, in Dayton, when she whispered, *Ben, we're the 5th Wave*, determined to convince me, desperate for me to believe.

"How do you know she's one of us, Ringer?" I ask. Well, more like beg. "How *can* you know?"

"Because I'm alive," she answers. She holds out her hand.

The safest thing—for me, for her, for the people I left behind in the safe house—is to ignore Ringer and kill the stranger. I have no choice. Which means I have no responsibility. I can't be blamed for following the rules that the enemy set down.

"Step aside, Ringer."

She shakes her head. Her dark bangs slide back and forth.

"Not going to happen, Sergeant."

Her dark unblinking eyes, her mouth firmly set, her whole body leaning toward me, and her hand waiting for the weapon that quivers in mine. I risked everything to rescue her and damn if she isn't risking it to save me.

The Others have loosed more than one kind of Silencer on the world, more than one kind of infested. I feel him inside me, the one who would rip my soul in two. And they didn't need to come a gazillion light-years to bring him here. He's always been there, inside, the Silencer Within.

"What's happening to us, Ringer?"

She nods: She knows exactly where I'm coming from. Always has.

"We still have a choice," she answers. "They want us to believe we don't, but it's a lie, Zombie. Their biggest one."

Behind her, Constance whimpers, "I am human."

That's how it'll go down. Those will be the last words of the last one left. I am human.

"I don't even know what that means anymore," I say to Ringer, to myself, to nobody at all.

But I drop the gun into Ringer's open hand.

37

SAM

THE FRONT DOOR flew open and Cassie lunged in from the porch, holding her rifle.

"Sam! Quick, go wake up Evan. Someone's—"

He didn't wait for the rest. He raced down the hall to Evan's room. Zombie had come back; Sam was sure of it.

Evan wasn't asleep. He was sitting up in bed, staring at the ceiling.

"What is it, Sam?"

"Zombie's back."

Evan shook his head. *How could that be?* Then he slid from the bed, grabbed his rifle, and followed Sam down the hall and into the living room.

And Cassie was saying, "What do you mean, Dumbo's gone?"

There was Zombie and Ringer and a stranger in the room with Cassie. Dumbo wasn't there. Teacup wasn't there.

"He's dead," Ringer answered, and Sam asked, "Teacup, too?"

And Ringer nodded. *Teacup, too.*

Behind him, Evan Walker asked, "Who is this?" He was talking about the stranger, a blond older lady with a nice face, about the age of Sam's mother when she died.

"She's with me," Ringer said. "She's okay."

The lady was looking at Sam. She was smiling. "My name is Constance. And you must be Sam. Private Nugget. It's very nice to meet you."

She held out her hand. His daddy taught him to always shake hands firmly. *A good, strong grip, Sam my man, but don't squeeze too hard.*

The smiling lady did, though—very hard. She yanked Sam into her chest, wrapping an arm around his neck, and then he felt the end of a gun pressing against his temple.

147

38

"THIS IS GOING to go smooth and easy," the lady yelled over the jumbled-up shouts of Zombie and Cassie. *"Smooth and easy,"* Zombie was looking at Ringer, who was looking at Evan Walker, and Cassie was looking at Ringer, too, and then his sister said, "You bitch."

"Weapons, over there," the lady said. Her voice still had a smile in it. "Stack 'em by the fireplace. *Now."*

They disarmed, one by one. Cassie said, "Don't hurt him."

"Nobody's getting hurt, sweetheart," the lady said, smiley-voiced. "Where's the other one?"

"The other what?" Cassie asked.

"Human. There's one more. Where is it?"

"I don't know what you're—"

"Cassie," Evan Walker said. But he was looking over Sam's head at the lady's face. "Go get Megan."

He saw his sister mouth to Evan Walker, *Do something.*

Evan Walker shook his head no.

"She won't come out of her room," Cassie said.

"Maybe she'll change her mind if you tell her I'm going to blow your little brother's brains out."

Zombie's face was pale and caked in dried blood, so he looked like a real zombie. "That's not going to happen," Zombie said. "So what now?"

"Oh, sure," Cassie said. "Terrific idea. Let's all trust Ringer."

"Then she shoots Nugget and keeps shooting people until Megan comes out," Ringer said. "Zombie, trust me on this."

148

"She's not here to hurt anyone," Ringer said. "But she will if she has to. Tell them, Constance."

"Me," Evan Walker said. "You've come for me, haven't you?"

"The girl first," Constance said. "Then we talk."

Cassie said, "That's fine. Talking's one of my favorite things. But first maybe you could let my little brother go . . . take me instead?" Cassie's hands were up and she was putting on her fake smile. It wasn't a good fake smile. You could always tell when she was faking, because she didn't look friendly; she looked like she was going to throw up.

The lady's arm like an iron bar pressing against his windpipe, hard to breathe now, and something else pressing against the small of his back, his special secret, nobody knew, not Zombie or even Cassie, and not this lady, either.

Sam slipped his hand behind his back, into the space between him and Constance.

He was a soldier. He had forgotten his ABCs but he remembered the lessons of combat. *Your squad before God*, that's what they taught him. He could remember only the vaguest outline of his mother's face, but he knew their faces, Dumbo's and Teacup's, Poundcake's and Oompa's and Flintstone's. His squad. His brothers and sisters. He couldn't recall the name of his school or what the street he lived on looked like. Those things and the hundred other forever-gone things didn't matter anymore. Only one thing mattered now, the cry of the firing range and the obstacle course rising from the throats of his squad: *No mercy ever!*

"You now have fifteen seconds," the lady holding him said. "Don't make me count them down; it's so *melodramatic*."

Then the gun was in his hand and he did not hesitate. He knew what to do. He was a soldier.

The gun kicked in his hand when he fired; he almost dropped it. The bullet ripped through the lady's abdomen and exited her lower back, the slug burying itself in the dusty sofa cushions. The noise was very loud in the small space, and Cassie cried out: For an awful second, she must have thought it was the lady's gun that went off.

The shot failed to drop the Constance lady or break her hold on his neck. Her grip loosened, though, at the shock of impact, and Sam heard the tiniest of gasps, a startled *huh*, and before he could blink, Ringer was flying over the coffee table, arm drawn back, hand curled into a fist. Her knuckles grazed his cheek before landing against the side of Constance's head, and then a hand he didn't see flung off the arm around his neck and he stumbled free. His sister reached for him, but he spun away, holding the gun with both hands, and Ringer yanked Constance completely off her feet and swung her body high into the air like an axman cutting firewood, smashing her down onto the coffee table. The table exploded, wood and glass and pieces of jigsaw puzzle spewing in every direction.

Constance sat up; Ringer rammed the heel of her hand into Constance's nose. *Pop!* You could hear it break. Blood burst from her open mouth.

Fingers clawing at his shirt: Cassie's. He pulled away. Cassie wasn't part of a squad. She didn't know what it meant to be a soldier. He did. He knew exactly what it meant.

No mercy ever.

He stepped over the broken pieces of the table and pointed the gun at the middle of the lady's face. Her bloody mouth pulled into a soulless snarl of a smile, bloody lips and bloody teeth, and

150

then he was back in his mother's room, and she was dying of the plague, the Red Death, Cassie called it, and he was standing by her bed and she was smiling at him with bloody teeth, face stained with bloody tears; he saw it so clearly, the face he'd forgotten in the face he saw now.

In the instant before he pulled the trigger, Sammy Sullivan remembered his mother's face, the face *they* had given her, and the bullet that tore down the barrel held his rage, bore his grief, contained the sum of all he had lost. It connected them as if by a silver cord. When her face blew apart, they became one, victim and perpetrator, predator and prey.

ABCDEFGHIJKLMNOPQRSTUVWXYZ

39

RINGER

THE BLOOD SPRAY blinds me for a second, but the hub retains the data of Nugget's location and the precise position of the gun. By the time that second expires, his hand is empty and mine isn't.

At the end of the next second, the gun is trained at the face of Evan Walker.

Walker is the linchpin, the fulcrum upon which our survival rests. Alive, he's an unacceptable risk. Pulling the trigger might cost my own life; I know that. Cassie—even Zombie—might kill me for killing him, but I don't have a choice. We're out of time.

None of them can hear it yet, but I can—the sound of the chopper bearing down from the north, loaded with Hellfire missiles and a squad of Vosch's best sharpshooters. The loss of Constance's signal can only mean one thing.

"Ringer," Zombie cries hoarsely. "What the fuck?"

A tiny figure rushes from my right. Nugget. I pull the punch so I don't break his sternum, but the blow sends him flying off his feet and into Sullivan's chest. They plop to the floor in a sprawl of arms and legs.

I stay focused on the target.

"Ben, don't," Walker says calmly, though Zombie hasn't moved. "Let's hear what she wants."

"You know what I want." Finger tightening on the trigger. There's no question that Walker has to die. It's so obvious, even Nugget would agree if he knew the facts. His sister, too. Well, maybe not. Love blinds more than it reveals. Razor taught me that.

"Ben!" Walker shouts. "No."

Zombie doesn't dive for a weapon. He doesn't leap toward me. He takes two very slow, very deliberate steps to put his body between me and Evan Walker.

"Sorry, Ringer," Zombie says. Incredibly, he's decided to whip out the slayer smile. "Not going to happen." He raises his arms as if to offer a better target.

"Zombie, you don't know . . ."

"Well, that's a given. I don't know shit."

If it were anyone else.

Sullivan, even Nugget.

What is the cost, Marika? What is the price? "Zombie, there's no time."

"No time for what?"

He heard it then; they all heard it; it had come within range of normal human hearing. The chopper.

"Holy shit," Sullivan gasped. "What have you done? *What the hell have you done?*"

I ignore her. Only Zombie matters. "They don't want us," I tell him. "They want him. We can't let them have him, Zombie."

If Zombie would just dip his head a half inch. That's all I need, half an inch. The 12th System will do the rest.

I'm sorry, Zombie. There's no time.

The hub locks in. I let loose the round. The bullet smashes into Zombie's thigh.

He's supposed to go down to clear the way for the next round—the kill shot to Evan Walker's head. He doesn't.

Instead, he falls back into Walker's chest and Walker wraps his arms around him, holding him up or using him as a human shield. Beneath the faint sound of the rotors outside, an even fainter sound, the *thu-wapp* of a parachute deploying. Then another. Then another. *Thu-wapp, thu-wapp, thu-wapp, thu-wapp, thu-wapp.* Five in all.

It hits me I've been appealing to the wrong person.

"Drop him," I say to Evan Walker. "If you care at all about what happens to Cassie, *drop him.*"

But he doesn't and now I'm out of time. Drawn out any further, this stalemate will cost all our lives.

The 5th Wave is coming.

153

40

EVAN WALKER

THERE CAN BE only one explanation.

Her leap across the room. The speed of her hands, the acuity of her vision and hearing. Only one possibility.

She had been enhanced. A human had received the gift.

Why?

She propelled herself toward the front window, covering the length of the room in three strides, rolling her body in midair to strike the glass with her shoulder, then disappearing into a halo of pulverized glass and wood.

Cassie immediately started toward him—or toward Ben, whom he still held upright. "Megan," Evan said. "Get her down to the basement."

Cassie nodded. She understood. She grabbed her little brother's wrist and yanked him toward the hallway.

"No! I'm staying with Zombie!"

"Jesus Christ, Sam, *come on* . . . "

They fled down the hall. The chopper was getting closer; the sound of its engines flowed through the broken window like waves crashing on the beach. First things first, though. He heaved Ben over his shoulder and carried him toward the sofa, stepping over the body that lay amid the shattered remnants of the coffee table. He laid Ben on the sofa and glanced about for something to tie off the leg. The dead woman's hoodie. Evan knelt beside her and ripped the hoodie open. He tore off a strip, from collar to

154

hem, and swung back around. Ben was eyeing him from a colorless face, breath high in his chest, going into shock.

The bullet had entered Ben's leg just above the kneecap. Any lower and he'd never walk again. Ben wasn't lucky. Ringer had placed the shot carefully.

Ben opened his mouth and said, "My bad. I shouldn't have brought them here."

"You couldn't know," Evan assured him.

Ben shook his head violently. "No excuse." He slammed his open palm against the cushions and dust exploded into the air. He coughed.

Evan lifted his eyes toward the ceiling and listened. How much time did they have? Hard to tell. Two minutes? Less? He looked back down at Ben, who said, "Basement."

Evan nodded. "Basement."

He pulled Ben from the sofa and slung him over his shoulder. Where was Cassie? He trotted down the stairs, Ben's cheek bouncing against his back. He carried him to the far corner of the room and eased him onto the concrete floor.

"Don't wait, Walker." Ben jerked his head toward the weapons cache. "If you don't take out that bird fast, it won't matter if they're down here."

Evan lifted the missile launcher from the hook on the wall. The chopper must be in range by now. He raced back up the stairs, taking them two at a time, the launcher heavy as a steel girder in his hands. His bad ankle sang with pain. He pushed through it.

The hallway was empty. The air thrummed against his skin. The Black Hawk was circling directly above the house. Leave them up here and risk the shot? Or get them downstairs and risk the missile? He dropped the launcher onto the floor.

155

41

CASSIE WAS POUNDING on the closet door and screaming Megan's name. She whirled around when Evan burst into the room.

"She's barricaded herself inside, the little bitch!"

He shoved Cassie out of the way and slammed his shoulder into the door. It jerked on its hinges but did not give way.

"Cassie, Sam, basement, *now*," he shouted.

They fled from the room. He brought up his good foot and slammed it into the middle of the door. The wood cracked. Again. *Crack. Again. Crack!* Three steps back and he lowered his shoulder into the crack. The door ripped down the middle and he stumbled through the opening into darkness. A pair of eyes wide with terror regarded him from the corner. He held out his hand.

"We're about to be blown up, Megan."

She shook her head. She wasn't leaving. No way. He reached for her and her hands balled into fists and pummeled his face. She scratched at his eyes. She screamed as if she were being beaten to death.

He grabbed her wrist and yanked. She flew into his chest, then kicked his groin *hard* while reaching toward the back of the closet with her free hand. A teddy bear lay among the wads of clothes.

"*Captain!*"

He grabbed the bear. "Here, I've got him."

The first Hellfire missile struck the house precisely two minutes and twenty-two seconds later.

156

42

CARRYING MEGAN, Evan was halfway down the basement stairs when the concussion from the blast hurled them into the air. He whipped his body around as he fell: He would take the force of the impact, not the little girl.

Slamming into the concrete floor knocked the wind out of him. Megan rolled off his chest and lay still.

Then the second missile struck.

Flames roared down from above. He saw them coming, a bright orange and red battering ram. He threw himself over the girl; the fire passed over them; he smelled his hair singe, felt the furnace-hot breath through his shirt.

He lifted his head. Across the basement he could see Cassie and Sam crouching beside Ben. He crawled over to them, dragging Megan behind him. Cassie's eyes met his: *Is she . . . ?*

He shook his head: *No.*

"Where's the launcher?" Ben asked.

Evan pointed at the ceiling. *Upstairs. Or it used to be, when there was an upstairs.*

Dislodged cobwebs and dust swirled around them. The ceiling was holding for now. He doubted it could withstand another hit. Ben Parish must have been thinking the same thing.

"Oh, that's great." Ben turned to Cassie. "Let's everybody form a prayer circle, quick, because we have just been royally fucked."

"It'll be okay," Evan assured him. He touched Cassie's cheek. "It's not the end. Not yet." He stood up. "They came here for one thing," he said quietly, his voice barely audible above the inferno over them. "They opened fire because they assumed they'd failed. They think I'm dead. I'm going to show them that they're wrong." Mystified, Ben shook his head. He didn't understand. Cassie did, though, and her face darkened with anger.

"Evan Walker, don't you dare do this again."

"Last time, Mayfly, I promise."

43

HE PAUSED AT the base of the stairs that led up into the smoke and flame. Behind him, Cassie was screaming, calling his name, cursing him.

He climbed anyway.

Ringer called it: *They don't want us. They want him.*

Halfway up, he wondered if he should have killed Ben Parish.

He would be a liability to Cassie. Slow her down. Be a burden she may not be able to bear.

He pushed the thought from his mind. Too late now. Too late to turn back. Too late to run, too late to hide. Like Cassie beneath the car that day, like Ben beneath the imploding death camp, he had reached the moment of facing that which he thought he could not face. He had risked everything to save her before, but those times the risk was measured, calculated, and a small chance always remained that he would endure.

Not this time. This time he was marching straight into the belly of the beast.

158

He turned once, at the top of the stairs, but he could not see her and he could not hear her. She was lost in a haze of dust and smoke and the slowly spinning gossamer strands of cobweb.

A cyclone whipped through the wreckage, the chopper making a pass, and the wind from its blades slung aside the smoke and tamped down the fire, flattening it out like a rolling red sea. He looked up and saw the pilot at the controls, looking down.

He raised his hands and shuffled forward. The fire encircled him. The smoke engulfed him. He walked through the maelstrom into clear, clean air.

Evan Walker stood still in the middle of the road, hands up, as the helicopter came down.

44

SQUAD ONE-NINE

FROM THEIR POSITION three hundred yards to the north, the five-member strike team from Squad 19 watch the chopper fire two missiles, then it's *bye-bye, house,* blasted down to its concrete foundation in an orgasm of fire and smoke.

In Milk's earpiece, the pilot's voice: "Hold your position, One-nine. Repeat: Hold position."

Milk raises his fist to signal his team: *We hold.*

The chopper makes a wide arc to circle back over the target.

Crouched beside Milk, Pixie sighs loudly, fussing with his eyepiece.

The strap's too big for his little head, and he can't keep it snug. Swizz whispers for him to shut up and Pix instructs him to kiss his ass. Milk tells them both to shut up.

The team huddles beneath a faded Havoline sign beside an old brick building that had been a body shop before the world went FUBAR. Stacks of used tires and piles of rims, discarded engine parts and tools, all scattered around the lot like wind-driven leaves; the cars and trucks and SUVs and minivans are coated in dust and grime, with shattered windows and mildewed upholstery, relics of the irrelevant past. The generation that followed Squad 19—if there was a generation to follow—would not recognize the strange symbols attached to the trunks and grills of these rusting hulks. In a hundred years, no one would be able to read the sign over their heads or even understand that the letters symbolized sounds.

Like it matters anymore. Like anyone cares. Better not to remember. Better not to know. You can't mourn what you never had.

The chopper hovers over the wreckage, and the downdraft from its blades flattens the smoke and pushes the flames sideways. They squint through their eyepieces, Milk and Pix to the south toward the chopper, Swizz and Snicks to the west, Gummy to the north, scanning the terrain for the green glow of an alien-infested enemy. They will wait for the Black Hawk to pull out, then move south down the highway, clearing the area as they go—if there's any damn thing to clear. Unless the Teds took off when they heard the chopper's approach, anything caught in that house was toast.

Pix saw it first: a tiny neon-green spark that bobbed about in the flames like a firefly in the summer dusk. He poked Milk in the leg and pointed. Milk nodded with a grim smile. *Oh yeah.* They've drilled for this, dear Jesus, they can't remember how often, but this is the first time in a real combat situation. A living, breathing, honest-to-God, in-the-flesh infested.

Six months, two weeks, and three days since the buses brought them together, the girls and boys of Squad 19. One hundred and ninety-nine days. Four thousand, seven hundred and seventy-six hours. Two hundred eighty-six thousand, five hundred and sixty minutes since Pix was Ryan, cowering in a drainage ditch, covered in scabs and sores and lice, with a bloated stomach and stick-thin arms and bulging, buggy eyes, brought onto the bus sobbing tearlessly because his body was starved for water. And Milk was called Kyle then, rescued from a camp a couple miles from the Canadian border, a big kid, sullen and angry and itching for payback, hard to control, difficult to break, but in the end they broke him.

They broke all of them.

Jeremy to *Swizz*, Luis to Gummy, Emily to Snickers. A bunch of candy-assed names for a bunch of candy-assed recruits.

The ones they could not break, the ones Wonderland told them were unfit, and the ones whose minds or bodies gave way in basic disappeared into incinerators or into secret holding rooms to retrofit their bodies into bombs. It was easy. It was absurdly easy. Empty the vessel of hope and faith and trust and you can fill it with anything you like. They could have told the kids in Squad 19 that two plus two equals five and they would have believed it. No, not just believed it; they would have killed anyone who claimed otherwise.

A tall figure topped in green fire emerges from the smoke and flame—arms up, hands empty, crossing the blackened rubble onto the road—and the chopper dips its nose and begins descending.

What the hell? Why don't they waste him?

Pix, you dumbass, he's gotta be the frigging *target*. Sonofabitch *made* it.

The chopper sets down and now Milk can see Hersh and Reese hop from the hold. He can't hear them, but he knows what they're screaming at the Ted over the cacophony of the engine: *Down, down, down! Hands on your head!* The figure drops to its knees; its hands are swallowed by the green fire dancing around its face. They drag the prisoner over to the bird and haul him inside.

The pilot's voice squawks in Milk's ear: "Returning target to base. See you on the back side, soldiers."

The Hawk roars directly over them, northbound. The Havoline sign quivers at its passing. Gummy watches the chopper shrink toward the horizon, and the world goes quiet fast, leaving only the wind and fire and his own heavy breath. *This will be quick,* he tells himself. Absently, he presses his hand against his shoulder, still tender from the night before, the wounds still fresh: *VQP.*

It was Milk's idea. Milk had seen Razor's body with his own eyes, and it was Milk who figured out what the letters stood for. *Vincit qui patitur. He conquers who endures.* They carved the same letters into their own arms—*VQP*—in honor of the fallen.

Milk gives the signal and they move out. Milk on the point, Pix right behind, Swizz and Snick the flankers, and Gummy bringing up the rear. Mark those windows across the street there, Snick. Check those cars, Swizz.

They've drilled this a thousand times, house to house, room to room, basement to roof. You clear the block, then move to the next one. Don't rush. Watch your back. Watch your buddy's back. If you have the shot, take the shot. Simple. Easy. So easy a child could do it, which is one of the chief reasons they picked children to do it.

Six months, two weeks, and three days after the school bus rolled to a stop and a voice called out, *Don't be afraid. You're safe now, perfectly safe,* Gummy hears something other than the wind and the fire and his own breath: a high-pitched whine like the squealing of that bus's brakes. That's the last sound he hears before the twenty-inch steel rim smashes into the back of his head, snapping his spinal cord. He's dead before he hits the ground.

One hundred and eighty-four days after rolling into camp, Snicks is next. She and Swizz drop to the ground when Gummy falls, that's the training, that's the memory their muscles hold, and their adversary knows it. She anticipated it.

Lying on his belly, Swizz looks to his right. Snicks is making a strangled gurgling sound, her rifle abandoned on the road next to her, both hands clutching the handle of the twenty-five-inch screwdriver embedded in her neck. Her jugular has been severed. She will be dead in less than a minute.

Four thousand, four hundred and sixteen hours after he saw the lights of the bus's headlamps stabbing through the woods in which he hid, Swizz scrambles on his hands and knees to the roadside—and sees the green light through his eyepiece for a split second before it vanishes behind the old garage: the pale fire of an infested. *Got you now, you sonofabitch.* Swizz doesn't know what happened to Milk and Pix, and he doesn't turn around to find out. He's running on instinct and adrenaline and a rage that cannot be measured or exhausted. He heaves himself to his feet and takes off for the garage. She's already on the roof by the time he reaches the southeast corner of the building, waiting for him, ready to leap.

At least it'll be quick.

Milk and Pix hear his rifle's report from their hiding place behind the overturned Tahoe that straddles the shoulder of the road. Three short, staccato bursts: *tat-tat-tat!*

Then silence.

With a soft, disgusted cry, Pix rips off the eyepiece, screw this, fucker won't stay up, and Milk calmly orders him to put it back on while he scans their surroundings. Pix ignores him. Broad daylight, he can see fine, and who cares whether they're human or infested anymore?

Wind and fire and their own breath. Don't get pinned. Don't go down any dead ends. Don't split up. Lying on his side, his shoulder pressing against the comforting steel of the SUV, Pix looks up into Milk's face. Milk's the sarge. Milk won't let him down. VQP.

Hell yes. VQP.

The girl's bullet travels across the road, shatters the driver's window, passes through the interior and exits on the other side, ripping through Pix's jacket and burrowing into his back until it reaches his spine. There the bullet stops.

Two hundred sixty-four thousand, nine hundred and sixty-three minutes from his rescue to this moment, and Milk scoots toward the front bumper, dragging Pix's body with him. The upper half jerks in his hands; the lower half is paralyzed, dead already, and what the fuck were they thinking, carving those stupid letters into their arms? Pix's small fingers clawing at Milk's face as the light drains from his eyes. *Protect me, cover me, keep the bastards off me, Sarge.*

That's right, that's right, Pix. VQP. V Q fucking P. He's still whispering to him when she steps around the hood of the car. He doesn't look up. He doesn't even hear her.

Fifteen million, eight hundred ninety-seven thousand, seven hundred and ninety-two ticks of the clock, and Milk follows the rest of Squad 19 down.

164

45

RINGER

I WON'T LEAVE these boys to rot where they fell.

I won't leave them for the rats and the crows and the blowflies, the buzzards and packs of feral dogs.

I will not abandon their bones to be picked over and scattered by vultures and vermin.

I will not burn them, either.

With my bare hands, I will dig a grave for them in the cold earth. The sun slips toward the horizon. The wind picks up, whipping my hair across my face, and the ground breaks between my fingers, my hands the plow that breaks the stubborn soil for the planting.

I know Zombie's watching me. I can see him at the edge of the black, blasted-out ruins of the house. He's leaning on a piece of charred two-by-four, holding his rifle and watching me. Twilight settles around us and still he watches as I carry the bodies one by one to the hole I've dug.

He hobbles over. He's going to shoot me. He's going to kick my body into the hole and bury me with my victims. He won't wait for me to explain. There will be no questions, because everything out of my mouth will be a lie.

He stops. I'm kneeling beside the grave and their faces are looking sightlessly up at me. The oldest—the squad leader, I'm guessing—could not be older than twenty.

The sound of the bolt on Zombie's rifle drawing back is enhanced and the hub orders a defensive response. I ignore it.

"I shot Teacup," I say into the face of the dead recruit. "I thought she was the enemy and I shot her. She had one chance and I had no choice. I let them take us, Zombie. It was the only way to save her."

His voice is as dry as dead leaves rattling on winter boughs. "Then where is she?"

"Gone."

The word hangs. Even the wind can't move it.

"What did they do to you, Ringer?"

I look up. Not at him. Straight up. The first stars peek at me through the gloaming.

Above me, the stars shine down unblinking. I blink, and my tears fall silver in their light. Vosch's gift allows me to see to the very edge of the universe, but I couldn't see the prison walls on every side.

"The same thing they did to Walker. The same thing they did to Constance and that priest and the cat lady."

The truth. The 12th System enhances all others, including the one that's been tearing my body apart since I returned from the wilderness. I refused to face the truth. I knew it, and I refused. A man blind from birth reaches out and touches an elephant's ear. *An elephant is flat like a sheet.* Another blind man touches its trunk. *An elephant is shaped like a snake.* A third strokes its leg. *An elephant is like a tree.*

I lower my head to the grave and speak the truth aloud:

"I'm pregnant."

166

46

CASSIE

BEN'S DEAD.

He left us, saying he'd be right back. But he hasn't come right back. He hasn't come back at all.

I huddle in the far corner of the basement with Sam and Megan. I've got a rifle, Megan's got Bear, and Sam's got an attitude. Grace's gun collection is six feet away. So many pretty shiny things, Sam can hardly contain himself. The most delightful thing he's discovered about shooting someone is how ridiculously easy it is. Tying your shoes is harder.

I grab a heavy wool blanket from the stack beside the workbench and throw it over all three of them, Sams, Megs, and Bear.

"I'm not cold!" he cries—Sam, not Bear.

"It isn't for warmth," I mutter at him. I start to explain, but the words peter out into meaningless dribble. What happened to Evan? What happened to Ben? What happened to Ringer? Finding out the answer to any of those questions would require me to rise from this floor, cross the length of this basement, climb those stairs, and possibly shoot someone or be shot myself, all of which calls for something I haven't got right now.

Last time, Mayfly. I promise.

Oh, that stupid, gag-worthy pet name. I should have called him something equally demeaning and cloying. *Sharkboy* is a good one. *Jawsie.*

167

The wooden stairs creak. I stay put. Cassiopeia's last stand. I have a full magazine and a heart full of hate; you don't need much of anything else.

Beside me, Sam hisses, "Cassie, it's Zombie."

Sure enough. Clumping awkwardly and badly off balance, too, like a real zombie. He's out of breath by the time he reaches the bottom. He leans against the wall, lips parted, face drained of color.

"Well?" I call across the room at him. "Did you find him?"

He shakes his head. He glances up the stairs. He looks back at me.

"Chopper," he says.

"What about the chopper? Evan blew it up?" Stupid question. I would have heard it.

"He got *on* it."

Ben needs to sit. A wound like his hurts like a mother; I should know. Why won't he sit? Why is he hanging there by the stairs?

"What do you mean, he got on it?"

"I mean he got on it. They took him, Cassie." Another look up the stairs, so I ask him why he keeps looking up the stairs. He goes, "There was a strike team . . ."

"There's a strike team?"

"There *was* a strike team." He wipes the back of his hand across his mouth. "Not anymore." His voice shakes—and I don't think it's from the pain or the cold. Ben Parish appears to be scared shitless.

"Ringer?" *Duh, Sullivan, who else?* "Ringer."

He nods. Then glances again topside. That's when I stand up. Sam, too. I tell him to stay. He tells me no. Ben holds up a hand.

"There's an explanation, Cassie."

"I'm sure there is."

"You need to hear her out."

"Or what? She snaps my neck with her super-ninja powers?" Ben, what's the matter with you? *She brought them to us.*"

"You gotta trust me on this."

"No, *you* need to trust *me*. I told you before she left—there's something not right about her. Now she's back and there's something *really* not right. What else do you need, Ben? What does she have to do for you to accept the fact she isn't on your side?"

"Cassie . . ." Trying very hard to keep it together. "I want you to put down that weapon . . ."

"That's not going to happen."

Trying very hard to be patient. "I won't let you hurt her, Cassie." And Sam goes, "Zombie's the sarge. You have to do what he says."

The stairs creak again. Ringer stops halfway down. She's not looking at me; she's looking at Ben. For a horrible second, I think about shooting them both, grabbing Sam and Megan, and running until we run out of land to run on. Picking sides, deciding who you can trust, deciding what's truth and what's not, you reach a point where chucking it all seems like the least intolerable option. Like people who commit suicide, you just get sick of the hassle.

"It's all right," Ben says to her or maybe to me or maybe to both of us. "It's going to be fine."

"She leaves the gun on the stairs," I call over.

Ringer drops her rifle right away. Why am I not comforted? Then she descends to the last step and sits.

47

THERE'S BEEN A SHITLOAD of *huh?* moments since the Others came, but this one has gotta be the *huh*-est of them all.

After the first go-around, I figure I must be missing something, so I ask Ringer to explain herself again, slower this time, with a little more detail and a lot more evidence.

"They aren't here," she says. "I'm not even sure they're *there*." With a nod toward the basement ceiling—and the unseen sky beyond.

"How could they not be there?" Ben wonders. There he goes again, deferring to her like the mealymouthiest courtier in Queen Ringer's court. I'm starting to wonder about Ben's ability to judge character. Since this war began, he's been shot twice—both times by the person who claimed to be on his side.

"The mothership could be completely automated," Ringer explains. "Obviously some form of sentient life built it, but the builders themselves could be light-years from here—or nowhere."

"Nowhere?" Ben echoes.

"Dead. Extinct."

"Sure, why not?" I'm fiddling with the bolt catch of my M16. Ben might still trust her after she lied about Teacup and where she was and what happened while she was there, *plus* her delivering an assassin to our doorstep, *plus* being shot by her, *twice*; I'm not so gobsmacked by her feminine charm, which, by the way, you could fit on the head of a pin and still leave room for angels to dance. "A couple thousand years ago, their probes find us. They

170

watch. They wait. At some point they figure out we're no good for the Earth or ourselves, so they build the mothership and load it down with bombs and drones and viral plague and proceed to wipe out ninety-nine point nine percent of the population with the help of human thralls who've been brainwashed since birth . . . because that's our medicine, that's what *good* for us—"

"Cassie," Ben says. "Take a breath."

"That's one scenario," Ringer says calmly. "Actually, it's the best-case scenario."

I shake my head and look over at Sam and Megan huddled under a big blanket in the corner. Incredibly, both have fallen asleep, their heads pressed together, Bear tucked beneath their chins, in a tableau that would be cute beyond words if it wasn't so heart-breakingly symbolic of something. Well, of *everything.*

"Just like your Silencer theory," I snap at her. "A computer program downloaded into fetuses that boots up when the kid hits puberty. A *scenario.*"

"No, that's a fact. Vosch confirmed it."

"Right. The maniac who orchestrated the murder of seven billion people. Well, sure, if *he* said it, then it must be true."

"Why else would he want Walker so badly?"

"Oh, I don't know. Maybe because Evan betrayed his entire civilization and is the one person on the planet who can stop them?"

Ringer is looking at me like I'm something disgusting she found growing on her toothbrush. "If that's all there is to it, your boyfriend would be dead right now."

"He *could* be dead right now. It kills me how you claim to know so much despite the fact that you don't know much at all. Theories, scenarios, possibilities, odds, *whatever.* And for your information,

171

just so you know, and this is no supposition based on the theory that *I-am-Ringer-ergo-I-know-all*, he isn't my boyfriend."

My face is hot. I'm thinking of the night I landed on the shores of Evanland and planted my flag upon that sculpted beach. Ben says something at that point, which I totally miss, because my mind has a way of scolding its own thoughts. Like, how could *I* be the flag-planter? Shouldn't that be Evan?

"Evan is human," Ringer insists. "His purpose is obvious. What isn't so obvious—and why Vosch needs to deconstruct his programming—is what triggered Evan's mind to rebel. He didn't just betray his 'people.' He betrayed *himself*."

"Well," Ben sighs, "that's fucked up." He shifts his weight against the wall, trying to find a more comfortable position. That's not possible with a bullet in your leg. Believe me, I've tried. "So there are no escape pods coming to evac the Silencers," Ben says slowly. "No pods, so no way to the mothership. No way to the mothership, so no way to blow it up. Shoots *that* plan all to hell. What about bombing the cities? Or is that a lie his programming told him, too?"

Ringer doesn't answer for a long time. I have no clue what she's thinking. Then *I* start thinking maybe this whole deal is a trick—of Vosch's. *Something* happened to Ringer after she checked out of the Walker Hotel. *Somebody* implanted her with bionics that turned her into a part-human, part-machine weapon of mass destruction. How do we know she *hasn't* flipped to the other side? A certain Brawny-paper-towel-looking guy did. How do we know she wasn't *always* on the other side?

My thumb's working that bolt catch again.

"I think they *are* going to bomb the cities," she finally says.

"Why?" I demand. "What's the point?"

"A lot of reasons. For one, it evens the playing field before the launch of the 5th Wave—urban combat gives the Silencers every advantage, and you can't tip favor too far to one side. But the most important reason is cities hold our memories."

Whaaaaa? Then I get it, and getting it makes my stomach hurt. My father and that damned wagon and those damned books. Libraries, museums, universities, everything we designed and built over six thousand years. Cities are more than the sum of their infrastructure. They transcend brick and mortar, concrete and steel. They're the vessels into which human knowledge is poured. Blowing them up will be the final reset of the clock back to the Neolithic.

"Not enough to reduce the population to a sustainable level," Ringer says softly. "Not enough to level what we built. We'll repopulate. We'll rebuild. To save the planet, to save our species, they have to change *us*." She touches her chest. "Here. If the Others can take away trust, they take away cooperation. Take away cooperation, and civilization is impossible."

48

"OKAY," BEN SAYS. Time to get down to the gnarly nub of it. "No on the pods but yes on the bombs. Which means we can't stay here—too close to Urbana. That's fine with me, because I really fucking hate Urbana. So where? South? My vote is south.

Find a source of fresh water, miles from anywhere, as in the middle of nowhere."

"And?" Ringer asks.

"And what?"

"And what then?"

"What then?"

"Yes. After we get to nowhere, then what?"

Ben lifts a hand. Lets it fall. His mouth curls into a smile. He looks so boyishly cute in this moment that I feel like bursting into tears. "There's five of us. I say we form a band."

I laugh out loud. Sometimes Ben's like a bracing mountain stream I dip my toe into.

"Anyway," Ben says after two seconds of Ringer staring blankly at him. "What the hell else are we going to do?"

He looks at her. He looks at me.

"Oh Christ, Sullivan," he moans, tapping the back of his head against the wall. "Don't even go there."

"He came for *me*," I tell him. He knows I'm thinking it, so I might as well say it. We're both a little surprised that I've gone there. "He saved your life—twice. He saved mine three times."

"Ben's right," Ringer butts in. "It's suicide, Sullivan."

I roll my eyes. I've heard this shit before—from Evan Walker himself, when he realized I was bulling my way into a death camp to find my baby brother. Why must I always be the isle of crazy alone in an ocean of sensibility? The *should* to everybody else's *shouldn't*? The *I-will* to their *better-nots*?

"Staying here is suicide, too," I argue. "So is running to nowhere. Anything we do now is suicide. We're at the point in the story where we have to choose, Ringer—a meaningful death, or a senseless one. Besides," I add, "he'd do it for us."

174

"No," Ben says quietly. "He would do it for *you.*"

"The base they're taking him to is over a hundred miles away," Ringer says. "Even if you reached it, you won't reach it in time. Vosch will be finished with him and Evan will be dead."

"You don't know that."

"I do know that."

"No, you *say* you know that, but you don't really know that, just like you don't know everything else you say you know, but we're just supposed to believe it because, hell, you're just brilliant little you."

And Ben goes, "Huh?"

"Whatever we do," Ringer says coolly to Ben, as if nothing I just said wasn't a major-league smackdown, "staying is not an option. As soon as that chopper delivers its cargo, it's coming back."

"Cargo?" Ben asks.

"She means Evan," I translate.

"Why would it . . . ?" Then he gets it. Ringer's victims buried down the road. The chopper's coming back to extract the strike team. "Oh." He wipes the back of his hand across his mouth. "Crap."

And I'm thinking, *Hey, Chopper!* and Ringer is watching me and thinking she knows what I'm thinking, which she does, but that doesn't prove she's always right.

"Forget it, Sullivan."

"Forget what?" And right away I acknowledge my coyness: "You did it. Or at least you *said* you did it."

"Did what?" Ben asks.

"That was different," Ringer says.

"Different how?"

"Different in that the pilot was in on it. My 'escape' from Vosch wasn't an escape; it was a test of the 12th System."

175

"Well, we can pretend this is a test, too, if that helps."

"Pretend *what* is a test?" Ben's voice rises an octave in his frustration. "What the hell are you two talking about?"

Ringer sighs. "She wants to hijack the Black Hawk."

Ben's mouth drops open. I don't know what or why it is, but when he's around Ringer, the smart drains out of him like spaghetti water through a colander.

"What about him?" Ringer nods toward Sams. "He's coming, too?"

"That's your business?" I ask.

"Well, I'm not babysitting while you go all Don Quixote on this."

"You know, making obscure literary references doesn't impress me. And yes, I happen to know who Don Quixote is."

"Okay, wait a minute," Ben says. "He's from *The Godfather*, right?" Straight-faced, so I'm not sure if he's joking. Back in the day, there was serious talk about Ben becoming a Rhodes Scholar. No lie. "You're gonna make Vosch an offer he can't refuse?"

"Ben can stay with the kids," I inform Ringer, as if I've thought it all out, as if the plan for rescuing Evan has been in the works for months. "We go, just you and me."

She's shaking her head. "Why would I do that?"

"Why *wouldn't* you do that?"

She stiffens and then, for some unclear reason, she looks over at Ben. So I look over at Ben, and Ben is looking straight down at the floor like he's never seen one before. *What is this amazing hard surface under my feet?*

"How about this." I won't stop trying. Why won't I stop? I try to stop, and then I fail. "Forget me. Forget Evan. Do it for *yourself*."

"Myself?" She's genuinely puzzled. Ha! For once she can't pretend she knows what I'm thinking.

"He's finished with you. He's done. So you have to go to him if you want to end it."

Ringer recoils like somebody slapped her. She wants to pretend she doesn't know who I'm talking about. Fat chance.

I saw it in her face when she told the story. I heard it in her voice. Between the frowns and long silences, it was there. When she said his name and when she couldn't bring herself to say his name, it was there: He's the reason she hasn't given up, why she hangs on, her *raison d'être*.

The thing worth dying for.

"Vosch thinks you're going to zig—so you zag. He thinks you're going to run away—so you run toward. You can't undo what he's done, but you can undo *him*."

"It won't solve anything," she whispers.

"Probably not. But he'll be dead. There's that."

I hold out my hand. I'm not sure why. It really isn't my deal to make because I can't promise final delivery of the goods. That little, rational, calm, ancient, wise voice in my head chirps, *She's right, it's suicide, Cassie. Evan's gone and this time there'll be no miracles. Let him go.*

My place is with Sam; it's always been with Sam. Sam is my *raison d'être*. Not some delusional Ohio farm boy crazy all the way down to the bottom of his bones. Jesus, if Ringer is right, even Evan's love may be part of the crazy. He *thinks* he's in love with me like he *thinks* he's an Other.

So what's the difference between thinking it and actually being it? Is there a difference?

177

There are times I hate my own brain.

"The dead," Ringer says in a voice that reflects the word: nothing there, gone, empty. "I came here to kill one innocent person. I killed five. If I go back, I'll kill until I lose count. I'll kill until counting doesn't matter." She isn't looking at me. She's looking at Ben. "And it'll be easy." She turns to me. "You don't understand. I *am what he made me.*"

I wish she'd cry. I want her to shout, scream, shake her fist, punch something, howl until her voice gave out. Anything would be better than the scooped-out, empty way she talked. What she said didn't match how she said it, and that's scary.

"And in the end, we'll both fail," she tells me. "Evan will die and Vosch will live."

She takes my hand anyway.

Even scarier.

49

BY THIS POINT, Ben has reached the end of his endurance—physical and mental. He can't remain standing any longer or keep up with this very strange, very quick turnabout, from *She's a traitor!* to *She's my partner!* He hops over to the stairs and lowers himself down, stretching his bad leg out in front of him. He stares at the ceiling, stroking the underside of his chin.

"Ringer, maybe you better get up there again. In case you missed somebody."

She shakes her head and her shiny black hair swings back and forth, a silky obsidian curtain. "I didn't miss anybody."

"Well. In case somebody else comes along."

"Like who?"

His head turns slowly in her direction. "Bad people."

She looks at me. Then she nods. She steps around him and stoops halfway up to retrieve her rifle. I hear her whisper, "Don't," to him, before disappearing from view.

Don't? "What is it with you two?" I ask.

"What's what?"

"The little looks. The 'don't' just now."

"It's nothing, Cassie."

"Nothing would be no little looks and no 'don'ts.'"

He shrugs, then glances up the stairs to the hole that opened to bare sky where the house used to be. "No getting there," he says. He smiles as if he's embarrassed for saying something stupid. "No matter how well you know someone, there's still a part of them you won't. You can't. Like, ever. A locked room. I don't know." He shakes his head and laughs. The laugh collapses the moment it's born.

"With Ringer, that's more like all the rooms in the Louvre," I point out.

Ben hauls himself to his feet and limps over to me, using his rifle as a crutch. By the time he arrives, his face is a study in exhaustion and pain. There you go. Parish heals up from one Ringer-inflicted wound, so she gives him another. Gotta keep the streak going.

"Have you lost your mind?" he asks.

"What do you think?"

"I think you have."

179

"How can you tell?" I'm fully confident he won't understand my question.

"The Cassie Sullivan I know would never leave her little brother."

"Maybe I'm not the Cassie Sullivan you know."

"So you're just gonna leave him—"

"With you."

"Maybe you haven't noticed, but when it comes to protecting people, I suck."

"It's not about you, Parish."

He slides down the wall beside me. Takes a few deep breaths. Then he blurts out, "Let's get real, okay? She won't get to Vosch and you won't get to Evan. That part's done. Time for the next part."

"The next part?"

"Them." He nods toward Sammy and Megan curled beneath the blanket. "It's always been about them, from day one. The enemy always knew it. The really sad and freaky part is why it's been so easy for us to forget."

"I haven't forgotten," I tell him. "Why do you think I'm going? This isn't about Evan Walker. And it isn't about you or me. If Ringer is right, Evan's our last hope." I look at my baby brother's face, angelic in sleep. "*His* last hope."

"Then I'll go with Ringer. You stay here."

I shake my head. "You're broken. I'm not."

"Bullshit. I can get around . . ."

"I'm not talking about your leg."

He flinches. His jaw tightens. "That's not fair, Cassie."

"I'm not worried about fair. This isn't about *fair*. This is about the odds. And risk. This is about my brother living to see next

Christmas. It would be great if there were someone I could tag to do it for me, but I'm it, Parish. It's down to me. Because I'm still there, Ben, under that car on the highway—I never got out and I never got up. I'm still there waiting for the bogeyman to come get me. And if I run now, anywhere or nowhere, he's going to find me. He's going to find Sam." I tug Bear from the blanket and hug him to my chest. "I don't care about whether Evan Walker is an alien or a human or an alien-human or a freaking turnip. I don't care about your baggage or Ringer's baggage, and I especially don't care about my baggage. The world existed for a very long time before this particular set of seven billion billion atoms came along, and it will go right on after they're scattered up, down, and sideways."

Ben reaches out and touches my wet cheek. I push his hand away. "Don't touch me." *You Has-Ben. You What-Might-Have-Ben.*

"Look, Cassie. I'm not your boss and I'm not your daddy. I can't stop you any more than you could have stopped me from going to the caves."

I press my face into the top of Bear's ratty old head. Bear smells like smoke and sweat and dirt and my little brother. "He loves you, Ben. More than me, I think. But that—"

"Not true, Cassie."

"Don't. Interrupt. Me. That's, like, one of my things. Just so you know. And now I would like to say something."

"Okay."

"There is something I'd like to say."

"I'm listening."

Looking away. Looking at nothing. Deep breath. *Don't say it, Cass. What's the point now?* There is no point. Maybe that's something we both need to understand.

181

"I've had a crush on you since the third grade," I whisper, "I wrote your name in notebooks. I drew hearts around it. I decorated it with flowers. Mostly daisies. I had daydreams and dreamdreams, and nobody knew except my best friend. Who is dead. Like everybody else."

Looking away. Looking at nothing. "But you were where you were and I was where I was. You could have been in China for all it mattered. When you showed up out of nowhere at Sammy's camp—I thought it had to mean something. Because you lived when you should have died, and I lived when I should have died, and we were both there for Sam, who also should have died. Just—just too many coincidences to be just a coincidence, you know? But that's all it is, a coincidence. There's no divine plan. There's nothing fated in our stars. No meant-to-be in any of it. We are accidental people occupying an accidental planet in an accidental universe. And that's okay. These seven billion billion atoms are good with that."

I press my lips onto that nasty stuffed animal's head. Really neat that human beings conquered the Earth, invented poetry and mathematics and the combustion engine, discovered that time and space are relative, built machines big and small to ferry us to the moon for some rocks or carry us to McDonald's for a strawberry-banana smoothie. Very cool we split the atom and bestowed upon the Earth the Internet and smartphones and, of course, the selfie stick.

But the most wonderful thing of all, our highest achievement and the one thing for which I pray we will always be remembered, is stuffing wads of polyester into an anatomically incorrect, cartoonish ideal of one of nature's most fearsome predators for no other reason than to soothe a child.

50

THERE ARE PREPARATIONS to make. Details to work out.

First, I'll need a uniform. Ben sits with the kids while Ringer and I dig up the bodies. There's the smallest recruit, whose uniform seems like the right size, but there's a bullet hole in the back of the jacket. Might be hard to explain. Ringer hauls out the next body, whose duds are dirty but unmarred by bullet holes and nearly blood-free. She explains that she crushed his skull with a twenty-inch steel rim. He didn't feel it, she assures me. Didn't see it coming. It's okay. I feel my gorge rise. *It's okay.* I change right there by the side of the road under the naked sky. Ha. *Naked sky.* And there is Cassiopeia above me, chained to her chair, watching her namesake bare herself and the dead boy, too. I catch Ringer looking at him, and her face is even paler than usual. I follow her gaze to the kid's arm, where cruddy-looking scabs glisten in the starlight. What are those? Letters?

"What is that?" I ask while rolling up the pant legs; they're a good four inches too long.

"It's Latin," she answers. "It means 'he conquers who endures.'"

"Why is it cut into his arm like that?"

She shakes her head. Her hand wanders to her own shoulder. She thinks I don't notice.

"You have one, too, don't you?"

"No." She kneels beside the boy, his combat knife in her hand. She slices along the tiny scar on the back of his neck and gingerly digs the tracking device from the cut.

"Here. Put this in your mouth."

"Like fuck."

She cups it in the palm of her hand and spits on it. Rolls the rice-sized pellet around in her spit to clean off the blood.

"Better?"

"In what way could that possibly be *better*?"

She grabs my hand and deposits the gooey pellet into my palm.

"You clean it, then."

I lace up the boots as she cuts into another kid's neck, dips out the tracker with the tip of the knife, then slides the blade between her lips. There is something matter-of-factly savage about it, and her words echo in my head: *I am what he made me.*

51

PREPARATIONS. DETAILS.

I'll need gear, but only what I can fit into the pockets and pouches of the uniform. Extra magazines for the rifle and side-arm, a knife, a penlight, a couple of grenades, two bottles of water, and three power bars, at Ben's insistence. Parish has this weird, superstitious faith in power bars, which is totally bogus, unlike my belief in the talismanic force of teddy bears.

"What if you're wrong?" I ask Ringer. "What if nobody comes looking for the strike team?"

She shrugs. "Then we're screwed."

So bright and cheerful. Such a ray of sunshine. I wake Sam and Megan and make them eat while Ben and Ringer prep for the assault outside. Something's up between those two. Something

184

they're keeping from me. Kind of makes me wish I had Evan's old mind-mining abilities. I'd plunge into Ben Parish's head and hack my way to the truth. I thought I busted Ringer with that part of her Silencers-are-ordinary-people-like-us-only-more-so theory. How did Evan's spirit enter and mix with mine if he's human? Her answer required advanced degrees in robotics, bionics, and electromagnetic physics to understand. The CPU attached to his brain interpreting my physiological biofeedback, creating an informational loop in which my data commingled with his, blah, blah, blah. Really, science is wonderful, but why does it tend to suck all the joyous mystery from the world? Love may be nothing more than a complex interaction of hormones, conditioned behavior, and positive reinforcement, but try writing a poem or song about *that*.

Preparations. Details.

I brief Sam and Megs on the plan. Sam's all in. Although infiltrating the base would be his top choice, at least he'll have some quality time with his beloved Zombie. Megan doesn't say a word and I'm worried she might balk at the critical moment. Can't blame her, though. The last time she trusted grown-ups, they stuffed a bomb down her throat.

I hand Bear to Sam for safekeeping, Sam's as much as the bear's. He hands it over to Megan. Oh Jesus. Too big for Bear now; they grow up so fast.

Blankets, I tell them. Everybody except Ringer gets a blanket.

Then there's nothing left to do but climb the stairs one last time. I take Sammy's hand, Sammy takes Megan's, Megan takes Bear's, and together we rise toward the surface. The stairs jiggle and moan. They may collapse.

We won't.

185

52

ZOMBIE

I WATCH AS Ringer carries the last two bodies into the bay of the old garage, one under each arm. I understand how that's possible; still, it's a little freaky to watch. I wait by the empty grave for her to come out. It doesn't happen. *Oh, boy. Now what?*

Inside the garage the smell of gasoline and grease brings home the past. Before there was Zombie, there was this kid named Ben Parish who worked on cars with his old man on Saturday afternoons, the last being a cherry-red '69 Corvette, his seventeenth birthday present from his dad, a guy who really couldn't afford it and pretended it was for his only son, but they both knew the truth. Ben's birthday was an excuse to buy the car, and the car was an excuse to spend time with his son as the clock wound down to graduation and then college and then grandkids and then the retirement home and then the grave. The grave leapt unexpectedly to the front of the line, not before the car, though; at least for a few Saturday afternoons, they had that car.

She'd laid her victims side by side in the center of the bay, crossing each one's arms across their chest. Ringer herself is nowhere in sight. For a second, I panic. Every time I expect a zig, there's a zag. I shift my weight to my good leg and drop the rifle from my shoulder into my hands.

From the deep shadows in the back, a low-pitched whine punctuated by a snuffling. I limp past rows of toolboxes and a cluster of oil drums, behind which I find her, sitting against the cinder-block wall, hugging her knees to her chest.

I can't stay upright; the pain's too much. I sit beside her. She wipes her cheeks. It's the first time I've seen Ringer cry. I've never seen her smile and probably never will, but now I've seen her cry. That's messed up.

"You didn't have a choice," I tell her. Digging up those bodies must have gotten to her. "And, anyway, they don't know the difference, right?"

She shakes her head. "Oh, Zombie."

"It isn't too late, Ringer. We can call it off. Sullivan can't do this without you."

"She'd have nothing to do if you hadn't stepped in front of Walker like that."

"Maybe I wouldn't have if you'd trusted me with the truth."

"The truth," she echoes.

"The important word here is *trusted*."

"I trust you, Zombie."

"Funny way of showing it."

She shakes her head. *That dumb Zombie, wrong again.* "I know you won't tell."

She stretches out her legs, and a plastic container flops from her chest onto her thighs. The bright green liquid inside it sloshes. It's a jug of antifreeze.

"A capful should be enough," she says, so softly I don't think the words are directed at me. "The 12th System—it'll protect me. Protect *me* . . ."

I grab the jug from her lap. "Goddamn it, Ringer, you didn't already drink this, did you?"

187

"Give that back, Zombie."

I let out my breath. I'll take that as a no. "You told me what happened but you didn't tell me how."

"Well. You know." She twirls a hand in the air. "The usual way."

Okay. I deserved that.

"His name was Razor." She frowns. "No. His name was Alex."

"The recruit who shot Teacup."

"For me. So I could escape."

"The one who helped Vosch set you up."

"Yes."

"And then Vosch kind of set the two of you up."

She gives me the patented impassive Ringer stare. "What does that mean?"

"Vosch left him with you that night. He must have known Razor had . . . that leaving the two of you alone might lead to . . ."

"That's crazy, Zombie. If Vosch thought that for a second, he never would have left Alex to guard me."

"How come?"

"Because love is the most dangerous weapon in the world. It's more unstable than uranium."

I swallow. My throat is dry. "Love."

"Yes, love. Can I have that back now?"

"No."

"I could take it from you." She's staring at me across a space no thicker than a fist with eyes only slightly lighter than the dark around them.

"I know you could."

188

I tense. I have a feeling she could knock me out with a flick of her little finger.

"You want to know if I loved him. You want to ask me that," she says.

"It's none of my business."

"I don't love anyone, Zombie."

"Well, that's okay. You're still young."

"Stop that. Stop trying to make me smile. It's cruel."

There's a knife twisting in my gut. The pain makes the bullet wound feel like a mosquito bite. For whatever reason, whenever I'm around this girl, pain follows, and not just the physical variety. Being intimately acquainted with both kinds, I'd rather be shot a dozen times than have my heart torn in half.

"You're a prick," she informs me. She pulls the jug from my hands. "I always thought so." She unscrews the cap and fills it halfway to the lip. The liquid shimmers a neon green. *Their* color.

"This is what they've done, Zombie. This is the world they've made, where giving life is crueler than taking it. I am being kind. I am being wise."

She raises the cup toward her lips. Her hand shakes; the bright green fluid sloshes over the edge and runs over her fingers. And in her eyes the same darkness that floods my core.

She doesn't pull away when I wrap my fingers around her wrist. She doesn't unleash her enhancement upon me and tear my head off my shoulders. She offers hardly any resistance when I force her hand down.

"I'm lost, Zombie."

"I'll find you."

"I can't move."

"I'll carry you."

She topples sideways into me. I wrap my arms around her. I cup her face; I run my fingers through her hair.

The darkness slips; it cannot hold.

53

WE'RE HEADING BACK to the hole when Cassie and the kids emerge from the basement of the demolished safe house, loaded down with blankets.

"Zombie," Nugget calls out. He races over, the stack of blankets in his arms bopping up and down as he runs. He pulls up when he gets a close look at Ringer's face. Right away he knows something's wrong; only dogs read faces better than little kids.

"What is it, Private?" I ask.

"Cassie won't let me have a gun."

"I'm working on that."

His face screws up. He's dubious.

I poke him in the arm with a loose fist and add, "Lemme bury Ringer first. Then we'll talk about weapons."

Cassie comes up, half leading, half dragging Megan by the wrist. I hope she hangs on tight. I have a feeling if she lets go, that girl's taking off. Ringer jerks her head toward the garage, *in there*, and says, "Ten minutes till the chopper."

"How do you know?" Sullivan asks.

"I can hear it."

Cassie shoots me a look accompanied by a raised eyebrow. *Get that? She says she can hear it.* While all anyone else can hear is the wind driving over the barren fields.

"What's the hose for?" she asks me.

"So I don't black out or suffocate," Ringer answers.

"I thought you were—what did you call it?—enhanced."

"I am. But I still need oxygen."

"Like a shark," Cassie says.

Ringer nods. "Like that."

Sullivan leads the kids into the garage. Ringer drops into the hole and lies flat on her back in the dirt. I pick up the rifle where she dropped it and lower it toward her. She shakes her head.

"Leave it up there."

"You sure?"

She nods. Her face is bathed in starlight. I catch my breath.

"What?" she asks.

I look away. "Nothing."

"Zombie."

I clear my throat. "It's not important. I just thought—for a minute there—flashed across my mind . . ."

"Zombie."

"Okay. You're beautiful. That's all. I mean—you wanted to know . . ."

"You get sentimental at the weirdest times. Hose."

I drop one end down. She closes her mouth over the opening and gives me the thumbs-up.

I can hear the chopper now, faint but growing louder. I shovel the dirt over her, sweeping it into the hole with my right hand while I hang on to the hose with my left. She doesn't need to say the words; I can read them in her eyes. *Hurry, Zombie.*

The sickening sound of the dirt hitting her body. I decide not to look. I watch the sky as I bury her, gripping the end of the hose so hard, my knuckles turn white. The nearly endless number of ways this can go wrong races through my mind. What if there's a full squad on board that chopper? What if it isn't just one Black Hawk but two? Or three, or four? What if, what if, what if, *whatever*.

I'm not going to make it back to the garage in time. Ringer is completely covered now, but I'm out in the open with a shot-up leg and a hundred yards to cross before the chopper—which I can see silhouetted against the backdrop of stars, a black naught against the glittering white—is in range. Never tried to run with a bullet in my leg. Never had to. Guess there's a first time for everything.

I don't make it very far. Maybe forty-five, fifty yards. I pitch forward, landing face-first in the dirt. Why the hell didn't *Cassie bury Ringer*? Would make more sense for me to hunker down with the kids, and besides, Sullivan would probably leap at the chance.

I heave myself upright. I'm vertical maybe five seconds, and then I'm down again. It's too late. I have to be within range of their infrared by now.

A pair of boots pounds toward me. A pair of hands haul me up. Cassie throws my arm around her neck and pulls me forward as I swing my bad leg around, hop with my good one, swing the bad one, but she bears most of the load. Who needs a 12th System when you have a heart like Cassie Sullivan's?

We fall into the bay of the garage and Cassie hurls a blanket at me. The kids are already covered, and I shout "Not yet!" Their body heat will gather beneath the material, defeating the purpose.

"Wait for my go," I tell them. Then, to Cassie: "You've got this." Incredibly, she smiles at me and nods. "I know."

54

CASSIE

"NOW!" BEN SHOUTS, probably too late: The chopper thunders over us. We dive under the blankets, and I begin the countdown.

How will I know when it's time? I asked Ringer.

After two minutes.

Why two?

If we can't do it in two minutes, it can't be done.

What did that mean? I didn't ask, but now I suspect that two is just a random number she pulled out of her ass.

I count it out anyway.

. . . 58 one thousand, 59 one thousand, 60 one thousand . . .

The old blanket stinks of mildew and rat piss. I can't see a damn thing. What I hear—all I hear—is the helicopter, which sounds like it's two feet away. Has it landed? Has the recovery team been deployed to check out the mysterious mound of dirt that looks suspiciously like a grave? The questions roll across the landscape of my mind like a slow-crawling fog; it's hard to think when you're counting—maybe that's why it's a recommended sleeping aid.

. . . 92 one thousand, 93 one thousand, 94 one thousand . . .

I'm having trouble breathing. This may have something to do with the fact that I'm slowly suffocating.

Somewhere around 75 one thousand, the chopper's engines had revved down. Not stopped, just the pitch and volume dipped. Landed? At 95 one thousand, the engines pick up again. Do I stay here until Ringer's arbitrary two minutes are up or do I listen to that wise little voice screeching in my ear, *Go, go, go, go now!*

At 97 one thousand, I go.

And damn does the world seem blindingly bright after bursting from my woolen cocoon.

Clear the bay doors, sharp right, then fields, trees, stars, road, and *chopper,* six feet off the ground.

And rising.

Crap.

Beside the Ringer-hole, a whirling shadow by the broken earth and another shadow that moves so slow in comparison, it seems as if it isn't moving at all. Ringer's sprung her trap on the search party. *Sayonara, search party!*

I'm running full out toward the Black Hawk, and the supplies in my uniform make me feel like I'm weighed down with bricks, the rifle bouncing against my back, and, shit, it's too far away and rising too fast, *pull up, Cassie, pull up, you're not going to make it,* time for Plan B only we don't have a Plan B, *and two minutes, what was that, Ringer? If you're the tactical genius in this operation, then we're so totally screwed,* and the space shrinks between me and the chopper while its nose dips slightly, and *how good's your vertical, Sullivan?*

I leap. Time stops. The chopper hangs suspended like a mobile above my fully extended body—even my toes are pointed—and there is no sound anymore or draft from the blades lifting the Black Hawk up or pushing my body down.

There was this little girl—she's gone now—with skinny little arms and bony little legs and a head topped with bouncy red curls and a (very straight) nose with a special talent only she and her daddy knew about.

She could fly.

My outstretched fingers banged on the edge of the open cargo doorway. I caught hold of something cold and metallic, and I locked down on it with both hands as the chopper soared straight up and the ground sped away from my kicking feet. Fifty feet up, a hundred, and I sway back and forth, trying to swing my foot onto the platform. Two hundred feet, two-fifty, and my right hand slips, I'm hanging on with just the left now, and the noise is deafening, so I can't hear myself scream. Looking down, I see the garage and the house across the street from the garage and down the road the black smudge of where Grace's house once stood. Starlight-bathed fields and woods shining silver-gray and the road stretching from horizon to horizon.

I'm going to fall.

At least it will be quick. *Splat*, like a bug against a windshield.

My left hand slips; thumb, pinky, and ring fingers thrum empty air; I'm attached to the chopper by two fingers now.

Then those fingers slide off, too.

55

I'VE LEARNED it *is* possible to hear yourself scream over the jet engines of a Black Hawk helicopter after all.

Also, it isn't true that your life flashes before your eyes when you're about to die. The only things that flash before mine are Bear's eyes, unblinking plastic, bottomless, soullessly soulful.

There's several hundred feet to fall. I fall less than one, jerking to a stop so hard, my shoulder's nearly ripped from its socket. I caught nothing to abort the plunge; someone caught *me*, and now that someone is hauling me on board.

I'm slung facedown onto the floor of the chopper's hold. First it's like, *I'm alive!* Then it's all, *I'm going to die!* Because whoever rescued me is yanking me upright, and I have basically three choices, four if you include the false choice of the gun, because firing a gun within the metallic cocoon of a helicopter is a very bad idea.

I've got my fists, the pepper spray contained in one of the twenty-nine million pockets of my new uniform, or the hardest, most terrifying weapon in all of Cassie Sullivan's formidable arsenal: her head.

I whip around and smash my forehead into the center of the face, *crunch!*, breaking a nose, and then there is blood. As in a lot of blood, practically a geyser, but the blow has no other effect. She doesn't move an inch. She doesn't even blink. She's been—what word did she use to describe the incredibly creepy and scary thing Vosch did to her?—*enhanced.*

"Easy there, Sullivan," Ringer says, turning her head to spit out a golf-ball-sized wad of blood.

56

RINGER

I PUSH SULLIVAN down into a seat and shout in her ear, "Get ready to bail!" She doesn't say anything, just stares up into my bloody face uncomprehendingly. Arteries cauterized by the microscopic drones swarming in my bloodstream, pain receptors shut down by the hub; I may look horrible, but I feel great.

I climb over her to the cockpit and plop into the copilot's seat. The pilot recognizes me immediately.

It's Lieutenant Bob. The same Lieutenant Bob whose finger I broke in my "escape" with Razor and Teacup.

"Holy shit," he shouts. "*You!*"

"Back from the grave!" I yell, which is literally true. I jab my finger at our feet. "Put her down!"

"Fuck you!"

I react without thinking. The hub decides for me—and that's the terrifying thing about the 12th System: I don't know anymore where it ends and I begin. Not fully human, not wholly alien, neither, both, something loosed within me, something unbound.

Afterward I realize the brilliance of it: The most precious commodity of any pilot is his sight.

I rip off his helmet and shove my thumb into his eye. His legs kick; his hand flies up to grab my wrist; and the chopper's nose dips. I intercept his hand and guide it back to the stick as I pour myself into him: Where there is panic, calm. Where there is fear, peace. Where there is pain, comfort.

I know he won't go all kamikaze on us, because no part of him is hidden from me. I know the desires he would deny even to himself, and there is no desire within him to die.

As there is no doubt in his mind that he needs me to live.

197

57

ZOMBIE WAS RIGHT all those months ago: As sanctuaries in the apocalypse went, the caverns of West Liberty were damn hard to beat.

No wonder the Silencer priest claimed them for his own.

Gallons of fresh water. An entire chamber stocked with dry and canned goods. Medical supplies, bedding, cans of heating fuel, kerosene, and gasoline. Clothes, tools, and enough weapons and explosives to outfit a small army. A perfect place to hide, even cozy, if you ignored the smell.

The Ohio Caverns reeked of blood.

The largest chamber was the worst. Deep underground and humid, with very little ventilation. The smell—and the blood—had nowhere to go. The stone floor still shimmers crimson in our lights.

A slaughter took place here. Either the false priest picked up the spent shell casings or he sliced his victims open, one by one. We find a spot against the wall with a sleeping bag, a stack of books (including a well-worn Bible), a kerosene lantern, a bag full of toiletries, and several rosaries.

"Of all the places he could bunk, he chose *this* spot," Zombie breathes. He's pressing a cloth against his face to filter the air. "Crazy SOB."

"Not crazy, Zombie," I tell him. "Sick. Infected with a virus before he was even born. That's the best way to think of it."

Zombie nods slowly. "You're right. That is the *best* way to think of it."

We've left Bob the pilot with Cassie and the two kids in another chamber, after packing and bandaging his wound and giving him antibiotics and a massive dose of morphine. He's in no condition to fly any farther tonight. Just getting us as far as the caverns exceeded his endurance, but I sat beside him and kept him focused and calm, his ballast and his anchor.

Zombie and I retreat toward higher ground, and he navigates the narrow passages with one hand on my shoulder, awkwardly swinging his bad leg, wincing with every step. I make a mental note to check the wound before I leave. The round should probably be removed, but I worry the procedure will do more harm than good. Even with antibiotics, the risk of infection is high, and nicking a major artery would be catastrophic.

"Only two ways down here," he says. "That works for us. We can block off one end, which leaves a single entrance to watch."

"Right."

"Think we're far enough from Urbana?"

"Far enough from Urbana to what?"

"To avoid getting vaporized." He smiles, and his teeth shine unusually bright in the lamplight.

I shake my head. "I don't know."

"You know what's scary, Ringer? You seem to know more than any of us, but whenever a critical question comes up, like the issue of whether or not we'll be vaporized in a couple of days, you never know the answer."

The path is steep. He needs to rest. I'm not certain he knows that I can feel what he feels through the conduit of his hand touching my shoulder. I don't know if that would comfort or terrify him. Maybe both.

"Hang on, Zombie." Acting as if I need to catch my breath.

"Gotta rest a minute."

I lean against an outcropping. At first he tries to be tough and stay upright. But after a minute or two he can't maintain the act; he eases himself onto the floor, grunting from the effort. Since we met, his near-constant companion has been pain, most of which I have delivered.

"Does it hurt?" he asks.

"What?"

He points at my nose. "Sullivan said she got you good."

"She did."

"It's not even swollen. And no black eyes."

I look away. "Thank Vosch."

"Kind of hoping you'll thank him for all of us."

I nod. Then I shake my head. Then I nod again.

Zombie knows he's on dangerous ground. He moves to safer territory quickly. "And it doesn't hurt? There's no pain?"

I look right into his eyes. "No, Zombie. There's no pain."

I squat, resting on my heels, and set the lamp on the floor. The space between us, less than a foot, feels more like a mile.

"Did you notice on our way in?" I ask. "Somebody built an outdoor shower. I think I'm going to take one before I leave." Blood's caked on my face, there's dirt in my hair, and damp earth is smeared over every exposed inch. An eternity passed after Zombie buried me. I can still see their faces blank with astonishment and horror as I burst from the grave, the two recruits sent back to pick up the squadmates they left behind to kill us. Sullivan had a similar look after she smashed her head into my nose. I've become the stuff of wonder and nightmares.

200

So I want to be clean. I want to feel human again.

"Won't matter if the water's cold?" Zombie asks.

"I won't feel it."

He nods like he understands. "It should be me. Not in the shower. Ha, ha. I mean going with you. Not Cassie. I'm sorry, Ringer." He pretends to study the cave's jagged teeth jutting down over our heads, a dragon's mouth frozen in midchomp. "What was he like? I mean. That guy. You know."

I know. "Tough. Funny. Smart. He loved to talk. And he loved baseball."

"What about you?" Zombie asks.

"I have no opinion about baseball."

"Not what I meant and you know it."

"It doesn't matter," I answer. "He's dead."

"Still matters."

"It's something you'd have to ask him."

"I can't. He's dead. So I'm asking you."

"What do you want from me, Zombie? Seriously, what do you *want*? He was kind to me—"

"He lied to you."

"Not when it mattered. Not about the important things."

"He betrayed you to Vosch."

"He sacrificed his life for me."

"He murdered Teacup."

"That's it, Zombie. No more." I rise. "I shouldn't have told you."

"Why did you?"

Because you're my bullshit-free zone, but I'm not giving him that. Because you're the one I came out of the wilderness for, no, not that, either. And not Because you're the one person I still trust.

201

Instead, I say, "You caught me at a weak moment."

"Well." Then the Ben Parish smile, the smile it almost hurts to look at. "If you're ever in need of an egotistical prick, I'm your man." He waits two breaths, then adds, "Oh, come on, Ringer. Come on. Smile. That joke works on so many levels, it isn't even funny."

"You're right," I answer. "It's not funny."

58

I SLIDE OUT of my clothes beside the outdoor shower. The overhead container was empty, so I had to fill it from the cistern next to the welcome center. The cistern must have weighed over a hundred pounds, but I hoisted it onto my shoulder as if it weighed no more than little Nugget.

I know the water is cold, but like I told Zombie, I'm protected by Vosch's gift. I feel nothing but wetness. The water bears away the blood and dirt.

I run my hands over my stomach. *He sacrificed his life for me.* The boy in the doorway lit up by a funeral pyre, carving letters into his arm.

I touch my shoulder. The skin is smooth and soft. The 12th System repaired the damage minutes after I inflicted it. I am like the water that runs over me, immune to permanence, recycling endlessly. I am water; I am life. The form may change, but the substance stays the same. Strike me down and I will rise again. *Vincit qui patitur.*

I close my eyes and see *his*. Sharp, glittering, brilliant blue, eyes that knife deeper than your bones. *You created me, and now your creation is coming back for you. Like rain to parched earth, I come back.*

And water bears away the blood and dirt.

59

CASSIE

HERE'S SOMETHING to chew on. Here's the charming truth about the world the Others are creating:

My little brother has forgotten the alphabet, but he knows how to make bombs.

A year ago it was crayons and coloring books, construction paper and Elmer's glue. Now it's fuses and blasting caps, wires and black powder.

Who wants to read a book when you can blow something up?

Beside me, Megan watches him the way she watches everything else: silently. She clutches Bear to her chest, another silent witness to the evolution of Samuel J. Sullivan.

He's working with Ringer, the two of them kneeling next to each other, a two-person assembly line. I guess they took the same IED class at camp. Ringer's damp hair shines like a blacksnake's skin in the lamplight. Her ivory skin gleams. A couple of hours ago, I smashed my forehead into her nose and broke it, but there's no swelling, no sign I inflicted any damage at all. Unlike my nose, which will be crooked till the day I die. Life is not fair.

"How'd you get on that chopper?" I ask her. It's been bugging me.

"Same way you did," she answers. "I jumped."

"The plan was for *me* to jump."

"Which you did. You were hanging on by a fingernail," she said. "I didn't think I had a choice at that point."

In other words, *I saved your worthless, freckly, crooked-nosed ass. What are you bitching about?*

Not that my nose has an ass. I really should stop putting thoughts into other people's heads.

She tucks a strand of her silky locks behind her ear. There's something so effortlessly and inexplicably graceful about the gesture that it borders on creepy. *What the hell happened to you, Ringer?*

Of course, I know what happened to her. *The gift,* Evan called it. All human potential times a hundred. *I have the heart to do what I have to do,* Evan told me once. He neglected to say at the time he meant that both literally and figuratively. He neglected to say a lot of things, the bastard who doesn't even deserve rescuing.

What the hell am I thinking? Looking at Ringer's delicate fingers dance in the complicated ballet of constructing a bomb, I realize the scariest thing about her isn't what Vosch has done to her body; it's what that amped-up body has done to her mind. When you tear down our physical limitations, what happens to our moral ones? I'm pretty certain the pre-enhanced Ringer couldn't have single-handedly massacred five heavily armed, well-trained recruits. I also suspect pre-enhanced Ringer couldn't have shoved her thumb into another human being's eyeball. That required a leap in evolution of an entirely different kind.

Speaking of Bob.

"You people are wacked," he goes. He's been watching, too, with his good eye.

"No, Bob," Ringer says without looking up from her task. "The world is wacked. We just happen to be occupying it."

"Not for long! You won't get within a hundred miles of the base." His panicky voice fills the little chamber, which smells of chemicals and old blood. "They know where you are—there's a fucking GPS on that chopper—and they're coming after you with everything they've got."

Ringer looks up at him. A flip of the bangs. A flash of the dark eyes. "That's what I'm counting on."

"How much longer?" I ask her. Everything depends on our reaching the base before sunrise.

"A couple more and we'll be ready."

"Yeah!" Bob shouts. "Get ready! Say your prayers, because it's goin' *down*, Dorothy!"

"She's not a Dorothy!" Sam shouts at him. "*You're* a Dorothy!"

"You shut the fuck up!" Bob yells back.

"Hey, Bob," I call over to him. "Leave my brother alone."

Bob's all balled up in the corner, quivering, sweating, the buttload of morphine apparently not enough. He couldn't be older than twenty-five. Young by pre-Arrival standards. Middle-aged by the new ones.

"What's gonna stop me from crashing us into a fucking cornfield, huh?" he demands. "Whatcha gonna do—punch out my other eye?" Then he laughs.

Ringer ignores him, which throws gas on Bob's fire.

"Not that it matters. Not that you have a chance in *hell*. They'll cut you down the minute we land. They'll carve you up like fucking Halloween pumpkins. So make your little bombs and hatch your little plots; you're all dead meat."

"You're right, Bob," I tell him. "That pretty much sums it up."

I'm not being snarky (for once). I mean every word. Assuming he doesn't crash us into a cornfield, assuming we aren't shot down by the armada that's surely on its way, assuming we aren't captured or killed inside the camp by the thousands of soldiers *who will be expecting us*, assuming by some miracle Evan is still alive and by some bigger miracle I find him, and assuming Ringer kills Vosch, the closest thing our species has to the indestructible cockroach, we still have no exit strategy. We're buying a one-way ticket to oblivion.

And those tickets don't come cheap, I think while I watch my Sams put the finishing touches on a bomb.

Oh, Sam. Crayons and coloring books. Construction paper and glue. Teddy bears and footy pajamas, swing sets and storybooks and everything else we knew you'd leave behind, though not this soon, not this way. Oh, Sam, you have the face of a child but the eyes of an old man.

I was too late. I risked everything to rescue you from the end, but the end already had you.

I push myself to my feet. Everybody looks at me except Sam. He's humming softly, slightly off-key. Theme music to build explosives by. He's the happiest I've seen him in a long time.

"I need to talk to Sam," I tell Ringer.

"That's fine," she says. "I can spare him."

"I wasn't asking for permission."

I grab his wrist and pull him from the chamber, into the narrow corridor, up the path toward the surface until I'm sure they can't hear us. Fairly sure, anyway. Ringer can probably hear a butterfly beating its wings in Mexico.

"What is it?" he asks, frowning, or maybe-frowning. I didn't bring a light; I can barely see his face.

That's a damn good question, kid. Once again, here I go, half-cocked and winging it. This should be a speech weeks in the making.

"You know I'm doing this for you," I tell him.

"Doing what?"

"Leaving you."

He shrugs. Shrugs! "You're coming back, aren't you?"

There it is: the invitation to a promise I cannot make. I take his hand and say, "Remember that summer you chased the rainbow?"

He looks up at me, utterly baffled. "Well, maybe not. I think you were still in diapers. We were in the backyard and I had the sprayer. When the sunlight hit the water . . . you know, a rainbow. And I was making you chase it. Telling you to catch the rainbow . . ." I'm about to let loose with some waterworks of my own. "Kind of cruel when I think about it."

"Why are you thinking about it, then?"

"I just don't want . . . I don't want you to forget things, Sam."

"Things like what?"

"You need to remember it wasn't always like this." Making bombs and hiding in caves and watching everyone you know die. "I remember things," he argues. "I remember what Mommy looked like now."

"You do?"

He nods emphatically. "I remembered right before I shot that lady."

207

Something in my expression must give me away. I'm guessing a mixture of shock and horror and a sadness that has no bottom. Because he turns on his heel and barrels back to the weapons chamber only to return after a minute with Bear in his arms.

Oh, that goddamned bear.

"No, Sams," I whisper.

"He brought you luck last time."

"He's . . . he's Megan's now."

"No, he's mine. He's always been mine." Holding him out to me.

I gently push Bear back into his chest. "And you need to keep him. I know you've outgrown him. I know you're a soldier or commando or whatever now. But one day, maybe there'll be a little kid who really needs Bear. Because . . . well, just because."

I kneel at his feet. "So hang on to him, understand? You take care of him and protect him and don't let anybody hurt him. Bear is very important to the grand scheme of things. He's like gravity. Without him, the universe would fall apart."

He stares at his big sister's face for a long, silent moment. *Memorize it, Sams. Study every bruised, scratched-up, scarred, crooked inch of it. So you don't forget. So you never forget. Remember my face no matter what. No. Matter. What.*

"That's crazy, Cassie," he says, and for an instant—and only an instant—the little boy is back, and I see in his nowface his then-face, hysterical with wonder and laughter, chasing rainbows.

208

60

RINGER

I HOP DOWN from the chopper. Zombie watches me sling the rucksack over my shoulder and says, "All done?"

"Done."

"How many you got left?" Nodding at the bag.

"Five."

He frowns. "Think it'll be enough?"

"It'll have to be. So, yes."

"Time to go, then," he says.

"Time to go."

Our eyes meet. He knows what I'm thinking. "I won't make that promise," he says.

"You can't come after me, Zombie."

"I won't make that promise," he says again.

"And you can't stay here. After the mothership drops the bombs, head south. Use the trackers I gave you. They won't mask you from IR or hide you from Silencers, but—"

"Ringer."

"I'm not finished."

"I know what to do."

"Remember Dumbo. Remember what coming after me cost. Some things you have to let go, Zombie. Some things—"

He grabs my face in both his hands and kisses me hard on the mouth.

"One smile," he whispers. "One smile and I'll let you go." My face in his hands and my hands on his hips. His forehead touching mine and the stars turning over us and the Earth beneath us, and time slipping, slipping.

"It wouldn't be real," I tell him.

"At this point, I don't care."

I push him away. Gently. "I still do."

—— **61** ——

THE BOMBS HAVE BEEN LOADED. Time to load Bob.

"You think I'm not ready to die?" he asks me as I escort him to his seat.

"I know you're not."

I strap him in. Through the open hatch, I can see Sullivan with Zombie, and she's trying very hard to stay composed. Cassie Sullivan is sentimental and immature and self-absorbed beyond belief, but even she knows we're crossing a threshold that we can't come back from.

"No plan," she whispers to Zombie. She doesn't want me to hear her and I don't really want to. Vosch's gift is a curse, too. "Nothing fated."

"No meant-to-be," Zombie says.

No plan. Nothing fated. No meant-to-be. Like a catechism or an affirmation of faith—or faith's opposite.

She rises on her toes and kisses his cheek. "You know what I'm gonna say now."

Zombie smiles. "He'll be fine, Cassie." He grabs her hand and squeezes hard. "With my life."

Her response is immediate and fierce. "Not with your life, Parish. With your death."

She notices me over his shoulder and pulls her hand away.

I nod. It's time. I turn to our one-eyed pilot. "Boot her up, Bob."

62

THE GROUND RECEDES. Zombie dwindles, becomes a black dot against gray earth. The road swivels to the right like the second hand of the terrestrial clock, marking the time that's lost, the time that cannot be taken back. Turning north, climbing, the explosion of countless stars, and the burning center of the galaxy a backdrop for the mothership glowing phosphorescent green, its belly full of the bombs that will erase the last remaining footprint of civilization. How many cities in the world? Five thousand? Ten? I don't know, but *they* do. In less than three hours, in the utter silence of the void, the bay doors will slide open and thousands of guided missiles carrying warheads no larger than a loaf of bread will vomit forth. A single orbit around the planet. After ten centuries, all we had built will be gone in a day.

The debris will settle. Rains will bathe the scorched and barren ground. Rivers will revert to their natural course. Forests and meadows and marsh and grasslands will reclaim what was cut and razed, filled and leveled and buried beneath tons of asphalt and concrete. Animal populations will explode. Wolves will return from the north and herds of bison, thirty million strong, will again darken the plains. It will be as if we never were, paradise reborn, and there is something ancient inside me, buried deep in the memory of my genes, that rejoices.

A savior? Vosch asked me. *Is that what I am?*

Across the aisle, Sullivan is watching me. She looks so small in that oversized uniform, like a little kid playing dress-up. How odd we ended up together like this. She disliked me from the moment she laid eyes on me. About her, I just thought there wasn't much *there* there. I'd known a lot of girls like Cassie Sullivan, shy but arrogant, timid but impulsive, naïve but serious, sensitive but flippant. Feelings matter to her more than facts, particularly the fact that her mission is a futile one.

Mine is hopeless. Both are suicidal. And neither is avoidable.

My headset crackles. It's Bob. "We've got company."

"How many?"

"Um. Six."

"I'm coming up."

Sullivan starts when I unbuckle. I pat her shoulder on my way to the copilot's seat. *It's okay. We were expecting this.*

Up front, Bob points out the incoming choppers on his screen. "Orders, boss?" With only a hint of sarcasm. "Engage or evade, or you want me to set her down?"

"Hold course. They're going to hail—"

"Wait. They're hailing us." He listens. I have a visual on them now, dead ahead, flying in attack formation. "Okay," he says, turning to me. "Three guesses. First two don't count."

"They're ordering us to land."

"Now it's my turn: 'Up yours.' Right?"

I shake my head. "Say nothing. Keep flying."

"You do realize they'll shoot us down, right?"

"Just let me know when they're in range."

"Oh, so that's the plan. *We're* shooting *them* down. All six of them."

"My bad, Bob. I meant let me know when *we're* in range. What's our speed?"

"A hundred and forty knots. Why?"

"Double it."

"I can't double it. Max is one-ninety."

"Then max it. Same heading." *Right down your throats, here we come.*

We leap forward; a shiver ripples down the chopper's skin; the engines howl; the wind screams in the hold. After a couple of minutes, even Bob's unenhanced eye can see the lead chopper coming straight at us.

"Ordering us down again," Bob yells. "In range in thirty!"

"What's going on?" Sullivan's head pokes between us. Her mouth drops open when she focuses on what's bearing down.

"Twenty!" Bob calls.

"Twenty *what?*" she shouts.

They'll pull up, I'm sure of it. Pull up or break formation to let us pass. They won't shoot us down, either. Because of the risk. *The risk is the key,* Vosch told me. By now he knows about the dead strike team and the commandeered chopper. Constance wouldn't have done that and Walker's been captured. That leaves just one person who could have pulled off something like this: his creation.

"Ten seconds!"

I close my eyes. The hub, my ever-faithful companion, shuts down my senses, plunging me into that space without sound, without light.

I'm coming, you son of a bitch. You wanted to create a human without humanity. Now you're going to get one.

IV

THE LAST DAY

63

EVAN WALKER

THE ROOM into which they threw him was small, bare, and very cold. When they pulled off the hood covering his head, the severity of the light blinded him. Instinctively, he covered his eyes.

One of his captors demanded his clothes. He stripped down to his briefs. *No, those too.* He dropped the shorts and kicked them toward the doorway, where the two boys wearing camouflage stood. One of them—the younger one—giggled.

They stepped out of the room. The door clanged shut. The cold and the silence and the blaring light were intense. He looked down and saw a large drain in the center of the tiled floor. He looked up, and as if looking up was the signal, water burst from the overhead sprayers.

He staggered back against the wall and covered his head with his hands. The cold bored into him, through skin to muscle to bone to marrow, until his knees buckled and he sank to the floor, head balanced on his upraised knees, arms wrapped around his legs. A disembodied voice boomed in the tiny space. *"STAND. UP."* He ignored it.

Instantly, the water changed from freezing cold to scalding hot, and Evan leapt to his feet, mouth hanging open in shock and pain. The blazing light cut through the steaming mist and splintered into countless rainbows that bobbed and spun, radiant against the colorless tile. The spray turned cold again, then abruptly stopped.

He leaned against the wall, gasping, and the voice boomed, "DON'T TOUCH THE WALL. STAND WITH YOUR FEET TOGETHER AND YOUR HANDS AT YOUR SIDES."

He pushed off from the wall. Never, not even on the bitterest winter day on the farm when the wind roared across the fields and tree branches broke under the weight of ice, never had he been this cold. This cold was a living thing, a beast with his body clamped between its jaws, and those jaws were slowly crushing him. Every instinct told him to move; physical exertion would increase his blood pressure, raise his heart rate, speed warmth to his extremities.

"DON'T MOVE."

He couldn't concentrate. His thoughts spun like the uncountable rainbows let loose by the spray. Closing his eyes might help.

"DON'T CLOSE YOUR EYES."

The *cold*. He imagined the water on his naked body freezing solid, ice crystals forming in his hair. He will go into hypothermic shock. His heart will stop. His hands balled into fists and he dug his nails into his palms. The pain will focus his mind. Pain always does.

"OPEN YOUR HANDS. OPEN YOUR EYES. DON'T MOVE."

He obeyed. If he did everything they said, followed every order, complied with every demand, they would have no excuse to use the one weapon for which he had no defense.

He would bear any burden, endure any hardship, suffer any torment if that suffering added a single moment to her life.

He had been willing to sacrifice an entire civilization for her sake. His own life was infinitely small and meaningless, the cost-less price. He always knew, from the day he found her half buried in the snow, what saving her meant. What loving her meant. The cell door slamming shut, the death sentence handed down.

But they had not brought him to this room of cold and shattered light to kill him.

That would come later.

After they had broken his body and crushed his will and dissected his mind down to the last synapse.

The undoing of Evan Walker had begun.

64

HOURS PASSED. His body grew numb. He seemed to float inside his own insensate skin. The white wall in front of him stretched to infinity; he was floating in an endless nothingness, and his thoughts became fragmented. His mind, starved for stimuli, flung out random images from his childhood, Christmases with his human family, sitting with his brothers on the front porch, squirming in the pew at church. And much older scenes, from a different life: the breathtaking sunsets of a failing star, skimming over mountain ranges three times the height of the Himalayas in silver fliers, cresting a hill and seeing beneath him a valley devoid of life, the crop destroyed by the ultraviolet poison of their dying sun.

If he closed his eyes, the voice screamed at him to open them. If he swayed, the voice screamed for him to stand still.

But it was only a matter of time before he collapsed.

He didn't remember falling. Or the voice screaming at him to get up. One moment he was upright, the next he was curled into

221

a ball in a back corner of the white room. He had no idea how much time had passed—or if any had passed at all. Time did not exist in the white room.

He opened his eyes. A man was standing in the doorway. Tall, athletic, with deep-set eyes of striking blue, wearing a colonel's uniform. He knew this man, though they had never met. Knew his face and the face behind the face. Knew his given name and knew his human name. He had never seen him before; he had known him for ten thousand years.

"Do you know why I've brought you here?" the man asked him. Evan's mouth opened. His lips cracked and began to bleed. His tongue moved clumsily; he could not feel it.

"Betrayed."

"Betrayed? Oh no, quite the opposite. If there is one word to describe you, it is *devoted*." He stepped to one side and a woman wearing a white smock wheeled a gurney into the room. Two soldiers followed. They scooped him from the floor and dumped him onto the gurney. Above him, a single drop of water clung to a sprayer nozzle. He watched it quiver there, unable to look away. A cuff was wrapped around his arm; he didn't feel it. A thermometer was run across his forehead; he didn't feel it.

A bright light was shone in his eyes. The woman probed his naked body, pressing on his stomach, massaging his neck and pelvis, and her hands were deliciously warm.

"What is my name?" the colonel asked.

"Vosch."

"No, Evan. What is my *name*?"

He swallowed. He was very thirsty. "It can't be pronounced."

"Try."

He shook his head. It was impossible. Their language had

evolved as a result of a very different anatomy. Vosch might as well ask a chimpanzee to recite Shakespeare.

The woman in the white smock with the warm hands slid a needle into his arm. His body relaxed. He wasn't cold or thirsty anymore, and his mind was clear.

"Where are you from?" Vosch asked.

"Ohio."

"Before that."

"Can't be pronounced—"

"Never mind the name. Tell me where."

"In the constellation Lyra, the second planet from the dwarf star. The humans discovered it in 2014 and named it Kepler 438b."

Vosch smiled. "Of course. Kepler 438b. And of all places from which you could choose, why the Earth? Why did you come here?"

Evan turned his head to look at the man. "You already know the answer. You know all the answers."

The colonel smiled. His eyes remained hard, though, and humorless. He turned to the woman. "Get him dressed. It's time for Alice to take a trip down the rabbit hole."

65

THEY BROUGHT HIM a blue jumpsuit and a pair of flimsy white shoes. He told the soldiers watching him, "It's a lie. What he's told you. He's like me. He's using you to murder your own kind."

The boys said nothing. They nervously caressed the triggers of their guns.

"The war you're about to wage isn't real. You'll be killing innocent people, survivors like you, until the last one falls and then we will kill *you*. You're participating in your own genocide."

"Yeah, well, you're a fucking piece of infested horseshit," the younger boy blurted out. "And when the commander's done with you, he's giving you to *us*."

Evan sighed. There was no breaking through the lie because accepting the truth would break *them*.

Vices are virtues now, and virtues vices.

Out of the room, down a long corridor, then descending three flights of stairs to the lowest level. Another long corridor, turning right into a third that spanned the length of the base, passing door after unmarked door, walls of gray cinder block and the sterile glow of fluorescent bulbs. Here night never fell; here the light was everlasting.

They came to the last door at the end of the gray tunnel. The hundreds of doors he had passed had been white; this door was green. It swung open as they approached.

Inside the room was a reclining chair with straps on the arms and the footrest. An array of monitors and a keyboard. A technician was waiting for him, blank-faced, standing at attention.

And Vosch.

"You know what this is," he said.

Evan nodded. "Wonderland."

"And what might I expect to find there?"

"Very little that you don't already know."

"If I knew what I needed to know, I wouldn't have gone to so much trouble to bring you here."

The technician strapped him into the chair. Evan closed his

224

eyes. He knew the uploading of his memories would be physically painless. He also knew it could be psychologically devastating. The human brain has a marvelous capacity to screen and sort experience, protecting itself against the unbearable. Wonderland laid bare experience without the brain's interference, extracting life's record with no interpretation of the data. Nothing in context, no cause and effect, life unfiltered, without the brain's gift of rationalization, denial, and creating convenient gaps.

We remember our lives. Wonderland forces us to relive them.

It lasted two minutes. Two very long minutes.

From the disaster of silence and light that followed, Vosch's voice: "There is a flaw in you. You know this. Something has gone awry and it's important that we understand the reason."

His wrists were worn raw from pulling against the straps. "You will never understand."

"You may be right. But it is my human imperative to try."

On the monitors columns of numbers flowed, his life organized into sequences of qubits, what he saw, felt, heard, said, tasted, and thought, and the most complex packets of information in the universe: human emotion.

"It will take some time to run the diagnostics," Vosch said. "Come with me. I want to show you something."

He almost fell coming out of the chair. Vosch caught him and gently pulled him upright.

"What has happened to you?" he asked Evan. "Why are you so weak?"

"Ask *them*." With a nod toward the monitors.

"The 12th System crashed? When did it crash?"

He'd made a promise. He had to find her before Grace did.

Running down the highway, running until the gift within him collapsed. Because nothing mattered but the promise, nothing mattered but her.

Evan looked into Vosch's bright blue, birdlike eyes and said, "What are you going to show me?"

Vosch smiled. "Come and see."

66

TURNING LEFT off the stairs brought you down the mile-long hallway to Wonderland's green door. Turning right brought you to a dead end, a blank wall.

Vosch pressed his thumb against the wall. Gears whined, a seam appeared, and the wall split down the middle, the two halves pulling back to reveal a narrow corridor that faded past the sterile glow of fluorescents into utter black.

A recording sprang from a hidden speaker: "*Warning! You are entering an area restricted to authorized personnel pursuant to Special Order Eleven. All unauthorized persons found in this area will be subject to immediate disciplinary action. Warning! You are entering an area restricted to authorized personnel . . .*"

The voice followed them into the dark. *Warning!* A smudge of sickly green light bathed the end of the narrow corridor. They stopped there, at a door with no handle. Vosch pressed his thumb against the middle of the door and it swung silently open. He turned to Evan.

"We call this Area 51," Vosch informed him without a trace of irony.

Lights flickered on as they crossed the threshold. The first thing that caught Evan's eye was the egg-shaped pod, identical to the pod in which he escaped Camp Haven, except for its size: This pod was twice as large. It dominated half the chamber. Above it, he could see the concrete-reinforced launch shaft that led to the surface.

"This is what you wanted to show me?" He didn't understand. He knew Vosch would have a pod on base to return to their vessel after the 5th Wave was unleashed. In a matter of hours, identical pods would be dispatched from the mothership to retrieve the rest of their embedded people. Why did Vosch want him to see his?

"It's unique," Vosch said. "There are only twelve others like it in the world. One for each of us."

"Why are you doing this?" He was losing his temper. "Why do you speak in riddles and lies as if I am one of your human victims? There are more than twelve. There are tens of thousands."

"No. Only twelve." He gestured toward their right. "Come over here. I think you're going to find this very interesting."

Hanging at eye level from the ceiling, its skin a glistening greenish gray, a twenty-foot-long cigar-shaped object. After the 3rd Wave, drones like this one filled the sky. *Vosch's eyes*, he had told Cassie. *It's how he sees you.*

"An important component of the war," Vosch said. "Important, but not critical. Their loss demanded a bit of improvisation in our hunt for you—you have wondered why it was necessary to enhance an ordinary human, yes?"

He was referring to Ringer. But Evan didn't see the connection.

"Why did you?"

"The purpose of the drones was not to pinpoint the location of survivors—it was to track *you*. You and the thousands like you who will abandon your assigned territories in the days ahead as the 5th Wave is launched and you realize that there will be no rescue, no escape to the mothership."

Evan shook his head. For the first time it occurred to him that Vosch may have gone mad. It was their greatest fear when designing the purification of the Earth. Sharing the body with a human consciousness might prove to be an overwhelming burden, a strain that could not be borne.

"Now you are wondering if I am not altogether in my right mind," Vosch said with a small smile. "I don't sound like the person you've known most of your ten-thousand-year-old life. The truth is we have never met, Evan. Until today, I did not even know what you looked like." Vosch took him by the elbow, gently, and guided him toward the back of the chamber.

Evan's unease deepened. There was something profoundly disturbing about this. He didn't understand why Vosch had brought him here, why he simply hadn't killed him—what did it matter if his human body died? His consciousness still existed on the mothership. What was the point of this bizarre show-and-tell?

In the corner was a wooden stand, and on the stand perched a large bird of prey, its head tilted forward, its eyes closed, apparently asleep. Evan's stomach fluttered. The years collapsed and he was a boy again, lying in his bed in that hazy space between dreaming and waking, watching the owl on the windowsill watching him, bright round eyes shining in the dark, and his body feeling as if it had been frozen in amber, unable to move, unable to look away.

Behind him, Vosch murmured, "*Bubo virginianus*. The great

horned owl. Magnificent, isn't he? A fearsome predator, nocturnal, solitary—his prey rarely know he's coming until it's too late. He is your demon, your spirit animal in a sense. You were designed to be his human equivalent."

The wings stirred. The thick chest heaved. The head lifted, the eyes came open, and their eyes met.

"Of course, it isn't real," Vosch went on. "It is a delivery device. A machine. One came to your mother while you were still in her womb, bearing the program that was transmitted into your developing brain. Another visited you after that program booted up. Your *awakening*, I think it's called, to endow you with the 12th System."

He could not turn away. The owl's eyes filled his vision, engulfed him.

"There is no alien entity inside you," Vosch said. "None inside any of us and none aboard the mothership. It is completely automated, like your old friend here, designed by its makers after centuries of careful study and deliberation and sent to this planet to wean the human population to a sustainable level. And, of course, to keep it there indefinitely by changing human nature itself."

Evan found his voice, and said, "I don't believe you." *The eyes.*

He could not look away.

"A flawless, self-sustaining loop, an immaculate system in which trust and cooperation can never take root. Progress becomes impossible, for all strangers are potential enemies, the 'other' who must be hunted down until the last bullet is spent. You were never meant to be an agent of destruction, Evan. You are part of Earth's salvation—or you were until something in your programming went wrong. *That* is why I've brought you here. Not to torture you or kill you. I have brought you here to save you."

He placed a consoling hand on Evan's shoulder, and his touch broke the hold of the owl's eyes. Evan whirled upon his captor. He would kill him. He would choke the life out of him with his bare hands.

His fist punched empty air. The momentum nearly carried him off his feet.

Vosch had vanished.

67

THOUGH HE REMAINED UPRIGHT, he had the sensation of falling from a great height. The room spun, the walls faded in and out of focus. Across the chamber, a figure stood in the doorway, a visual anchor that steadied him. He took a hesitant step forward and stopped.

"What do you remember?" Vosch called from the threshold.

"Was I standing right beside you? Did I place my hand upon your shoulder? What are our memories but the ultimate proof that we exist? What if I were to tell you that everything you remember since we stepped into this room, *all of it*, is a lie, a false memory transmitted into your brain by that 'owl' behind you?"

"I know it's a lie," Evan answered. "I know who I am." He was shaking. He was colder than he'd been in the white room beneath the icy spray.

"Oh, what you 'heard' was the truth. It's the memory that's false." Vosch sighed. "You are a stubborn one, aren't you?"

"Why should I believe you?" Evan cried. "Who are *you* that I should believe?"

"Because I am one of the chosen. I have been entrusted with the greatest mission in human history: the salvation of our species. Like you, I've known since I was a boy what was coming. Unlike you, I knew the truth."

Vosch's eyes strayed to the pod. His tone shifted from stern to wistful. "It's impossible to express how lonely I have been. Only a handful of us know the truth. In a blind world, only we had eyes to see. We were not given a choice—you must understand—*there was no choice*. I am not responsible. I am a victim as much as they are, as much as you!" His voice rose in fury. "This is the cost! This is the price! And I have paid. I have done everything that was demanded of me. I have fulfilled my promise, and now my work is done."

He held out his hand.

"Come with me. Allow me to grant you one last gift. Come with me, Evan Walker, and lay down your burden."

68

HE FOLLOWED VOSCH—what choice did he have?—back down the long corridor to the green door. The technician rose when they entered and said, "I've run the test three times, Commander, and I still can't find any anomalies in the program. Do you want me to run it again?"

"Yes," Vosch answered. "But not now." He turned to Evan.

"Please sit."

He nodded to the tech, who strapped Evan back into the reclining chair. The hydraulics whined; he rotated back, his face toward the featureless white ceiling. He heard the door open. The same woman who had examined him in the white room entered, wheeling before her a gleaming stainless-steel cart. On it, laid out in a neat row, were thirteen syringes filled with an amber-colored fluid.

"You know what this is," Vosch said.

Evan nodded. The 12th System. *The gift.* But why return it?

"Because I'm an optimist, an incurable romantic, like you," Vosch said, as if he had read Evan's mind. "I believe where there is life, there is hope." He smiled. "But mostly because five young men are dead, which means she may still be alive. And if she lives, there is only one option left for her."

"Ringer?"

Vosch nodded. "She is what I have made her; and she is coming to demand that I answer for what I've done."

He leaned over Evan's face, and his eyes burned with iridescent fire, and the blue flames seared him down to his bones.

"*You will be my answer.*"

He turned to the tech, who flinched under the intensity of his glare. "She may be right: Love may be the singularity, the inexplicable, ungovernable, ineffable mystery, impossible to predict or control, the virus that crashed a program designed by beings next to which we are no more evolved than a cockroach." Then back to Evan: "So I will do my duty; I will burn down the village in order to save it."

He stepped back. "Download him again. Then erase it."

"Erase it, sir?"

"Erase the human. Leave the rest." The commander's voice filled the tiny room. "We cannot love what we do not remember."

69

IN THE AUTUMN WOODS there was a tent, and in that tent there was a girl who slept with a rifle in one hand and a teddy bear in the other. And while she slept, a hunter kept vigil over her, an unseen companion who retreated when she woke. He had come to end her life; she was there to save his.

And the endless arguments with himself, the vanity of his own reason posing the unanswerable question, *Why must one live while the world itself perished?* The more he reached for that answer, the farther the answer retreated from his grasp.

He was a finisher who could not finish. His was the heart of a hunter who lacked the heart to kill.

In her journal she had written *I am humanity,* and something in those three words splintered him in two.

She was the mayfly, here for a day, then gone. She was the last star, burning bright in a sea of limitless black.

Erase the human.

In a burst of blinding light, the star Cassiopeia exploded, and the world went black.

Evan Walker had been undone.

233

70

CASSIE

NOT TEN MINUTES into it and I'm starting to think this whole mission-impossible, killing-Vosch-and-rescuing-Evan thingy was a very bad idea.

Bob the one-eyed pilot shouts, *"Ten seconds!"* Ringer closes her eyes, and in an awful, sickening instant, I'm convinced we've been set up. This has been her plan all along. Leave Ben and the kids defenseless, then get the two of us killed kamikaze style at five thousand feet, because who gives a shit? There's a copy of her that lives in Wonderland. She'll just be downloaded into a new body once we're all dead.

Now's your chance, Cass. Take out your knife and cut out her treacherous heart . . . if you can find it. If she has one.

"They're breaking formation!" Bob announces.

Ringer's eyes snap open. My chance slips away. "Hold our course, Bob," she says evenly.

The choppers bear down on us, spreading out so everybody gets a fair shot, so no one feels left out or cheated of the chance to blow us into a gazillion pieces.

Bob holds our course but hedges our bets, locking a missile on the lead copter. His thumb hovers over the button. The thing that blows my mind about Bob is how quickly he switched sides. When he opened his eyes this morning, both of them, he was pretty certain which team he was batting for. Then, in the batting of an eye

234

(ha! sorry, Bob), he's locked and loaded, ready to annihilate his fellow brothers and sisters-in-arms.

So there you go. You can love the good in us and hate the bad, but the bad is in us, too. Without it, we wouldn't be *us*.

All I want to do in this moment is give Bob a big hug.

"They're going to ram us!" Bob screams. "We gotta dive, we gotta dive!"

"No," Ringer says. "Trust me, Bob."

Bob laughs hysterically. We barrel toward the lead chopper as it barrels toward us, both at full throttle. "Oh, sure! Why wouldn't I trust *you*?" White-knuckled on the stick, thumb caressing the button, in a few seconds it won't matter what Ringer tells him, he's going to fire. Ultimately, Bob is on nobody's side but Bob's.

"Break," Ringer whispers at the big black fist rocketing toward our face. "Break *now*."

Too late. Bob jams the button, the Black Hawk shudders like some gigantic foot kicked it, and a Hellfire missile explodes from its mount. The cockpit lights up like the noonday sun. Somebody screams (I think it might be me). A maelstrom of fire engulfs us for half a second—debris popping and smacking against our hull— and then we burst through the fireball to the other side.

"Hoooooolyyyy Mother of *God!*" Bob yells.

Ringer doesn't say anything at first. She's looking at his scope and the five remaining white dots. Four break off, two right and two left, and the third continues on, edging toward the bottom of the screen. *Oh no. Where is he going?*

"Hail them," Ringer tells Bob. "Tell them we're surrendering."

"We are?" Bob and I say at the same time.

"Then hold course. They're not going to force us down or fire on us."

"How do you know?" Bob asks.

"Because if they were, they would have done it by now."

"What about the other one?" I demand. "It's gone. It's not following us."

Ringer gives me a look. "Where do you think it's going?" Then she turns away. "It'll be all right, Sullivan. Zombie will know what to do."

Like I said, a very bad idea.

71

I SINK BACK into my seat and fight to get air into my lungs. I think I forgot to breathe back there. My mouth is bone-dry. I sip some water, but just enough to wet my mouth, because I'm a little concerned about having to pee during the operation. Ringer's described the base to me in some detail, including the location of the Wonderland room, but I never asked where the bathrooms were.

Ringer's voice crackles annoyingly in my ear. "Get some rest, Sullivan. We're in the air for another couple of hours."

And sunrise won't be far behind. We're cutting this too close. I'm no expert on covert ops, but I'm guessing they're a wee bit easier in the dark. Plus, if Evan was right, today is Green Day, the day the fireballs of hell rain from the sky.

I hunt around in my pockets until I locate one of Ben Parish's magical power bars. The alternative is bursting into tears. I'm determined not to cry until I see Sam again. He's the only thing left that's worthy of my tears.

And what the hell did she mean, *Zombie will know what to do?*

That's good, Sullivan, he'd better know, because you sure as hell don't. If you knew what to do, you wouldn't be on this damn chopper. You'd be with your little brother. Wise up. You know the real reason you're here. You can tell yourself it's for Sam, but you're not fooling anybody.

Oh God, I'm a horrible person. I'm worse than One-Eyed Bob. I abandoned my blood for a *guy*. And that's so wrong, it makes every other wrong thing I've ever done seem right. Ben told me Evan was lying or crazy or both, because who destroys their entire civilization for a girl? *Oh, I don't know, Ben. Maybe the same kind of person who would sacrifice her only flesh and blood to repay a debt she didn't owe.*

I mean, it isn't as if I *asked* him to save me all those times. Any more than I asked him to shoot me in the leg. I never asked him for anything. He just gave. Gave past the point where giving is sane. Is that what love is? And is that why it makes no sense to me, because I've never felt it, not for him, not for Ben Parish, not for anyone?

No, no, no, please, brain, don't. Don't serve up Vermont and that damned dog again. I promise I'll stop thinking so much. Thinking too much has been my problem for a very long time. I've overthought everything, from why the Others came to what Evan was to the very weird fact that I lived while practically all of humanity died. Down to why that girl in front of me has the

237

silkiest, most beautiful hair I've ever seen, and why I don't, and why she has perfect porcelain skin, which I don't. And the nose. Good Christ, how stupid. What a waste of time. It's just genes with a little alien technology thrown in, big whoop.

I finish the bar and crumple the wrapper in my fist. It just doesn't feel right to throw it down on the floor.

I lean back against the bulkhead and close my eyes. This would be an excellent time to pray, if I could think of a prayer, but my mind, so stuffed that my thoughts have to line up like crowds at Disney, can't think of anything to say to God.

Not sure I want to talk to him anyway, the enigmatic bastard. Like he's crossed his arms and turned his back, and I wonder if this is how Noah felt on the boat. *Okay, really appreciative about me, Lord, but what about them?* And God says, *Oh, don't ask so many questions, Noah. Look! I made you a rainbow!*

The only thing that bobs up is Sammy's bedtime prayer, so, a little desperate, I go with it.

Now I lay me down to sleep . . .

Well, not really.

When in the morning light I wake . . .

Well, probably won't happen, either.

Teach me the path of love to take.

Yes! Okay, that's good! Please, God. This one thing and don't fall down on the job.

Teach me.

238

72

ZOMBIE

KEEPING WATCH at the caves' entrance, admiring the night sky—except that one small green spot hovering above the horizon—when one of the stars breaks off from the field and descends toward us. Fast. *Very* fast. Nugget touches my sleeve and says, "Look, Zombie! A falling star!"

I push off the old, rickety handrail I've been leaning against.

"That's no star, kid."

"Is it a bomb?" His eyes are wide with fear.

For one gut-rolling second, I think it could be. They've stepped up the schedule for some reason, and the obliteration of the cities has begun.

"Come on, back downstairs, double time."

I don't have to tell him twice. He's already yards ahead of me when I hit the first chamber. I scoop Megan from the floor. She drops the teddy bear. Nugget picks it up. I carry her deeper into the caves, balancing her on the hip of my good leg, but each step sends a jolt of pain that makes the top of my head feel as if it's going to come off. There's a ledge down here, a three-foot-high, five-foot-deep gash in the rock cut out by an ancient river. I lift Megan into it and she crawls toward the back until the shadows engulf her. Shit. Nearly forgot. I motion for her to come back.

I pull one of the dead recruit's trackers from my pocket. Ringer's idea and a damn good one.

"Put this in your mouth," I tell Megan.

She is thunderstruck. The look in her eyes, like I asked her to chop off her head. I've broached a touchy subject.

"Look, Nugget'll do it." I press the tracker into his empty hand.

"Right here, Private," I say, pulling back my lip and pointing to a spot between my cheek and gums. Then I turn back to Megan. "See?" But Megan has faded back into the shadows. *Damn it.* I give Nugget another tracker. "Make sure she does it, okay? She listens to you."

"Oh, no, Zombie," Nugget says very seriously. "Megan doesn't listen to *anybody.*"

He shoves Bear into the space and calls softly to her, "Megan! Take Bear. He'll keep you safe, like gravity." After that piece of logic only a child could understand, he hitches up his pants, balls his fists, thrusts out his little chin, and says, "They're coming, aren't they?"

We both hear it then, like the answer to his question: the sound of a chopper's engines, doubling in volume with each of our rapid breaths. Toward the entrance the brilliant white of its searchlight slices through the dark.

"Go, Nugget. Get up there with Megan."

"But I'm fighting with you, Zombie."

He sure is. And at the worst possible time. Over his shoulder, I can see lamplight flickering in the weapons chamber. *Double damn it.*

"Here's what you can do—kill that light down there. Then meet me back here. If we're lucky, they won't even land."

"Lucky?" I get the feeling he *wants* them to land.

"Don't forget, Nugget, we're all on the same side."

He frowns. "How can we be on the same side if they want to kill us, Zombie?"

"Because they don't *know* we're on the same side. Go. Shut off that damn light—go!"

He scampers up the path. The chopper's light fades, but not so much its engines. Must be executing a sweep. We should be far enough underground to foil the IR, but there's no guarantees.

The lamp goes out and the caves plunge into darkness. I can't see an inch in front of my nose. After a few seconds, someone small bumps into me. I'm fairly confident it's him. Only fairly, though, because I whisper, "Nugget?"

"It's okay, Zombie," he informs me, all business. "I grabbed a gun."

73

THERE'S SOMETHING I'm forgetting. What is it?

"Here, Zombie, you forgot these." He pushes a gas mask into my chest. God bless Nugget. And God bless Silencers like Grace and Father Death, who knew how to stockpile for the end of the world.

Nugget's practiced; he's already got his strapped on. "You've got Megan's?" Dumb. Of course he'd grab one for her. "Okay, pal, up you go."

"Zombie, listen . . ."

"That's a direct order, Private."

"No, Zombie! *Listen.*"

I listen. Nothing except my own breath hissing and huffing in the mask.

"They left," Nugget says.

"Shhh."

Tink-tink-tink. The sound of metal striking stone.

Damn you, Ringer, being right all the time is incredibly annoying.

They've tossed in the gas.

74

ASSUMING YOU DON'T *draw them off, how will they come?* I asked Ringer while we were barricading the back entrance.

You never paid attention in class.

Do we always have to make it about me? Trying to tease a smile from her has segued from a hobby to a borderline obsession.

Gas first.

You think? I'd go with a few sticks of C-4 to seal off the exits, then finish us off with a couple of bunker-busters.

That's probably second.

Behind us, toward the main entrance, the tear gas detonates with four loud pops. I grab Nugget around the waist and heave him into the cleft with Megan. "*Get that mask on her now!*" I shout, then I'm hobbling up the path, thinking, *Thank God he remembered! That kid deserves a promotion.*

One thing's for certain, Ringer said. *They won't be settling in for a siege. If they attempt a dynamic CQC, they'll probably hit the main entrance, which will give you a slight advantage: It's narrow like a cow chute—they'll funnel right to you.*

I'm running blind. Well, calling it *running* would be generous. I've got massive amounts of painkiller in me at least, so the leg's not giving me much trouble. Adrenaline helps, too. Check the bolt catch on the rifle. Check the straps on the mask. In absolute dark. In absolute uncertainty.

If they bust through the back entrance in a kind of pincer maneuver, we're screwed. If they hit with overwhelming force up front, we're screwed. If I freeze up or screw up at the critical moment, we're screwed.

Freeze up like in Dayton. Screw up like in Urbana. I keep circling back to the same spot, and that spot is where I lost my baby sister, where I should have fought but ran instead. The chain that broke from her neck, lost now, still binds me. Oompa. Dumbo. Poundcake. Even Teacup, her, too: She'd still be alive if I'd done my job.

Now the chain dropping like a noose around Nugget and Megan, and now the noose tightens, the circle comes round.

Not this time, Parish, you zombie son of a bitch. This time you break the chain, you cut the noose. You save those kids no matter what.

I will kill them as they funnel down the chute. I'll kill them all. Doesn't matter that they're no different from me. Doesn't matter they're trapped in the same goddamned game, bound like me to play a part they did not choose. I will kill them one by one.

Absolute dark. Absolute certainty.

243

The explosion knocks me off my feet. I fly backward; my head crashes against stone; the universe spins like a top. The air boils with the sound of rock smashing against rock as the entrance collapses.

The mask got knocked sideways when I hit, and I take a huge breath of noxious gas. A knife plunges into my lungs, fire fills my mouth. I roll to my side, gagging and coughing.

I lost the rifle in my fall. I sweep the area around me, can't find it, never mind, doesn't matter, *know what matters*, hauling myself to my feet, yanking the mask back into place and tasting pulverized rock on my tongue, limping back the way I came, one hand searching the darkness, the other gripping my sidearm, knowing what's coming next because I called it and Ringer knew I called it, *that's probably second*, and I'm screaming through the mask, "*Don't move, Nugget! Don't move!*" but I don't think anybody can hear my voice but me.

The second explosion hits at the back entrance, and I stay on my feet though the floor ripples and stalactites break loose and smash down, a big one missing my head by a couple of inches. I can hear Nugget faintly calling my name. I lock in on the sound and follow it back to the crevice. I pull him out.

"They've sealed us in," I gasp. My throat burns. I've swallowed fire. "Where's Megan?"

"She's okay," I can feel him shaking. "She's got Bear." I call to her. A tiny voice muffled by a gas mask comes back. Nugget's clutching my jacket with both hands like the dark might snatch me away if he lets go.

"We shouldn't have stayed here," Nugget cries.

Out of the mouths of babes, but there was nowhere to run,

244

nowhere to hide. We rolled the dice that Bob's chopper would draw them off, and we lost. The bomber's gotta be on its way with a payload that will turn this 250,000-year-old cave into a swimming pool two miles long and a hundred feet deep.

We've got minutes.

I take Nugget by the shoulders. Squeeze hard. "Two things, Private," I tell him. "We need light and we need explosives."

"But Ringer took all the bombs with her!"

"So we'll make another one, real quick."

We shuffle toward the weapons chamber, Nugget leading the way, my hands still on his shoulders. I steady him, he steadies me, the chain that binds us, the chain that sets us free.

75

SOMETHING I'M FORGETTING. What is it?

Nugget bends low over his task. The chamber's choked with smoke and dust; it's like trying to put together a jigsaw puzzle in heavy fog, not unlike this whole freaking invasion. The familiar blasted into a million pieces, an impossible jumble where no piece seems to fit with another. The enemy is within us. The enemy is not. They're down here, they're up there, they're nowhere. They want the Earth, they want us to have it. They came to wipe us out, they came to save us. And the shattered truth forever receding from your grasp, the only certainty is uncertainty, and Vosch reminding me of the one truth worth hanging on to: *You're going to die. You're going to die, and there's nothing you or I or anyone else can do to stop it. That was true before they came and it's still true: The only certainty is uncertainty, except your own death, that's damn certain.*

His fingers are shaking. His breath is loud and fast inside the mask. One wrong move and he blows us both up. My life is now in the hands of a kindergartner.

Screwing on the blasting cap. Attaching the fuse. Sullivan might be upset he's forgotten his ABCs, but at least the little SOB knows how to make a bomb.

"Got it?" I ask.

"Got it!" He holds up the device triumphantly. I take it from him. *Oh Jesus, I hope so.*

Something I'm forgetting. Something important. What could it be?

76

NOW ON TO the next impossible dilemma: bust through the back door or the front?

One bomb. One chance. I leave Nugget with Megan and check the rear entrance first. A wall of rock maybe six feet thick, if I'm remembering my landmarks right. Then returning the length of the cave to the front entrance. Moving too damn slow. Taking too damn long. Finally there, I find exactly what I expected to find: another rock wall, who knows how thick, and no way of telling if this is the better way out.

Oh, screw it.

I jam the PVC pipe into the deepest, highest crack I can reach. The fuse seems too short; I might not have time to reach a safe distance.

The certainty of uncertainty.

I light the fuse and book back up the path, dragging my bad leg behind me like a reluctant kid on the first day of school. The bang of the explosion seems muted, a pitiful echo of the two that trapped us down here.

Ten minutes later, I've got Nugget by one hand and Megan by the other. It wasn't easy for Nugget to talk her out. She felt safe in that cozy little niche and the chain of command wasn't worth a hill of beans to her. The person in charge of Megan is Megan.

The hole at the top of the fall isn't very big and doesn't look very stable, but fresh air whistles through it and I can see a pinprick of light. Nugget says, "Maybe we should just stay here, Zombie." He's probably thinking the same thing: Seal the entry points, station sharpshooters at both ends, and then it's just a waiting game. Nobody makes bunker-busting bombs anymore. Why waste precious munitions needed for the real war on a couple little kids and a gimpy recruit? They'll come out. They *have* to come out. The risk of staying is unacceptable.

"Don't have a choice, Nugget." Also no choice in who goes first. I grab his sleeve and pull him away from Megan. I don't want her to hear this. "You wait for my signal, understand?" He nods. "What do you do if I don't come back?"

He shakes his head. The light's too weak and the lenses on the mask are too clouded for me to see his eyes, but his voice quivers in pre-cry mode. "But you *are* coming back."

"If I've got a heartbeat, you bet your ass I'm coming back. But in case I don't."

Up comes the chin. Out goes the chest. "I'll shoot 'em all in the head!"

I heave myself into the hole. My back smacks against the top, the sides squeeze against my shoulders: It's gonna be a tight fit. Halfway through, I decide to take off the mask. I can't take the feeling of being slowly smothered anymore. Fresh, cold air bathes my face. Christ, it feels good.

The opening to the outside isn't big enough for one of cat lady's dinners to wiggle through. I punch out the loose rocks with my bare hands. A smidgen of night sky, a swath of grass, and the one-lane access road slicing them down the middle. No sound but the wind. *Let's go.*

I crawl into the open. I reach for the rifle slung over my shoulder, only there is no rifle slung over my shoulder: I forgot to pick it up on my way back to the entrance. So that's what I was forgetting. That was it, my rifle. Right?

Squatting beside the hole, holding my sidearm between my legs, listening, looking, *Don't rush this; be sure.* Escaping the trap is fine and wonderful, but where to now? Dawn isn't far off and then the mothership begins her appointed rounds. I can see her balanced on the horizon, green like a traffic light signaling Go. I stand. A challenging maneuver given my leg's stiffened up and putting weight on it hurts like hell.

Here I am, boys. Take your best shot.

Nothing to see but the road and grass and the sky. Nothing to hear but the wind.

I whistle into the hole for Nugget. Two short toots, one long. After a hundred years his round little head pokes out, then his shoulders, I pull him the rest of the way. He rips off the gas mask and inhales the fresh air, then yanks the gun from the back of his pants. He swivels left to right, knees slightly bent, gun thrust forward, like countless boys before him with plastic guns and water pistols.

I whistle again for Megan. No answer, so I call down, "Megan, let's go, girl!" Beside me, Nugget sighs deeply.

"She's so annoying."

And he sounds so much like his sister that I actually laugh. He gives me a curious look, head tilted slightly to one side.

"Hey, Zombie? There's a red dot on the side of your head."

77

DUMBO DIDN'T THINK TWICE in Urbana. I don't now.

I dive into Nugget's chest, hurling him to the ground. The round slams into the rockfall behind us. A second later I hear the report of the sharpshooter's rifle. The shot came from the right, in the direction of the copse of trees by the main road.

Nugget starts to get up. I grab his ankle and yank him back down.

"Low crawl," I whisper in his ear. "Like they taught us in camp, remember?"

He starts to rotate a one-eighty—back toward the hole and the false security of the cave with its provisions and weapons. I don't blame him; it's my first instinct, too. Going back, though, only puts off the inevitable. If smoking us out and picking us off fails, they'll just call in the bunker-busters.

"Follow me, Nugget." I scuttle toward the welcome center. The roof is a perfect vantage point for a sharpshooter, but our best option is to head away from the shooter we know about.

"Megan . . . ," he gasps. "What about Megan?"

What about Megan?

"She won't come out," I whisper. *Please don't come out, kid.*

"She'll wait."

"Wait for what?"

For history to repeat itself. For the circle to come round.

Only one place I can think of that's reasonably safe. I'm not happy about it and I know he sure as hell won't be. But this kid is anything but soft; he'll deal. "Past the building, then straight on about twenty yards," I tell him as we scoot along on our bellies.

"Big hole. Full of bodies."

"Bodies?"

I imagine a red dot shimmering between my shoulder blades or on the back of Nugget's head. I've got eyes on him now, and if I see that red dot, I'm going Dumbo on it again. The ground rises slightly as we near the pit, and then we can smell it, and the stench makes Nugget retch. I lock down on his arm and tug him to the edge. He doesn't want to look, but he looks.

"It's just dead people," I choke out. "Come on, I'll lower you down."

He pulls against my grip. "I won't be able to get back out."

"It's safe, Nugget. Perfectly safe." Unfortunate choice of words.

"They'd have taken the shot by now if they knew where we were."

He nods. Makes sense to him. "But Megan . . ."

"I'm going back for her."

He looks at me as if I've lost my mind. I take his wrists and

250

lower him feetfirst into the hole. "You hear anything, you play dead," I remind Nugget.

"I'm going to be sick."

"Breathe through your mouth."

His lips part. I see the tiny pellet glistening inside his mouth. I give him a thumbs-up. He raises his right hand very slowly and puts it against his forehead in salute.

78

CRAWLING AWAY from the death pit, I know what's going to happen. I know I'm going to die.

My time's been borrowed and you can't cheat death forever. Sooner or later you have to pay up, with interest, only please don't let Nugget and Megan be the price for my abandoning my sister. So I say to God, *You took Dumbo for the debt, Poundcake and Teacup, that's enough, let that be enough. Take me but let them live.*

The ground explodes in front of me. Clods of dirt and stone fly into my face. *Well, shit, crawling's pointless now.* I heave myself up, but the bad leg buckles, and down I go. The next shot rips into my sleeve, nicking my biceps before exiting the opposite side; I hardly feel it. Instinctively I curl into a ball and wait for the finishing round. I know what's happening. These are soldiers of the 5th Wave. Their hearts have been filled with hate, their minds conditioned for cruelty. They're playing with me. *Gonna make it last, you infested sonofabitch. Gonna make it fun!*

And my sister's face before me, then Bo's and Cake's and Cup's, then more faces than I can count, faces I recognize and faces I don't, there's Nugget and Megan, Cassie and Ringer, there's the recruits in camp and the bodies in the processing hangar laid end to end, hundreds of faces, thousands, tens of thousands, living and dead but mostly dead. In the pit behind me, one living face among hundreds that aren't, and Vosch's rule applies to him, too.

Hand raised in salute. Mouth open and the tiny pellet that glistens inside.

Holy shit, Parish, the tracker. *That's what you forgot.*

I jam my hand into the pocket, pull out the pellet, and stuff it into my mouth. In the cluster of trees across the road, on the rooftop of the welcome center, and from wherever the hell else they might be, the shooters hold their fire when the green inferno that surrounds my head winks out.

79

Everything hurts. Even blinking hurts. But I'm getting up.

We rise.

That's what zombies do.

Maybe the shooters don't notice at first. Maybe they've turned their attention elsewhere, looking for green targets. Whatever the reason, when I get up, nobody takes me down. No hobbling this time, no dragging my wounded leg, no shuffling in the dirt like a damned zombie. I run full out through the pain, calling

252

Megan's name now, fingers clawing in the dark until they wrap around her wrist.

Then I've got her outside. Her arm around my neck. Her breath in my ear.

I know the circle's complete. I know the bill's come due. Just let me save her first, dear Christ, suffer her not to die.

I don't see it coming. Megan does. The teddy bear falls to the ground. Her mouth flies open in a silent scream.

Something smashes into the base of my skull. The world goes white, then there's nothing, nothing at all.

80

CASSIE

YOU CAN SEE IT from miles away: The air base is an island of blazing light in a dark, horizonless sea, a white-hot ember of civilization glowing in the middle of a wasteland of black, though *civilization* is too nice a word for what it is. After all we dreamed and all those dreams we made real, all that's left of us are these bases, the lighted fools to guide humanity's way to dusty death.

Macbeth was never my favorite, but there you go.

The chopper banks to the left, bringing us toward the base from the east. We pass over a river, black water reflecting the conflagration of stars above it. Then the treeless buffer zone surrounding the camp that's laced with trenches and razor wire and booby-trapped with land mines, protection against an enemy who will never come, who isn't even here and maybe not even *there*—in the mothership that swings into view when we turn for the final approach. I look at it. It looks back at me.

What are you? What are you? What are you? The Others, my father called you, but aren't we also that to you? *Other-than-us*, therefore *not-worthy-of-us.* Not worthy of life.

What are you? The shepherd culls the herd. The homemaker buys the bug spray. The blood of the lamb on its knees, the herky-jerky of the cockroach on its back. Neither has an inkling of the knife or the poison. The shepherd and the homemaker will lose no sleep. There's nothing immoral about it. It's murder without crime, killing without sin.

That's what they've done. That's the lesson they've brought home. We've been reminded who we are—not much—and what we were—too many. Roaches can scurry, sheep can run, it's no matter. We'll never get too big for our britches again; they'll see to that. I'm looking at an object in our sky that will be there until our sky is gone.

Our escorts peel off as we shoot straight toward the landing zone. They'll stay in the air to monitor the situation after we land. There's a swarm of activity beneath us, trucks and armored Humvees racing toward the strip, troops swarming like ants from a kicked-over mound. Sirens blare, searchlights stab into the sky, antiaircraft guns swing into position. This should be fun.

Ringer pats Bob on the shoulder. "Good job, Bob."

"Fuck you!"

Oh, Bob, Gonna miss you. Gonna miss you so bad.

Ringer climbs back into the hold with me, grabs the bag of Sammy-bombs, and plops into the seat across the aisle. Her dark eyes shine. She's the bullet in the chamber, the powder in the

254

hole. You can't blame her. Evan pointed it out a long time ago: For any of this shit to mean anything, you gotta live long enough for your death to matter. Not necessarily make a difference— neither her death nor mine will—just to *matter*.

Suddenly I need to pee.

"VQP, Sullivan!" she shouts. We've taken off our headsets.

I nod. Give her the thumbs-up. *VQP, you bet.*

Our descent begins. The hold is lit up by searchlights. Motes of dust sparkle and spin around her head: Saint Ringer, the raven-haired angel of death. Outside the blue circle upon which Bob puts us down, a ring of soldiers inside a barricade of armored vehicles, surrounded by watchtowers manned by snipers, beneath four attack helicopters patrolling overhead.

We are so doomed.

81

RINGER LEANS BACK in the seat and closes her eyes like she's going to grab a quick power nap before the big final exam. Bag in one hand, detonator in the other. I've got a rifle, a handgun, a very large knife, a couple of grenades, a half-full (think positive!) bottle of water, two high-energy bars, and a full bladder. Bob throttles the chopper down and now you can really hear those sirens blasting. Ringer's eyes pop open and she stares at me like she's memorizing my face—I decide that so I don't obsess about my crooked nose.

Then she says so softly I can barely hear her: "See you at the checkpoint, Sullivan."

One-Eyed Bob throws off his harness. He whips around and screams in Ringer's face, "He *wanted* you to come back, you stupid bitch! Why do you think you're still alive?" Then he flies out of the cockpit, his legs pumping cartoon-fast before his feet even touch the ground, waving his hands over his head and screaming loud enough to be heard over the sirens.

"*Pull back! Pull back! She's gonna blow! SHE'S GONNA BLOW!*"

Ringer goes right, and I go left toward a terraced garden of fatigues identical to the ones I'm wearing, rifles pointed at my head, the front row kneeling, back row standing, and then Ringer hits the detonator and the chopper hops five feet in the air with an emphatic *whuuu-uuump*. The concussion shoves me right into the line of soldiers, the heat from the blast singeing their faces and burning away the hairs on the back of my neck. I bowl into the pack while the pack reverts to its instincts, just like Ringer said it would, everybody flattening on the tarmac and covering their heads with their hands.

You'll want to run but you gotta hold, Ringer told me back at the cave. *Once the chopper blows, they'll lose you, so you have to wait for me.*

So here I am, just another recruit lying on her belly like the hundred others around her, hands over her head, her cheek pressed against the freezing concrete. Dress just like 'em, look just like 'em, act just like 'em: It's Vosch's own game turned against him.

People are screaming orders but nobody can hear them over the sirens. I wait until somebody taps me on the shoulder, but I'm no higher than hands-and-knees when Ringer sets off the IED somewhere in the vicinity of the hangar fifty yards away. That sets off full-panic mode. Any semblance of order breaks down as troops run for the nearest cover. I take off toward the control tower and the cluster of white buildings beyond it.

A hand grabs my shoulder, whips me around, and then I'm face-to-face with some random teenager who, as bad luck would have it, I'm going to kill.

"Who the fuck are you?" he screams in my face.

His body stiffens, welcoming the bullet. Not my bullet. I don't even have the gun out of the holster. The kill belongs to Ringer, Vosch's inhuman human firing from half a football field away. The kid's dead before he hits the ground. I take off again.

I turn back once, at the base of the control tower. Searchlights crisscrossing the field, the chopper burning, squads running willy-nilly, Humvees screeching in every direction. Chaos is what Ringer promised and chaos is what we got.

I sling the rifle into my hands and sprint toward the white buildings, heading for the command center located in the middle of the complex. There I'll find (I hope) the key that will open the lock that bars the door that leads to the room that will keep my baby brother safe.

As I fall in behind a cluster of recruits crowding the door into the first building, Ringer sets off the second bomb. Somebody yells *Jesus Christ!* and the logjam breaks. We all tumble inside like clowns bursting from the car at the circus.

There's a part of me that hopes I find him first. Not Evan. Ringer's creator. I've invested a lot of time imagining what I'd do to him—how I'd pay him back for the blood of the seven billion. Most of it's too gross to talk about.

I'm moving through the lobby of the main administration building. Huge banners hang from the ceiling; WE ARE HUMANITY and WE ARE ONE. A sign that says UNITY and another that screams

257

COURAGE. The largest spans the length of an entire wall, VINCIT QUI PATITUR. I run beneath it.

A red light spins in the corridor on the other side of the lobby. I jump when a voice booms from the ceiling: "GENERAL ORDER FOUR IS NOW IN EFFECT. REPEAT: GENERAL ORDER FOUR IS NOW IN EFFECT. THIS IS NOT A DRILL. YOU HAVE FIVE MINUTES TO REPORT TO YOUR DESIGNATED SECURITY AREA. REPEAT. THIS IS NOT A DRILL. YOU HAVE FIVE MINUTES TO REPORT . . ."

Through the door at the end of the hall. Up the stairs straight ahead to the next door. Which is locked. With a keypad. I press my back against the wall beside the pad and wait. One thousand one, one thousand two, one thousand three . . . While I'm counting, the third bomb detonates outside, a muffled *pop!* like someone coughing in another room. Then I hear the *pop-pop, pop-pop-pop* of small-arms fire. At one thousand eight, the door bursts open and a squad lumbers through. Right past me, not even a backward glance. Now, that's too easy; I'm using up my quota of good luck way too soon.

I duck through the doorway and jog down another corridor, which is disconcertingly identical to the first corridor. Same spinning red light, same high-pitched *UUUH-UHHH* of the siren, same annoying Siri-on-dope voice, "GENERAL ORDER FOUR IS NOW IN EFFECT. YOU HAVE THREE MINUTES TO REPORT TO YOUR DESIGNATED SECURITY AREA . . ." It's like a dream from which you can't wake up. At the end of this hall is an identical door with an identical keypad. The only difference is the window right beside this door.

I open up with the M16 at full stride. The glass explodes and I dive through the blasted-out opening without missing a step. And

Defiance shall be my name! Back outside in the fresh, clean Canadian air, running across the narrow strip of land that separates the buildings. A voice springs from the dark, hollering, *"Halt!"* I fire in the voice's general direction. I don't even look. Then, off to my left, in the vicinity of the newly repaired armory, the fourth bomb detonates. A chopper roars right over my head, sweeping its lights back and forth, and I slam into the side of the building and press my body flat against the steel-reinforced concrete.

The chopper moves off and I move on, around the side of the building to the sliver of a path that cuts down its length, wall on one side, a ten-foot-high chain-link fence topped with razor wire on the other. There should be a padlocked gate at the far end.

So the lock—I shoot it off, I said to Ringer back in the caves.

That only works in the movies, Sullivan.

Yeah, you're right: It's good this isn't a movie, or the hectoring, self-important, annoying secondary character would definitely be dead by now.

"THIS IS NOT A DRILL. GENERAL ORDER FOUR IS NOW IN EFFECT. YOU HAVE TWO MINUTES TO REPORT . . ."

All right already, I get it. General Order Four is in effect. What the hell is General Order Four? Ringer never mentioned anything about general orders, four or otherwise. It must mean a lockdown of the base, all hands to battle stations, that kind of thing. That's what I decide. Anyway, what *they* do doesn't change what I have to do.

I jam a grenade into the diamond-shaped hole in the chain link, right above the lock, pull the pin, then hustle back the way I came, far enough not to get killed by the shrapnel, but not far enough to escape being peppered by a thousand tiny needles. If I hadn't turned away at the last second, my face would have been

259

shredded. The largest piece hits right in the middle of my back, wasp-sting sharp times ten. My left hand got a taste, too. I look down and see a wet glove of blood glistening in the starlight.

The grenade didn't just take out the lock; it blew the entire gate from its hinges. It's halfway across the courtyard, right next to the statue of some war hero from the days when wars had heroes. You know, the good ol' days when we slaughtered each other for all the *right* reasons.

I trot toward the building on the other side of the courtyard. There are three doors evenly spaced along the wall facing me, and out of one, two, or all of them I can expect a welcoming committee, according to Ringer. I'm not disappointed. The middle door flies open right before my second grenade flies toward it and, predictively, somebody yells, "*Grenade!*" They slam the door closed—*with the grenade inside.*

The blast hurls the entire door toward my head. I dive out of the way. *This is where it gets hard*, Ringer said. *There's gonna be blood.*

How much blood?

How much can you take?

What are you, my sensei or something? How many 5th Wavers am I going to have to kill?

As it turns out, at least three. I count that many semiautomatic rifles lying on the other side of the missing door, but it's an educated guess. Hard to tell when the troops have been blown to pieces. I slip through the mess and sprint down the hall, leaving bloody boot prints in my wake.

Red light. Siren. Voice. "GENERAL ORDER FOUR IS NOW IN EFFECT. YOU HAVE ONE MINUTE TO REPORT . . ." Somewhere on the base, the next bomb goes off, meaning two things:

Ringer's still at large, and she's got one bomb left. I'm a building away from the command center, beneath which is the bunker that houses the Wonderland room. It's also, as Ringer pointed out numerous times, a dead end. If we get trapped or cornered, there won't be any *vinciting* to our *patituring*.

Little Red Ridinghood Lost Her Way. The clever mnemonic device I came up with to navigate this next-to-last building. I hang a left at the first juncture, then a right, then another right, then a left. *Her* stands for *high*, meaning I hit the first stairwell after *Lost*. Of course, I could have just used the word *high*, but that would ruin the mnemonics. *Little Red Ridinghood's Lost Highway?* Come on.

I don't see anyone, don't hear anyone except the eerie General Order Four voice echoing down the empty halls—"YOU HAVE THIRTY SECONDS"—and now I'm starting to get a very bad feeling about this General Order Four business, and I'm cursing Ringer, because obviously General Order Four must be an important piece of intel she either should have known about or chose not to mention for reasons only clear to her.

As I race up the stairs, the final countdown begins: "TEN SECONDS . . . NINE . . . EIGHT . . . SEVEN . . . SIX . . ."

Landing. One more flight. Then straight ahead to the walkway that connects this building with the command center. *Almost there, Cassie. You've got this.*

"THREE . . . TWO . . . ONE."

I shove open the door.

Total darkness smashes down.

82

NO LIGHT. NO SIREN. No voice so soothing, it's unnerving. Total dark, utter silence. My first thought is that Ringer must have cut the power. My next thought is how odd that would be, since we never discussed cutting the power. My third thought? Same as the one on the chopper: Ringer's a plant, a double agent, working with Vosch to accomplish his nefarious scheme for total world domination. Probably a power-sharing arrangement: *Very well, it's decided. You will control all territory west of the Mississippi . . .*

I dig into my pockets for the penlight. I know I grabbed one. I specifically remember checking the batteries before tucking it away. In my panic—okay, not *panic, haste,* I am in haste—I pull out a power bar and thumb the switch that is not there. *Damn you and your damn bars, Ben Parish!* I hurl the bar into the void.

I'm not disoriented. I know where I am. Straight ahead is the walkway to the command center. I can hunt for the light as I go. No biggie. Once I'm in the center, there're a couple of heavily manned checkpoints to pass, several steel doors with electronic locks to breach, four flights of stairs, a mile-long hallway terminating at a green door, which I won't be able to tell is green *unless I can find my fucking penlight.*

I shuffle forward, one hand sweeping the air in front of me, the other patting, digging, fumbling, and clawing at my fatigues. Too many pockets. Too many damn *pockets.* My breath a tornado ripping across the prairie. My heart a freight train rumbling down the tracks. Should I stop and empty all my pockets? Wouldn't I end up saving time? I keep moving, part of me marveling at the fact that something like losing a penlight could throw me.

Chill, Cassie. In situations like this, darkness is your friend.

Unless they've got IR, which of course they do. They've blinded me; they're sure as hell not blind.

I keep moving. In haste. Not panic.

Halfway across the walkway now. I know I'm halfway across because I find the light and click on the damned elusive thing. The beam hits the frosted glass doors straight ahead, a blurry blob of shininess. I draw my sidearm. On the other side of those doors is the first checkpoint. I know this for a fact—or a Ringer-supplied fact. It's also our rendezvous spot, basically because this is as far as I was going to get as a non-enhanced, ordinary mortal.

The command center is the most heavily fortified building on base, manned by elite troops and protected by state-of-the-art sur-veillance technology. After she set off her last diversionary IED, Ringer was hitting the center from the opposite end (*penetrating* was the word she used, which made me feel all icky) and meeting me here, after Ringer did what Ringer does best: kill people.

Are you killing Vosch before meeting me? I asked.

If I find him first.

Well, don't go out of your way. The quicker we can get to Wonderland . . .

And she gave me a look like, *Don't tell me.* So I responded with a look that said, *I'm telling you.*

Nothing to do now but wait. I sidestep to the wall. Switch out the handgun for the rifle. Try not to worry about where she is, *if* she is, and what's taking her so long. Also, I need to pee.

So when I hear you set off the fifth bomb . . .

Fourth. I'm holding the fifth in reserve.

Reserve for what?

I'm going to stuff it in his mouth and light it.

She said it with no emotion. No hate or satisfaction or antici-pation or anything. Sure, she says most things unemotionally, but this was one of those things where you expect a little passion to permeate.

You must really hate him.

Hate isn't the answer.

I didn't ask a question.

It isn't hate and it isn't rage, Sullivan.

Okay, then. What is the answer? Feeling like I've been manipu-lated into asking the question.

She turned away.

I wait beside the frosted glass doors. The minutes crawl. Dear God, how long could it take a superhuman WMD to overcome a few guards and foil a high-tech security system? After the furious rush to reach this spot, nothing. I'd be bored out of my mind if I wasn't already scared out of it. *Where the hell is Ringer?*

Click. I turn off the light to save the batteries. The unfortunate by-product of my thriftiness is that darkness returns. *Click.* On.

Click. Off. *Click, click, click, click.*

Hissssss. I hear the sound before I feel the water.

It's raining.

264

83

CLICK. I SHINE THE LIGHT toward the ceiling. The sprinklers are running at full throttle. Cool water spatters my upturned face.

Great. One of Ringer's bombs must have triggered the system.

I'm soaked in minutes. It totally isn't fair, I know, but I blame her. I'm wet, I'm cold, I'm hyped on adrenaline, and now I *really* have to pee.

And still no Ringer.

How long do I wait for you?

I don't know how long it will take.

Sure, but at some point, won't it be obvious you're not coming?

That would be the point when you stop waiting, Sullivan.

Well, right. I'm really regretting not popping her in the nose when I had the chance. Wait. I *did* pop her in the nose when I had the chance. Good. One less thing.

I can't sit here forever hunched over in a wet, miserable ball. If it's my doom to be wet and miserable, I'm going to meet it standing up. I'll test those doors. Just a little push to see if they'll open. There can't be anyone close on the other side, otherwise they'd have seen my light or noticed my shadow and pounced on me in the dark.

The artificial rain drips down my forehead, hangs from the ends of my hair, traces my jaw like a lover's finger. Water squishes beneath my boots. My wounded hand has begun to sting, sting *bad*, a thousand tiny needles stabbing into my skin, and then I notice the burning sensation on my scalp. The feeling spreads. My neck, my back, my chest, my stomach, my face. My entire body is on fire. I stumble from the doors back to my cozy spot against the wall. Something is not right. The ancient part of my brain is screaming its lungs out. *Something is not right.*

I click on the penlight and shine it on my hand. Huge welts crisscross the skin. Fresh blood seeps from the shrapnel holes and quickly turns a deep, velvety purple, as if my blood is reacting to something in the water.

Something in the water.

The heat is nearly unbearable, like I've been doused with scalding-hot water, only the liquid falling on me isn't hot. I shine the light on my other hand. It's covered with bright, dime-sized red polka dots. Hastily—*not panicky*—I yank open the jacket, pull up my shirt, and see a starfield of crimson suns burning against a backdrop of pale pink.

I've got three options: stand here stupidly beneath the poisoned spray, stupidly bust through the frosted glass doors into God-knows-what, or wisely get out of this complex before my skin liquefies and sloughs off my bones.

I decide to go with Option Three.

My little light slices through the mist, cutting rainbows as I run. I bang into the stairwell, bounce against the wall, slip on the slick concrete, and tumble down to the landing. The penlight flies from my hand and winks out. *Gotta get outside, outside, outside.* Once there, I'll strip off my clothes and roll naked in the dirt like a pig. Hot matchsticks pressing against my eyes, tears streaming down my cheeks, hot coals searing my mouth and throat, and every other inch of my body puckering up into pestilential boils.

What's that, Cassie? What kind of boils?

Now I get it. Now I understand.

Cut the power. Open the floodgates. Unleash the pestilence. General Order Four is the invasion in microcosm, the acoustical version of the first three worldwide waves, same tune, different lyrics, and any intruder caught in their wake humanity's avatar.

Which would be me. I am humanity.

Outside, outside, outside! I'm on the main floor, the main *windowless* floor based on my memory since I have no light and no glowing red exit sign to guide the way. Not in haste anymore. In full-bore panic.

Because I've been here before. I know what comes after the 3rd Wave.

84

SILENCER

TEN MILLENNIA ADRIFT.

Ten thousand years unbounded by space or time, stripped of the senses, pure thought, substance without form, motion without gesture, paralyzed force.

Then the dark split open and there was light.

Air filling its lungs. Blood moving through its veins. Imprisoned for ten millennia inside its limitless mind, now finite. Now free.

It climbs the stairs toward the surface.

Red light pulsing. Siren blaring. A human voice assaulting its ears:

"GENERAL ORDER FOUR IS NOW IN EFFECT. YOU HAVE ONE MINUTE TO REPORT TO YOUR DESIGNATED SECURE AREA."

It rises from the deep.

The door above bangs open and a troop of the mammalian vermin thunders toward it. Juveniles carrying weapons. In the confined space of the stairwell, their human stench is overwhelming.

"What are you, fucking deaf?" one of them shouts. The voice is grating, the sound of their language ugly. "We're GO-Four, dipshit! Get your ass back down into that bunk—"

It snaps the juvenile's neck. The others it kills with equal efficiency and speed. Their bodies gather around its feet. Broken necks, burst hearts, shattered skulls. In the instant before they died, perhaps they looked into its eyes, blank and unblinking, a shark's eyes, the soulless predator rising from the depths.

"THREE . . . TWO . . . ONE."

The stairwell plunges into darkness. An ordinary human would be sightless. Its human container, though, is not ordinary.

It has been enhanced.

In the first-floor hallway of the command center, the sprinkler system bursts to life. The Silencer lifts its face and drinks the lukewarm spray. It has not tasted water in ten millennia, and the sensation is both jarring and exhilarating.

The corridor is deserted. The vermin have retreated into safe rooms, where they will remain until the two intruders have been silenced.

Silenced by the inhuman thing inside this human body.

In the downpour, the wet jumpsuit quickly molds to its powerful physique. It is unburdened by this body's history; it has no memory of childhood or the farm where its shell was raised, no

268

recollection of the human family who loved and nurtured it, the same who died, one by one, while it stood by and did nothing.

It found no girl hiding inside a tent in the woods, a rifle in one hand and a teddy bear in the other. It never carried her broken body across a sea of white, never pulled her back from the edge of death. There was no rescue of her or her brother, no vow to protect her at all costs.

There is nothing human left in it, nothing human at all.

It does not remember the past; therefore, the past does not exist. Its humanity does not exist.

It does not even have a name.

The enhancement informs it that a chemical agent has been introduced into the water. It will feel none of the poison's effects. It has been designed to endure pain, to be immune to suffering, its own and its victims'. The ancients had a saying for this, *vincit qui patitur*, and it applied to the vanquished as well as to the victor. To conquer, you must endure not just your own suffering but the suffering of others. Indifference is the ultimate evolutionary achievement, the highest rung on nature's ladder. The ones who created the program driving the human body that was once called Evan Walker understood this. They had studied the problem for thousands of years.

The fundamental flaw in humanity was its humanity. The useless, baffling, self-destructive human tendency to love, to empathize, to sacrifice, to trust, to imagine *anything* outside the boundaries of its own skin—these things had driven the species to the edge of destruction. Worse, this one organism threatened the survival of all life on Earth.

The Silencer's makers did not have to look far for a solution. The answer lay in another species that had conquered the entirety of its domain, ruling it with unquestioned authority for millions of years. Beyond their immaculate design, the reason sharks rule the ocean is their complete indifference to everything except feeding, procreation, and defending their territory. The shark does not love. It feels no empathy. It trusts nothing. It lives in perfect harmony with its environment because it has no aspirations or desires. And no pity. A shark feels no sorrow, no remorse, hopes for nothing, dreams of nothing, has no illusions about itself or anything beyond itself.

Once a human named Evan Walker had a dream—a dream it can no longer remember—and in that dream there was a tent in the woods and in that tent there was a girl who called herself humanity, and the girl was worth more to it than its own life.

No longer.

When it finds her, and it *will* find her, it will kill her. Without remorse, without pity. It will kill the one whom Evan Walker loved with all the emotion of a man stepping on a cockroach.

The Silencer has awakened.

85

ZOMBIE

THE FIRST PERSON I SEE is Dumbo.

That's how I know I'm dead.

I go where you go, Sarge.

Well, Bo, this time it looks like I've gone where you went.

I watch through a shimmering fog as he pulls a cold pack from his med kit and breaks the seal to mix the chemicals. The familiar serious look on his face—the mask of worry—like the welfare of the entire world rests on his shoulders, I've missed that.

"A cold pack?" I ask him. "What the hell kind of heaven is this, anyway?"

He gives me his *shut-up-I'm-working* look. Then he presses the pack into my hand and tells me to hold it against the back of my head. His ears look smaller in the shimmering fog. Maybe that's his heavenly reward: smaller ears.

"I shouldn't have left you, Bo," I confess. "I'm sorry."

He fades into the fog. I wonder who I'll see next. Teacup? Poundcake? Maybe Flintstone or Tank. I hope it isn't my old tentmate, Chris. My sister? Thinking of seeing her again makes my stomach tighten. Dear God, we have stomachs in heaven? I wonder what the food is like.

The face that swims into view isn't one I know. It's a black girl around my age, with model-perfect cheekbones and beautiful eyes, though there's no warmth in them. They shine hard as polished marble. She's wearing fatigues with sergeant's stripes on the sleeves.

Damn. So far the afterlife is depressingly like my forelife.

"Where is she?" the girl asks.

She squats in front of me and rests her forearms on her thighs. Lean body, like a runner's. Long, graceful fingers, nicely trimmed nails.

"I'm gonna make you a promise," she says. "I won't bullshit you if you don't bullshit me. Where is she?"

I shake my head. "I don't know who you're talking about." The cold pack feels deliciously good against my throbbing head, and that's about the only thing that does. It's starting to dawn on me that I might not be so dead after all.

She reaches into her breast pocket, pulls out a crinkled piece of paper, and tosses it into my lap. Dear God, there's Ringer lying in a hospital bed with tubes running everywhere, some kind of screenshot from a video camera. Must have been taken around the time Vosch loaded her up with the 12th System.

I look up at the sergeant and say, "I've never seen this person before in my life."

She sighs, then picks up the photo and stuffs it back into her pocket. She stares across the brown fields shimmering in the blaze of starlight. The fog lifts a little. A broken wooden railing, the faded white wall of a farmhouse, and the silhouette of a silo over her shoulder. I'm guessing we're on the front porch.

"Where was she going?" the girl asks. "And what was she going to do when she got there?"

"Judging from that picture, she's not going anywhere anytime soon."

The kids. What have you done with Megan and Nugget? I press my lips together to hold the question inside. They have Megan, no doubt about that—she was with me when Mount Rushmore fell on my head. Maybe not Nugget, though. Maybe he's still hiding in the pit.

"Your name is Benjamin Thomas Parish," she informs me. "Aka Zombie, former recruit and current sergeant of Squad 53, which went Dorothy last fall and has been on the run ever since the operation you led that took out Camp Haven. Your former squad is dead or MIA, with the exception of the private whose picture I just showed you. Marika Kimura, aka Ringer, who has commandeered one of our choppers and is now on a heading due north of this position. We think we know where she's going, but we would like to know why and what she intends to do once she gets there."

She waits. I'm thinking the pause has been offered for me to fill in the silence. Ringer's full name is Marika Kimura. Why did I have to learn her first *and* last name from total strangers?

The silence drags out. She's giving off the vibe that she could wait forever, even though we both know she doesn't have that long.

"I'm not Dorothy," I finally say. "One of us is, but it isn't me."

She shakes her head. "Dude, you're so far off the reservation, I can't see you with a frickin' telescope." She grabs my chin with those long fingers and squeezes. Hard. "I don't have the patience for this shit and you don't have the time. What's the plan, Sergeant Zombie? What's Ringer's game?"

Damn, she's strong. I have some trouble opening my mouth to talk. "Chess."

She holds on to my chin for another second, then lets go with a disgusted snort. She motions toward the front door of the farmhouse and two figures emerge, one tall, the other short—Nugget-sized short.

The sergeant stands up and pulls Nugget in front of her, two strong hands gripping his shoulders.

"Talk," she says.

Nugget's eyes staring into mine.

"Say something," she orders.

She unholsters her sidearm and presses the muzzle against the side of his head. Nugget doesn't even flinch. He doesn't whimper or cry out. His body is as still as his eyes, and his eyes are saying, *No, Zombie. No.*

"Do it and see what you get," I tell her.

"I'll do them both," she promises me. "First him, then the girl." She moves the gun to the back of Nugget's head. I don't understand at first, then I wish I didn't. When she pulls the trigger, I'll get a faceful of Nugget's brains.

"Okay," I say, keeping my voice level—or as level as possible.

"Then you can do me. Then we're all dead and you can explain that inconvenient fact to your CO."

And then I do something that totally throws her off guard, which is the purpose, the genius behind the design that's worked since I was twelve years old: I smile. The full-on Parish Special.

"What was it before all this shit went down?" I ask her. "Sprinter, right? Or was it long-distance? Me, it was football. Wide receiver. Not much speed but I had hands." I nod. "I had hands." I look over Nugget's head into her eyes. I can see starlight glinting in them, sparking like silver fire. "What happened to us, Sergeant Sprinter? What have they done to us? A year ago, could you imagine blowing out the brains of a little kid? I don't know you, but somehow I don't think so. Call me Dorothy, but I don't think there were ten out of seven billion people who could. Now we stuff bombs down their throats and put guns to their heads like it's the most natural thing on Earth, like putting on clothes or brushing our teeth. You wonder what's next. I mean, after you reach that point, can you go any lower?"

"This is what I need," she says, baring her teeth to mock the Parish Special. "You workin' your Dorothy shit."

"Marika's going back to the place where that picture was taken," I tell her, turning off the smile. Nugget's eyes grow wide: *Zombie! No!* "Once she gets there, she's going to find the asshole who fucked us over—her, you, me, and everybody else in this hemisphere—and when she finds him, she will kill him. Then she's

274

probably going to kill every brainwashed recruit on that base. And when you go back—if you make it back before that big green motherfucker up there starts shitting green bricks of death—she'll kill you, too."

I switch the smile back on. Dazzling. Brilliant. Irresistible. Well, at least that's what people told me back in the day. "Now put down that gun, Sergeant Sprinter, and let's get the fuck out of here."

86

I'M YANKED to my feet and shoved into the house with Nugget, Megan, and two offensive-lineman-sized guys who've removed their jackets just to show how tough they are. They have identical tattoos on their ripped biceps: *VQP.* We hang in the front parlor, Megan on the sofa holding the teddy bear, Nugget glued to my side, though he isn't happy with me right now.

"You *told*," he accuses me.

I shrug. "Bullet's left the chamber, Nugget. Not much they can do about it now."

He shakes his head. The metaphor's lost on him. I lean over and whisper in his ear: "At least I didn't tell them about Cassie, right?"

The mention of his sister's name nearly sends him over the edge. His bottom lip juts out; his eyes fill up.

"Hey, okay now, what's this? Huh? Private, your actions tonight have shown extraordinary courage above and beyond the call of duty. You know what a field promotion is?"

Nugget shakes his head solemnly. "No."

"Well, you just got one, Corporal Nugget."

I place the edge of my hand to my forehead. His chest pops out, his chin comes up, his eyes burn with the ol' Sullivan fire. He returns the salute smartly.

On the porch, the sarge is having a heated debate with her second-in-command. The topic's no mystery; you can hear them clearly through the open door. They've completed the mission, the 2IC argues, time to off these bastards and return to base. *Capture and contain*, the sarge shoots back. *My orders don't say nothing about offing anybody*. She's wavering, though; you can hear it in her voice. Her 2IC comes back with my point about the bomb-shitting beast in high orbit: Whatever she decides about the Dorothys, they have to return to base before dawn or enjoy a front-row seat to Armageddon.

The screen door bangs open and she charges right up to my face, close enough for me to catch a whiff of perfume. It's been so long since I smelled any that my headache disappears in a single, wondrous instant.

"How's she gonna do all this?" she shouts. "How can one person . . . ?"

"It only takes one." My quiet answer in counterpoint to her loud question. "Just one, and the world changes. It's not unheard-of, Sergeant."

She stares at me with those dark, flinty eyes filled with a hundred daggers of light. "Corporal," she snaps to her 2IC without looking away from my face, "we're bugging out. Escort the prisoners to the chopper. They're gonna take a little trip down the rabbit hole." Then to me: "You remember Wonderland."

I nod. "I sure do."

87

BLACK BIRD RISING, the Earth falling away—from the air, the caverns are invisible. The farmhouse and the fields shine silver, and the blast of cold wind is like the voice of the world screaming. The last time I rode in a chopper, I was heading back to a different camp, on a mission to save the kid who sits beside me now, whose once-round face is now lean and stern and full of grim purpose. One day he'll ask his grandkids, *Ever tell you about the time I was promoted to corporal at the age of six?*

His grandkids. According to Ringer, they'll be fighting the same war he is. So will *their* grandkids and their grandkids' grandkids. The war that can't end while the enemy's ship sails serenely over our heads. How could it end when all our descendants have to do is look up?

Like Sergeant Sprinter watching me from across the narrow aisle of the hold. The perfectly scary and scarily perfect thing about their plan is it doesn't matter that she knows I'm Ted-free. *Whoever's not with us is against us.* That kind of thinking nearly brought an end to history, more than once. This time it has.

I look away from her face to the screaming world outside the chopper. I can't see the ground. Just the thin black line of the horizon, the congregation of a million stars, and the green eye-shaped orb that hangs just above the line separating heaven from Earth.

Someone's touching my thigh. And it's not the someone I expect. Dirty, scratched-up hands, chipped nails, pencil-thin arms, pinched face, a headful of tangled hair despite Sullivan's valiant attempts to keep it combed. I touch that hair, drawing it back to tuck behind her ear, and Megan glances shyly at me but doesn't pull away. The last time she rode in a chopper, the people she trusted had just placed a bomb inside her throat. The same people she was going back to now. How do you deal with something like that? How do you make it make sense? I almost say it; the words push against my lips and almost escape. *Not going to let it happen, Megs. This time you're safe.*

The sergeant is shouting something over the headset. I catch only about 10 percent. *Go four? Go four, you sure?* And *We got the juice for that?* And a bunch of expletives you really can't include in the percentage. At hearing the words *Go four,* the other recruits in the hold tighten up. I don't know what the hell Go four means, but it doesn't sound good.

Not good at all.

88

RINGER

FROM THE ROOF of the command center, I hear the window shatter two hundred yards away. A body tumbles out and writhes in the dirt beneath the broken window, its uniform speckled with shards of glass, groaning in pain. I can't see her face—but even from this distance, I recognize the tangle of strawberry curls.

I sprint across the rooftop, leap forty feet to the roof of the adjacent building, then jump three stories to the ground. Sullivan sees my boots hit the grass a foot from her head and screams. She fumbles with her sidearm. I kick it out of her hand and haul her to her feet. Her uniform is soaked. Her eyes are swollen and red, her face pockmarked with angry crimson boils. She's shaking uncontrollably, going into shock. I'll have to act fast.

I throw her over my shoulder and sprint toward a small storage shed located on the back side of the building. The door's padlocked. I bust it apart with one kick and carry her inside. The hub processes the data transmitted by the olfactory drones: something in the water, something toxic.

I strip off her jacket. Rip off her shirt and undershirt. Slipping in and out of consciousness, she barely resists. Boots, socks, pants, underwear. Her skin's inflamed and clammy to the touch. I press my hand against her chest; her heart slams against my palm. I look into her weeping, unseeing eyes and shove my way into her. The toxin won't kill her—I hope—but her terror might.

I tamp down the panic to slow her heart. The primitive part of her brain pushes back: The fight-or-flight response is older and more powerful than the technology I contain. The struggle continues for several minutes.

Our hearts, the war.

Her body, the battlefield.

279

89

I THROW MY JACKET over her bare shoulders. She pulls it tight across her chest, a good sign that I haven't lost her yet.

"Where. The hell. Were you?"

"Watching this entire camp bunker-dive," I tell her. "They've cut the power . . ."

She laughs harshly, then turns her head and spits. Her spittle is flecked with blood, and I think of the plague. "Did they? I hadn't noticed."

"It's pretty smart," I say. "Flush us outside, where our options are limited, then dispatch enhanced personnel to finish—"

She's shaking her head. "We have no options, Ringer. Wonderland. We have to get to Wonderland . . ." She tries to stand. Her knees buckle and she goes down. "Where the fuck are my clothes?"

"Here, take mine. I'll wear yours."

For some reason she laughs. "*Commando. That's funny.*"

I don't get it.

I can feel the toxin worm its way into my legs after I pull on her fatigues, and thousands of microscopic bots swarm to neutralize its effects. I hand her my dry shirt, shrug into her wet one.

"The poison doesn't do anything to you?" she asks.

"I don't feel anything."

She rolls her eyes. "I already *knew* that."

"I'll take it from here," I tell her. "You stay."

"Like hell."

"Sullivan, the risk is—"

"I don't give a shit about your risk."

"I'm not talking about the risk to the mission. *Your* risk."

"That doesn't matter." She stands up. This time she stays up. "Where's my rifle?"

I shake my head. "Didn't see it."

"Okay then. What about my gun?"

I take a deep breath. This isn't going to work. She's more a liability now than an asset, and she's never been much of an asset. She'll slow me down. She might get me killed. I should leave her here. Knock her out if I have to. Screw our deal. Walker's dead; he must be; there's no reason Vosch would keep him alive once he's been downloaded into Wonderland. Which means Sullivan is risking everything for nothing.

I am, too. For something I can't even put into words. The same something I saw in her eyes that I cannot name. Something that has nothing to do with Vosch or avenging what he's done to me. It's more important than that. More solid. But that's about as close as I can come to describing it.

Something inviolable.

But I don't say any of that. My mouth comes open and these words come out instead: "You won't need a weapon, Sullivan. You'll have me."

90

I LEAVE HER for a little while. First I make her promise to stay. She's not interested in making promises; she wants to hear them.

So I promise I'll come back for her.

She seems better when I get back. Her face is still red, but the hives or boils or whatever they were have almost disappeared. She's not happy about it, but she throws her arm around my neck and leans against me on the way to the command center.

The entire base is eerily quiet. Our footsteps fall like thunder.

You're watching us, I silently tell Vosch. *I know you're watching.*

Sullivan pushes away when we reach the door.

"How're you gonna do this?" she demands. "We'll be burned alive by the toxin."

"Don't think so. I just shut off the water main."

I smash my fist through the steel door and push down the bar on the opposite side. No alarm sounds. No light blinds us. No bullets take us down. The silence is stifling.

Sullivan breathes in my ear, "It's the waves, Ringer. The power. The water. The plague. You know what's next. You know what's coming."

I nod. "I know."

We find the bodies in the stairwell that leads to the underground complex. Seven recruits, no blood, and not a scratch on them. Obviously, whoever did this was enhanced. Two of the kids have their heads completely twisted around so they stare up at us, though their bodies are facedown. I hand Sullivan one of their pistols. We pick our way through the pile and continue down. She holds the gun in one hand; the other is clutching my sleeve. She couldn't see the recruits and didn't ask what happened or what I saw. She either doesn't want to know or she figures it doesn't matter.

Only one thing matters, she said. She's right. I'm just not sure either one of us can explain what that is.

At the very bottom there is darkness and silence and a hallway even my enhanced eyes cannot see the end of. But I remember

282

where I am. I've been here before, beneath the constant glow. This is where Razor found me, rescued me, gave me hope, and then betrayed me.

I stop. Her hand grips my sleeve hard.

"I can't see a goddamned thing," Sullivan whispers. "Where's the green door?"

"You're standing in front of it."

I ease her to one side and trot down the hall a dozen yards to get a running start. For all I know, even an enhanced human being can't bust through that door's locking mechanism. No choice, though. Halfway to the door, I've reached full velocity and nearly don't have the space to pull up when Sullivan steps in front of me and tries the handle.

The door opens. I slide six feet to a stop. And I'm glad she can't see the startled expression on my face. She'd laugh.

"They don't need to lock the door if there's no power," she points out. "Wonderland needs juice, right?"

Of course she's right. I feel stupid for not foreseeing the obvious.

"I understand," she says, reading my mind. "You're not used to feeling stupid. Trust me, you get used to it." She smiles. "Maybe Wonderland has its own dedicated power system—just in case."

We step into the room. Sullivan closes the door behind us. Her fingertips brush over the dead keypad for a second before dropping to her side. After everything, her capacity to hope has not died.

"What now?" she asks after I've pressed several buttons on the console with no result.

I don't know, Sullivan. You're the one who demanded we come here when you knew they killed the power.

"There's no backup?" she asks. "You'd think it'd have batteries or something, in case they *accidentally* lost power."

Then she says, more to fill the silence than anything else, "I'll stay here. You go find the power station or whatever and get the lights back on."

"Sullivan. I'm thinking."

"You're thinking."

"Yes."

"That's what you're doing. Thinking."

"It's what I do best."

"And all this time I thought killing people was what you did best."

"Well, if I had to pick two things to be really good at . . ."

"Don't joke," she says.

"I never do."

"See? That's fundamental. That's a critical flaw."

"You're right. I should kill more and talk less."

"So is talking too much."

I'm running my hands along the tabletop. Nothing. I drop to the floor and crawl beneath the counter. A tangle of wires, couplings, extension cords. I stand up. On the wall, flat-screen monitors—no cords, probably wirelessly connected to the system. Nothing else to Wonderland except the keyboard, but there has to be something else. Where is the data stored? Where's the processor? Of course, this is alien technology. Vosch could be carrying the processor in his pocket. It could be on a chip the size of a single grain of sand embedded in his brain.

The most puzzling thing is the risk. Wonderland is a vital piece of machinery, an important component in the winnowing of the 5th Wave, key to picking out the bad apples, including Evan Walker, the most rotten apple in the barrel.

The room is dry. No sprinklers came on in here. So where's the power? The power might be out in every other part of the complex, but it should be on in this room. The risk is too great.

"Ringer?" Being unable to see me has unnerved her. I see her hand reaching out in my direction. "What are you thinking about now?"

"They can't risk losing power to Wonderland."

"Which is why I asked about backup batteries or—"

Stupid. Stupid, stupid, stupid. I hope Sullivan is right. I hope I can get used to feeling stupid. I step around her and hit the light switch.

Wonderland comes to life.

91

CASSIE SITS. The white chair whines. She rotates back to face the white ceiling. I fastened her in.

"I've never done this," she confesses. "Almost, back at Camp Haven."

"What happened?"

"I strangled Dr. Pam with one of these straps."

"Good for you," I say sincerely. "I'm impressed."

I step over to the keyboard. I'm certain I'll be asked for a password. I'm not. I touch a random key and the launch page pops up on the central monitor.

"What's going on?" she asks. She can't see anything from the chair except the white ceiling.

Data bank. "Found it." I click the button.

"Now what?" she demands.

Everything is in code. Thousands of numerical combinations, which I guess represent the individuals whose memories have been captured by the program. Impossible to know which sequence is Walker's. We could try the first one, and if that isn't him, work our way down the list, but—

"Ringer, you're not talking."

"I'm thinking."

She sighs loudly. She wants to say something like *I thought you said you were good at that,* but she doesn't.

"You can't figure out which one is Evan's," she says finally.

"We've gone over this," I remind her. "Even if I could locate his data, you don't know that his memories will lead you to him. After he was downloaded, Vosch probably—"

She lifts her head as far as she can from the chair and snaps, "He's in there somewhere. *Give me all of them.*"

At first I'm sure I didn't hear her correctly. "Sullivan, there are thousands of them."

"I don't care. I'll go through every goddamned one till I find him."

"I'm pretty sure it doesn't work that way."

"Oh, what the hell do you know, huh? How much do you really *know,* Ringer, and how much of what you 'know' is shit that Vosch wants you to know? The truth is you don't know shit. I don't know shit. Nobody knows shit."

Her head flops back. Her hands clutch the straps. Maybe she's thinking of strangling me with one.

"You said Vosch downloaded them all," she goes on. "And that's how he knew the way to manipulate you. *He* carries all those memories inside him, so it must be safe. *Perfectly safe.*"

I'm ready to execute the command, if for nothing else but to shut her up.

"Why are you afraid?" she asks.

I shake my head. "Why aren't you?"

I hit the execute button, sending tens of millions of unfiltered memories into Cassie Sullivan's brain.

92

HER BODY JERKS against the restraints. The fabric starts to tear; it may rip apart. Then she stiffens like someone suffering a seizure. Her eyes roll back in her head. Her jaw clenches. One of her fingernails snaps off and flies across the room.

On the monitors the sequences race by in a blur, too fast even for my enhanced vision to follow. How much data is contained in the minds of ten thousand people? What's happening to Sullivan is like trying to stuff the solar system into a walnut. It will kill her. Her mind will blow apart like the singularity at the moment of creation.

I've no doubt Vosch used Wonderland to download individuals' experiences—I'm certain he downloaded mine—I also have little doubt those experiences were purged somehow after they served their purpose. No single human being can contain the sum of all that human experience. At the least, it would shatter your personality. How can you hold on to the core of your reality in the midst of so many alternatives?

Sullivan moans. Her cries are soft, coming from deep in her gut. *She's weak. You knew better. You should have taken her place.*

The technology they've infected you with could handle this; the 12th System would have protected you. Why did you let her do it?

But I know the answer to that question. The 12th System can only enhance the human body—it is helpless against fear. It cannot give me the one thing that Cassie Sullivan has in abundance.

I thought I knew what courage was. I was even arrogant enough to lecture Zombie about it. But I had no idea what true, undiluted courage was until this moment. That unidentifiable something I saw in her eyes is part of it, the root from which her courage sprang.

My finger hovers over the abort button. Would it be an act of courage to push it? Or the final failure of my human side—the part of me that hopes when there is no hope, believes when there is no reason to believe, trusts when all trust has been broken? Would pushing the button be Vosch's ultimate victory over me? *See, Marika, even you belong to us now. Even you.*

It's over in less than five minutes. An eternal five minutes; the universe took shape in less time.

The monitors go blank. Cassie goes limp. I approach her gingerly. I'm afraid to touch her. Afraid of what I might feel. I'm in fear for my own mind, my own sanity. Plunging into a single human consciousness is dangerous enough; I can't fathom being immersed in thousands.

"Cassie?"

Her eyelids flutter. I see the white ceiling reflected in her green eyes. And something else. Something shocking. Not horror. Not sorrow. No confusion or pain or fear. None of the things she must have found in Wonderland.

Instead, her eyes, her face, her entire body has ignited with the opposite of all those things, there all along, unconquerable, undefeatable, immortal. The root of her courage. The foundation of all life, often obscured, never lost.

Joy.

She takes a long, shuddering breath and says, "We're here."

93

HER FACE GLOWS. Her eyes shine. A smile plays on her lips.

"You wouldn't believe . . .," she whispers. "You don't know . . ."

I shake my head. "No, I don't."

"It's so beautiful . . . so *beautiful* . . . I can't. Oh God, Marika, I *can't* . . ."

She's sobbing. I take her face in my hands, begging the hub to keep me out. I don't want to be where she is. I don't think I could bear it.

"Sammy's here," she cries. "Sammy's *here*." And she strains against the frayed restraints as if she could somehow wrap her arms around him. "And Ben, he's here, too. Oh God, oh Christ, I called him broken. Why did I do that? He's strong . . . he's so *strong*, no wonder they can't kill him . . ."

Her eyes roam the featureless white. Her shoulders shake. "They're all here. Dumbo and Teacup and Poundcake . . ."

I back away from her. I know what's coming. It's like watching a runaway train bearing down. I fight a nearly overwhelming urge to run.

"I'm sorry, Marika. About everything. I didn't know. I didn't understand."

"We don't have to go there, Cassie," I mutter weakly. *Please, don't go there.*

"He loved you, Razor . . . Alex. He couldn't admit it to anyone. He couldn't even admit it to himself. He knew before he did it that he would die for you."

"Walker," I say hoarsely. "What about Walker?"

She ignores me or she doesn't hear the question. She is here and she is not. She is Cassie Sullivan and she is everyone else.

She has become the sum of us.

"Rainbow fingers," she gasps, and I stop breathing. She's seeing my father's hand holding mine. She remembers the way that felt, the way it made *me* feel, my father's hand in mine.

"We're out of time," I say, to pull her out of my memories. "Cassie, listen to me. Is Walker there?"

She nods. She starts to cry again. "He was telling the truth. There *was* music. And the music was beautiful . . . I *see* it, Marika. His planet. The ship. What he *looked* like . . . oh my God, that's *disgusting*." She shakes her head to clear the image. "Marika, he was telling the truth. It's *real* . . . it's *real* . . ."

"No, Cassie. Listen to me. Those memories aren't real."

She screams. She thrashes against the restraints. Thank God I haven't untied her yet or she might tear out her own eyes.

I don't have a choice now. I'll have to risk it.

I grab her shoulders and force her back into the chair. A cacophonous blast of emotions explodes in my mind and for a second I'm afraid I'll black out. How does she endure it? How can one mind bear the weight of ten thousand others? It defies comprehension. It's like trying to define God.

Inside Cassie Sullivan is a horror so profound, there are no words. The people downloaded into Wonderland lost every person

290

who mattered to them, and most of those downloaded people were children. Their pain is hers now. Their confusion and sorrow, their anger and hopelessness and fear. It's too much. I can't stay within her. I stumble backward until I smack against the counter.

"I know where he is," she says, catching her breath. "Or at least where he might be, if they brought him back to the same place. Untie me, Marika."

I pick up the rifle leaning against the wall.

"Marika."

I walk to the door.

"*Marika.*"

"I'll be back," I manage to choke out.

She screams my name again and now I don't have a choice. If he hasn't heard us before, he's certain to have heard her now.

Because I have heard *him*.

Someone is descending the stairs at the other end of the mile-long corridor. I'm not sure who it is, but I know *what* it is.

And I know why it's coming.

"You'll be safe here," I lie. The hopeful kind of lie you tell children. "I won't let anything happen to you."

I open the door and stagger from light into darkness.

EVEN WITH MY ENHANCED SPEED, I won't be able to reach the stairway door before he does. But with a little luck, I can get within the firing range of an M16.

I'm certain it's Vosch. Who else could it be? He knows I'm here. He knows why I'm here. Creator to his creation, creature to her creator, that's our bond. Only one way for me to break it. Only one way to be free.

I explode down the hallway, a human missile. I hear him coming. He must hear me coming.

The range of an M16 is 550 meters, one-third of a mile. The hub calculates my speed and the distance to the stairwell. Not going to happen. I ignore the math and keep running. Nine hundred meters—eight—seven. The processor embedded in my cerebral cortex goes berserk, running the numbers over and over, coming up short, and sending me messages of escalating urgency. *Run back. Find cover. No time. No time, no time, notimenotimenotimenotime.*

I ignore it. I don't serve the 12th System. The 12th System serves me.

Unless it decides that it won't.

The hub pulls the plug on the drones that enhance my muscles: If it can't stop me, at least it can slow me down. My speed drops. Abandoned, I'm running like an ordinary human. I feel chained and unbound at the same time.

The lights in the hall blaze to life. The stairway door flies open and a tall figure lurches into view. I open fire, charging forward, closing the gap as fast as I can. The figure stumbles, careens against the far wall, and brings up its hands instinctively to cover its face.

I'm in range now—I know it, the enemy knows it, and the hub knows it. It's over. I lock in on the figure's head. My finger tightens on the trigger.

Then I see a blue jumpsuit, not a colonel's uniform. Wrong height. Wrong weight, too. I hesitate for an instant and in that instant the figure lowers its hands.

My first thought is for Cassie—that she suffered Wonderland when Wonderland wasn't necessary. She risked everything to find him . . . until he found her.

Evan Walker has a knack for finding her; he always has.

I stop a hundred meters away but I don't lower my rifle. Between his leaving and our reunion, there's no telling what happened. The hub agrees with me. No risk if he's dead, enormous risk if he's not. Whatever value he had is gone now, contained in the consciousness of Cassie Sullivan.

"Where's Vosch?" I ask.

Without a word, he lowers his head and charges. He's halved the distance before I open fire, first overriding the hub's insistence I aim for the head, then its demand I retreat before he reaches me. I put six rounds into his legs, thinking that will drop him. It doesn't. By the time I give in to the hub's shrieking command, it's too late.

He knocks the rifle from my hands. So fast I don't see the blow coming. Don't see the next one, either, the fist that smashes into the side of my neck, hurling me into the wall. The concrete cracks on impact.

I blink, and his fingers lock around my throat. Another blink and I break the hold with my left and punch as hard as I can with my right, dead center into his chest to break his sternum and drive the shattered bone into his heart. It's as if I rammed my fist into a three-inch-thick plate of steel. The bone cracks but does not break.

I blink again, and now my face is pressing against cool concrete and there's blood in my mouth and blood on the wall I've been rammed into—only it isn't a wall; it's the floor. I've been flung a hundred yards and landed flat on my stomach.

Too fast. He moves faster than the priest at the caverns, faster than Claire in the infirmary bathroom. Faster than Vosch, even. It defies the laws of physics for a human being to move that fast.

Before the alien processor in my brain uses the nanosecond it needs to calculate the odds, I know the outcome:

Evan Walker is going to kill me.

He lifts me from the floor by the ankle and slings me against the wall. The blocks splinter. So do a number of my bones. He doesn't let go. He smashes my body against the other wall. Back and forth until the concrete breaks apart and rains to the floor in a fall of dusty gray. I don't feel anything; the hub has shut down my pain receptors. He lifts my body over his head and slams it down against his upraised knee.

I don't feel my back break but I hear it magnified a thousand times by the auditory drones embedded in my ears.

He drops my limp body to the floor. I close my eyes, waiting for the coup de grâce. At least he'll make it quick. At least I know that the 12th System's final gift to me will be a painless death.

He kicks me onto my back. Then he kneels beside me, and his eyes are fathomless pits, black holes that no light can penetrate or escape. Nothing lives in those eyes, neither hate nor rage nor amusement nor the mildest curiosity. Evan Walker's eyes are as blank as a doll's, his stare as unblinking.

"There is another," he says. "Where is it?" His voice is affectless, without a trace of humanity. Whoever Evan Walker was before is gone.

When I don't answer, the thing that was Evan Walker, with obscene gentleness, cups my face in its hands and slices into my consciousness. The entity raping my soul is itself soulless, alien, *other*. I can't pull away; I can't move at all. With enough time—time that it doesn't have—the 12th System might be able to repair the damage to my spine, but for now I'm paralyzed. My mouth comes open. No sound comes out.

It knows. It releases me. It rises.

I find my voice, and I scream as loud as I can. *"Cassie! Cassie, it's coming!"*

It lumbers down the hall toward the green door.

And the green door will open. She will see him with eyes that have seen all that he's seen and a heart that's felt all he has felt. She'll think he has come to save her—that his love will deliver her once again.

My voice wilts into a pitiful whimper. *"Cassie, it's coming. It's coming . . ."*

No way she hears me. No way for her to know.

I pray she won't see it coming. I pray that the thing that was once Evan Walker will be quick.

95

SILENCER

AT THE END of the hall is a green door. On the other side of the green door is a white room. Inside that room its prey is bound to a white chair, the goat tied to a stake, the wounded seal trapped in a powerful current. It will crush her skull. It will rip her heart still beating from her chest with its bare hands. The one Evan Walker had saved on that first day so upon this final day his soulless remains can kill her. There is no irony in this cruelty; there is only cruelty.

But the chair is empty. Its prey has vanished. The Silencer examines the straps that held her arms. Hair, skin, blood. She must have ripped herself free.

It lowers its head, listening. Its hearing is exquisitely acute. It can hear the other human breathing nearly a mile away at the other end of the corridor, the one whose back it had broken, whose bones it had shattered against the concrete walls. It can hear the breaths of the soldiers huddled in safe rooms throughout the base, waiting for the all clear to sound, their quiet voices, the rustle of their uniforms, their galloping hearts. It can hear the electricity thrumming through the wires inside the walls of the room. It sifts through the confusing jumble of noise to isolate its prey. It seeks a single heartbeat, a solitary breath close by; she can't have gone far.

There is no satisfaction when it pinpoints her location. A shark feels no satisfaction at the detection of the baby seal in the surf.

It lunges from the room on legs it cannot feel: The processor in its brain has nullified the pain from the wounds, and the arterial drones have shut off the flow of blood to the bullets' entry points. Its legs are as numb as its heart, as insensitive as its mind.

Three doors down, on the right. It stands for a moment outside the door, frozen, hands loose at its sides, head bowed, listening. Somehow its prey had known the combination and entered this room. It does not ponder how she could know the code. It does not pause to consider why the girl was in the white room or what had happened to her there. Where the prey came from and its life before it got there—these things are irrelevant. Beneath the seal's silhouette on the surface, the beast rockets upward from the deep.

She is close—very close. It hears her breath on the other side of the door. It discerns the beat of her heart. She's pressing her ear against the door, listening.

The Silencer's hand draws back, fingers curled into a fist.

Rotating its hips into the blow to maximize force, it smashes its fist through the reinforced door. On the other side the prey recoils, but too late; it catches a handful of her hair. She rips free with a startled scream, leaving behind a wad of curls in its hand.

The Silencer tears the door from its hinges and springs inside.

The prey is scrambling across the wet floor, slipping as she goes, between two rows of junction boxes that line either side of the narrow aisle.

It has cornered her in one of the complex's electrical rooms. There is only one way out, and to escape, she must pass the Silencer—and that will be impossible.

The Silencer does not rush. There is no hurry. It glides across the puddled water deliberately, closing the gap. The prey pauses near the back wall; perhaps she realizes she has nowhere to run, no place to hide, no choice but to turn and face the thing that sooner or later must be faced. She veers to her right and jumps, reaching for a handhold in the three-foot space between the top of a box and the ceiling. Her hand wraps around one of the incoming lines and she hauls herself into the tiny niche.

She's trapped.

The oldest part of its human brain is alerted before the highly advanced processor embedded in its cerebral cortex: Something is not right.

The Silencer pauses in its charge.

Item: A thick, rust-colored high-voltage cord dangling loose—cut or pulled free from the junction box.

Item: A thin sheet of water covers the floor and pools around its feet.

The processor in its brain cannot slow down time but can slow

297

down the host's perception of it. In the ache of time grinding to a crawl, the power line falls from the prey's hand in a graceful, sweeping arc. The light sparks off the exposed wires as they descend languidly as snow.

Too far from the doorway to run. And the boxes on either side of the Silencer are flush with the ceiling; no open space into which it can jump.

The Silencer leaps, extending its body to its full length parallel to the ground, flying a foot above the floor, arm outstretched, fingers spread wide, its only hope to catch the crimson cord before it makes contact with the water.

The line that gracefully falls slips through the Silencer's fingers. The light glints off the wires as they touch ground, silently, like falling snow.

96

RINGER

I'VE BEEN HERE BEFORE, lying helplessly beneath the constant sterile glow.

Razor would come to me while my body fought the losing battle against the forty thousand invaders the enemy injected into it. Razor would come to me, and his coming would sustain me, the hope he offered the tether that kept me from hurtling endlessly through the void.

He died to save me, and now his child will die with me.

The stairway door slams. Boots echo on the stone floor. I know the sound. I recognize the rhythm of his stride.

That's why the Silencer didn't kill you. It was saving you for him.

"Marika."

Vosch towers over me. He is ten thousand feet tall, fashioned from solid rock, an impregnable battlement that cannot be broken, that cannot fall. His azure eyes shine as he looks down on me from unscalable heights.

"You've forgotten something," he tells me. "And now it's too late. What have you forgotten, Marika?"

A child bursts through the brittle stalks of winter-killed wheat, carrying a capsule-sized bomb within its mouth. Human breath enfolds the child and everything is engulfed in green fire, and afterward nothing remains.

The pill. His parting gift in the breast pocket of my jacket. I will my hand to rise and my hand won't move.

"I knew you would come back," Vosch says. "Who else would have the final answer but the one who created you?"

The words die on my lips. I can still speak, but what's the point? He already knows what I want to ask. It's the only question I have left.

"Yes, I have been inside their ship. And it's as remarkable as you've imagined. I have seen them—our saviors—and, yes, they are also as remarkable as you've imagined. They aren't physically there, of course, but you've already guessed that. They are not here, Marika. They never were."

His eyes glow with the transcendental joy of a prophet who has seen heaven.

"They are carbon-based like us, and that is where all similarities end. It took them a very long time to understand us, to accept what was happening here and devise the only viable solution to the problem. Likewise, it took *me* a very long time to understand and accept their solution. It's difficult to ignore your own humanity, to step outside yourself and see through the eyes of a wholly other species. That's been your particular problem from the beginning, Marika. I had hopes that one day you would conquer it. You are the closest I've ever come to seeing myself in another human being."

He notices something about my face and kneels beside me. His finger presses against my cheek, and my tear rolls over his knuckle.

"I am going away, Marika. You must have guessed that. My consciousness will be preserved for all time aboard the mothership, eternally free, eternally safe from whatever may happen here. That was my price. And they agreed to pay it." He smiles. The smile is kind, a father to his beloved child. "Are you satisfied now? Have I answered all your questions?"

"No," I whisper. "You haven't told me why."

He doesn't scold about having just told me why. He knows I'm not asking about his motivation.

"Because the universe has no limits, but life does. Life is rare, Marika, and therefore precious; it must be preserved. If they may be said to have anything resembling human faith, it is that. All life is worthy of existence. The Earth is not the first planet they have saved."

He cups my cheek in his hand. "I don't want to lose you," he says. "Virtues have become vices, and you've said it yourself: This particular vice follows no rules, even its own. I have committed a mortal sin, Marika, and only you can absolve me."

He slips his hand beneath my head and lifts it gently from the floor. He kneels beside me, creator, father, cradling my head in his hands.

"We found it, Marika. The anomaly in Walker's programming. The flaw in the system is that *there isn't one*.

"Do you understand? It's important that you understand. The singularity beyond space and time, the undefinable constant that transcends all understanding—they had no answer for it, so they gave none. How could they? How could love be contained in any algorithm?"

His eyes still sparkle, though now with tears. "Come with me, Marika. Let us go together, to a place where there is no more pain, no more sorrow. All of this will be gone in an instant." He waves his hand to indicate the base, the planet, the past. "They'll take away any memory that troubles you. You will be immortal, forever young, forever free. They will give me that. Grant me the grace to give *you* that."

I whisper, "Too late."

"No! This broken body, it's nothing. Worthless. It's not too late."

"It is for you," I tell him.

Behind him, Cassie Sullivan takes the cue. She presses the gun to the back of my creator's head and pulls the trigger.

—————— **97** ——————

THE GUN FALLS from her hand. She sways on her feet, staring down at Vosch's body and the semicircle of blood that slowly expands beneath his head, creating an obscene mockery of a halo. She's found herself in a moment she's dreamed of for a very long time, but she doesn't feel what she thought she would feel. It isn't the moment of triumph and revenge she thought it would be. What she feels, I can't tell; her face is expressionless, her gaze turned inward.

"Evan's gone," she says in a dead voice.

"I know," I tell her. "He's the one who did this to me." Her eyes slide from Vosch to me. "Did what?"

"Broke my back. I can't move my legs, Cassie."

She shakes her head. Evan. Vosch. Me. Too much to process.

"What happened?" I ask.

She glances down the hallway. "The electrical room. I knew exactly where it was. And the code to the door, I knew that, too." She turns back to me. "I know practically everything about this base."

Her eyes are dry but she's about to break; I can hear it in her voice, filled with sick wonder. "I killed him, Ringer. I killed Evan Walker."

"No, Cassie. Whatever attacked me wasn't human. I think Vosch erased his memory—his *human* memory and—"

"I know that," she snaps. "It's the last thing he heard before they took it from him: 'Erase the human.'" She catches her breath. His experiences are hers now. She shares the horror of that moment, the last moment of Evan Walker's life.

"And you're sure he's dead?" I ask.

She waves her hand helplessly in the air. "Pretty damn sure."

She frowns. "You left me tied to that fucking chair."

"I thought I had time . . ."

"Well, you didn't."

The overhead speakers pop. "GENERAL ORDER FOUR IS NOW RESCINDED. ALL ACTIVE-DUTY PERSONNEL TO REPORT IMMEDIATELY TO BATTLE STATIONS . . ."

I can hear the squads exiting their bunkers around the base.

Any moment the thunder of boots and the glint of steel and the rain of bullets. Cassie cocks her head as if she, too, can hear them with her unenhanced ears. But she has been enhanced in another, more profound way, a way I can only pretend to understand.

"I have to go," she says. She isn't looking at me. It's like she isn't even speaking to me. I can only watch as she yanks the knife from the sheath strapped to my thigh, steps over to Vosch, flattens his hand against the floor, and, with two hard whacks, chops off his right thumb.

She drops the bloody digit into the pocket of her fatigues. "It wouldn't be right to leave you here, Marika."

She slides her hands beneath my shoulders and drags me to the nearest door.

"No, forget about me, Cassie. I'm done."

"Oh, be quiet," she mutters. She punches the code into the keypad and pulls me into the room. "Am I hurting you?"

"No. Nothing hurts."

She props me up against the far wall facing the door and presses the gun into my hand. I shake my head. Hiding in this room, having the gun, it only delays the inevitable.

There is another way, though: I carry it in my breast pocket.

When the time comes—and the time will come—you'll wish that you had it.

"Get out of here," I tell her. My time has come, but not hers. "If you can make it out of the building, you might be able to reach the perimeter . . ."

She shakes her head impatiently. "That's not the way, Marika." Her eyes lose focus again. "It isn't far. Five minutes from here?" She nods as if someone has answered her question. "Yeah. At the end of the hall. About five minutes."

303

"The end of the hall?"

"Area 51."

She stands up. Steady on her feet now and her mouth firmly set.

"He's not going to understand. He's going to be pissed as hell, and you're going to explain it to him. You're going to tell him what happened and why, and you're going to take care of him, understand? You're going to keep him safe and make sure he bathes and brushes his teeth and trims his nails and wears clean underwear and *learns to read*. Teach him to be patient and to be kind and to trust everyone. Even strangers. Especially strangers."

She pauses. "There was something else. Oh yeah. Make him understand it isn't random. That there's no way seven billion billion atoms could accidentally coalesce into a person called Samuel Jackson Sullivan. What else? Oh! Nobody is allowed to call him Nugget ever again for the rest of his life. I mean, really. So stupid.

"Promise me, Marika. Promise me."

98

THE SEVEN BILLION BILLION

WE ARE HUMANITY.

We are one.

We are the girl with the broken back sprawled in an empty room, waiting for the end to come.

We are the man who's fallen a half mile away, and the only

thing still living in us is not alive, but an alien device that directs every resource at its disposal to saving our body lying on the cold stone, to shock our heart back to life. There is no difference between us and the system. The 12th System is us and we are the 12th System. If one should fail, the other will die.

We are the prisoners aboard the Black Hawk helicopter that circles the base while its fuel runs low, swinging over a broad river, its waters black and swift, and our voices are quelled by the wind that roars through the open hold, and our hands are clasped; we are bound to one another in an unbroken chain.

We are the recruits hustling to our battle stations, the rescued ones, the winnowed ones, the harvest gathered into buses and separated into groups in which our bodies were hardened and our souls emptied only to be filled with hate and hope, and we know as we break from our bunkers that dawn approaches and with it the war, and this is what we've longed for and dreaded, the end of winter, the end of us. We remember Razor and the price he paid; we carved the initials *VQP* into our bodies in his honor. We remember the dead but we can't remember our own names.

We are the lost ones, the solitary ones, the ones who did not board those buses chugging down the highways, the empty city streets, the lonely country roads. We dug in for the winter and watched the skies and trusted no stranger. Those of us who did not die from starvation or the bitter cold or simple infections that antibiotics we did not have could have relieved, we endured. We bent, but we did not break.

We are the lonely hunters designed by our makers to drive survivors onto the buses that scavenge the countryside and to kill those who refuse. We are special, we are apart, we are Other. We have been awakened into a lie so compelling that to not believe it would be madness. Now our work is done and we watch the skies, waiting for a deliverance that will never come.

We are the seven billion who were sacrificed, our bodies stripped down to our bones. We are the ones swept aside, the discarded ones, our names forgotten, our faces lost to wind and earth and sand. No one will remember us, our footprints erased, our legacies wiped out, our children and their children and their children's children at war against one another unto the last generation, to the end of the world.

We are humanity. Our name is Cassiopeia.

In us the rage, in us the grief, in us the fear.

In us the faith, the hope, the love.

We are the vessel of ten thousand souls. We carry them; we hold them; we keep them. We bear their burden, and through us, their lives are redeemed.

They rest in us and we in them. Our heart contains all others.

One heart, one life, on the advent of a mayfly's final flight.

CASSIE

ALIENS ARE STUPID.

Ten thousand years to pick us apart, to know us down to the last electron, and they still don't get it. They still don't understand. Dumbasses.

The pod rests on a raised platform three stairsteps off the floor. Egg-shaped, tortoiseshell-green, about the size of a big SUV, like a Suburban or an Escalade. The hatch is closed, but I've got the key. I press the pad of Vosch's severed thumb against the round sensor beside the door and the hatch soundlessly slides open. Lights flicker on, bathing the interior in a wash of iridescent green. Inside, a single seat and another touchpad and that's it. No instrument panel. No little monitors. Nothing but the chair, the pad, and a small window through which I guess you can wave good-bye.

Evan was wrong and he was right. He believed all their lies but he knew the only truth that matters. The one truth that mattered before they came, when they came, after they came.

They had no answer for love.

They thought they could crush it out of us, burn it from our brains, replace love with its opposite—not hate, indifference. They thought they could turn men into sharks.

But they couldn't account for that one little thing. They had no answer for it because it wasn't answerable. It wasn't even a question.

The problem of that damned bear.

RINGER

AFTER CASSIE LEAVES, I drop the gun.

I don't need it. I have Vosch's gift in my pocket.

I am the child in the wheat.

The slap of boots on pavement, on polished concrete floors, on metal risers, from the airstrip to the command center, the sound of thousands of feet running like the *scratch-scratch* of the rats behind the walls of the old hotel.

I'm surrounded.

I'll give her the only thing I can, I think, reaching for the green capsule in my pocket. *The only thing I've got left.*

My fingers dig into the jacket pocket.

The *empty* jacket pocket.

I pat my other pockets. No. Not *my* pockets. They're Cassie's pockets: I switched clothes with her in the supply shed before we entered the command center.

I don't have the green capsule. Cassie does.

The slap of boots on pavement, on polished concrete floors, on metal risers. I push myself from the wall and crawl toward the door.

He isn't far. Just across this room, through that door, a few feet down the hall. If I can get to him before they reach this level, I may still have a chance—*they* won't, but I will.

Cassie will.

Door. I yank the handle down, swing it halfway open, then quickly slide into the space between to prop it open with my body. I can see him, the faceless murderer of seven billion who should have killed me when he had the chance—and he had several—but couldn't. He couldn't, because even he was confounded by love's unpredictable trajectory.

Hall. He must still have the device. He carried it everywhere he went. Lightweight and no larger than a cell phone, it tracked every implanted recruit on the base. And with a swipe of the thumb, it can send a signal to the implants inside their necks, killing each one of them.

Vosch. Lying on my stomach, I reach for him, grab the back of his uniform, and roll him over. The bloody crater that was his face is turned to the sterile glow of the ceiling. I hear them on the stairs, boots on metal risers, growing louder. *Where is it? Give it up, you son of a bitch.*

Breast pocket. Right where he always kept it. The display screen swarms with green dots, a three-squad cluster's worth heading straight toward me. I highlight all of them—every recruit on the base, over five thousand people, and the green button beneath my thumb flashes, and this is why I didn't want to come back. I knew what would happen. I knew:

I'll kill until I lose count. I'll kill until counting doesn't matter.

I'm staring at the screen lit up with five thousand tiny pulsing lights, each a hapless victim, each a human being.

Telling myself I don't have a choice.

Telling myself I'm not his creation. I'm not what he has made me.

ZOMBIE

ON OUR SEVENTEENTH PASS around the perimeter—or maybe the eighteenth; I've lost count—the lights of the air base abruptly blaze back on, and across from me, Sergeant Sprinter barks into her headset, "*Status?*"

We've been circling for over an hour and our fuel must be low. We'll have to set down soon; the only question is where, inside the base or out. Right now we're approaching the river again. I expect the pilot to change course, bring us over some land, but she doesn't.

Megan is nestled under my arm, her head tucked beneath my chin. Nugget presses against the other arm, watching the base below. His sister is down there somewhere. Possibly alive, probably dead. The restoration of the lights is a bad sign.

We bank over the river, keeping the base on our left, and I can see other choppers circling over it, too, waiting for the all clear to land. Their spotlights cut through the predawn mist, pillars of glistening white. We're over the river now, swollen from an early spring thaw.

Above us, the sky lightens to gray and the stars begin to fade.

This is it. Green Day. The day the bombs fall. I look for the mothership but can't spot it in the brightening sky.

Conversation with the ground over, the sergeant pulls off her headset. Her eyes on my face, her hand resting on the butt of her sidearm. Nugget stiffens beside me; he knows what's coming before I do; his hands claw at his harness, though there's nowhere to run and nowhere to hide.

The orders have changed. She draws her weapon and levels it at his head.

I throw myself in front of him. Finally the circle comes round. Time to pay the debt.

CASSIE

THROUGH THE OPEN DOOR behind me, soldiers flood into the room. They quickly spread out shoulder to shoulder from wall to wall, in two rows, the closest one kneeling, two dozen rifles aimed at a single curly-headed, crooked-nosed target. I turn and face them. They don't know me, but I know them. I recognize each and every face of the ones who have come to kill me.

I know what they remember and what they can't. I hold them inside me. It's like I'm about to be murdered by a human mosaic of myself. Makes you wonder: Is this murder? Or suicide?

I close my eyes. *I'm sorry, Sams. I tried.*

He is with me now, my brother; I feel him.

And that's good. At least when I die, I will not be alone.

RINGER

THE STAIRWAY DOOR slams open and they pound into the hall, weapons drawn. Fingers tighten on triggers.

Too late for them.

Too late for me.

I press the button.

ZOMBIE

ACROSS THE AISLE, the sergeant jerks in her seat; her beautiful dark eyes roll back; her skull pops against the bulkhead; and then she slumps against her harness. Megan bolts upright with a startled cry. Every recruit in the hold has followed the sergeant's lead.

Including the pilot.

The chopper's nose dips, whipping hard to the right and slamming me into Nugget, who's not wasting any time unbuckling himself. The damn kid gets everything before I do. I play a fast, desperate game of slappies with Megan, struggling to free her first. Nugget's hurled from his seat—I catch hold of his sleeve and yank him into my chest. Then Megan's loose but I'm not, holding on to her with one hand and Nugget with the other.

311

"The river!" I scream at him.

He nods. He's the coolest one among us. His little fingers fly over the buckles to set me free.

The chopper barrels toward the water. "Hang on to me!" I shout. "Don't let go!"

We're falling sideways. The river is a featureless black wall rushing toward the open hatch on Nugget's side.

"ONE!"

Nugget closes his eyes.

"TWO!"

Megan screams.

"THREE!"

I swivel out of the seat, a kid under each arm, and drop feetfirst toward the opening.

CASSIE

THE SOLDIERS FALL to the ground. One second they're up, the next they're down. Somebody's fried their brains. I'm not sure how, but I'm pretty sure who.

I turn away. I've seen enough bodies to last my ten thousand lifetimes, from my mother drowning in her own blood to my father writhing gut-shot in the dirt, from the ones before and the ones after and the ones in between, my dead and their dead, *our* dead.

Yeah, I've seen enough.

Plus, those kids who just fell, they're *my* bodies, too, in a way. It's like looking down at your own corpse. Times twelve.

I step inside the pod. I lower myself into the chair. I buckle myself in, pulling tight the straps that cross my chest. In my hand a dead man's thumb. In my pocket a green capsule encased in plastic. In my head ten thousand voices that strangely sing as one. And in my heart, a stillness, a quiet place untouched by anything, beyond space, unbounded by time.

Cassie, do you want to fly?

The green pill fell out when I ripped myself from the Wonderland chair, and I picked it up without thinking about it, without even looking at it. Then I saw Ringer lying in that hallway and I remembered we'd swapped jackets. She'd been carrying around the bomb the whole time and didn't tell anyone. I think I know why. I know her as well as she knows herself. Better, even, because I can remember what she's forgotten.

I press Vosch's severed thumb against the launch button. The hatch door closes, the locking mechanism hums. The ventilation system kicks on; cool air brushes against my cheek.

The pod shivers. I feel like raising my hands.

Yes, Daddy, I want to fly.

ZOMBIE

I LOSE THE KIDS when we hit the water. The force of our landing snatches them away. The chopper tumbles into the river several hundred yards upstream and the fireball paints the surface a dusky orange. I see Megan first, her face breaking the surface enough to allow her a gurgling scream. I grab her wrist and yank her toward me.

"Captain!" she yells.

Huh?

"I lost Captain!"

She kicks against my legs, reaching with her free hand toward the teddy bear that spins lazily away from us. *Oh Christ. That damned bear.*

I look over my shoulder. *Nugget, where are you?* Then I see him at the shoreline, half in, half out, back arching as he coughs up a gallon of river water. The kid is truly indestructible.

"Okay, Megan. Climb aboard; I'll get him."

She hitches herself onto my back, wrapping her thin arms around my neck and her stick legs around my torso. I kick over to the bear. *Gotcha.* Then the long swim to shore, which isn't that far, but the water's freezing and Megan on my back bears me down. *Bears me down.* That's a good one.

We collapse on the shore beside Nugget. Nobody speaks for a few minutes. Then Nugget goes, "Zombie?"

"Somebody hit the kill switch. Only thing that makes sense, Private."

"Corporal," he corrects me. Then he says, "Ringer?"

I nod. "Ringer."

He processes for a second. Then, his voice shaking because he's afraid to ask: "Cassie?"

CASSIE

THE HAND OF GOD slams down as the pod explodes up the launch shaft, a massive fist flattens my body into the chair, and then the fist closes around me, *squeezing.* Some wiseass has dropped a two-ton rock on my chest and I'm finding it very difficult to breathe. Also, somebody with no regard whatsoever for my comfort and safety has turned off all the lights—I can't even see the eerie green glow that seemed to come from everywhere and nowhere. Either that or my eyes have been shoved to the back of my skull.

ZOMBIE

NO, NUGGET. She probably didn't make it. Before I can say the words, Megan slaps my chest and points toward the base. A shining ball of green light shoots over the treetops into the rose-colored sky. The afterimage lingers in our eyes long after it's lost in the atmosphere.

"It's a shooting star!" she says.

I shake my head. "Wrong direction."

I guess, in the end, *I* was wrong.

CASSIE

THE FEELING OF being slowly crushed to death in total darkness lasts for several minutes. In other words, forever. Okay, *forever* is one word.

A word we throw around like we can even grasp it, like *forever* is something the human mind can comprehend.

The straps across my chest loosen. The two-ton boulder dissolves.

I take a huge, shuddering breath and open my eyes. The pod is dark—gone is the green light and good riddance; I always hated Other-green, not my shade at all. I look out the window and gasp.

Hello, Earth.

So this is how God sees you, sparkling blue against the dullest black. No wonder he made you. No wonder he made the sun and the stars so he could see you.

Beautiful is another word we tossed around too casually, slopping it over everything from cars to nail polish until the word collapsed under the weight of all the banality. But the world is beautiful. I hope they never forget that. The world is beautiful.

A water droplet bobs before my eyes. Floating free, the oddest tear I've ever brushed away.

Never forget, Sams. Love is forever. If it wasn't, it wouldn't be love. The world is beautiful. If it wasn't, it wouldn't be the world.

The wildest thing about holding my brother's memories inside me? Seeing myself through his eyes, hearing myself with his ears, sailing the Cassiopeian sea in three dimensions, the way we experience practically everything except the one thing we're supposed to understand the best: ourselves. To Sam, there is the bundle of colors and smells and sensations that make up *Cassie,* and that *Cassie* is not Ben's Cassie or Marika's Cassie or Evan's Cassie or even Cassie's Cassie; she belongs to Sam and to Sam alone.

The pod rolls, the shining blue gem slips from sight, and for the last time in my life I am afraid, as if I've fallen off the edge of the world—which I guess in a sense I have. Instinctively, I reach for the vanished Earth; my fingertips bump against the window.

Good-bye.

Oh, I am too far away. And too close. There I am, hearing a tiny voice scratching in the wilderness, *Alone, alone, alone, Cassie, you're alone.* And there I am looking through Evan's eyes at the girl with the indispensable teddy bear and the useless M16, huddled in her sleeping bag deep in the woods, thinking she's the last person on Earth. I watch her night after night and go through her things while she's away foraging. What a bastard I am, touching her stuff and reading her journals, why can't I just kill her already?

That's my name. Cassie for Cassiopeia. Alone as the stars and lonely as the stars.

Now I discover myself in him and I am not the person I expected to find. His Cassie sears the darkness with the brightness of a billion suns. He's as baffled by this as I am, as humanity is, as the Others are. He can't say why. There's no reason, no neat explanation. It's impossible to understand and impossibly irrelevant, like asking why anything exists in the first place.

He had the answer, all right. It just wasn't the answer I was looking for.

I'm sorry, Evan; I was wrong. It wasn't the idea of me that you loved, I know that now. The stars outside the window fade, overtaken by that nauseating green glow, and after a minute the hull of the mothership slides into view.

Oh, you bitch. For a year, I've hated your green guts. I've watched you, filled with hate and fear, and now here we are, just the two of us, Other and humanity.

That's my name. Not Cassie for Cassandra. Or Cassie for Cassidy. And it's not Cassie for Cassiopeia. Not anymore. I am more than her now.

I am all of them, Evan and Ben and Marika and Megan and Sam. I am Dumbo and Poundcake and Teacup. I am all the ones you emptied, the ones you corrupted, the ones you discarded, the thousands you thought you had killed, but who live on in me.

But I am even more than this. I am all those they remember, the ones they loved, everyone they knew, and everyone they only heard about. How many are contained in me? Count the stars. Go on, number the grains of sand. That's me.

I am humanity.

ZOMBIE

WE MOVE TO the cover of the trees. If what I suspect has actually happened—that someone inside the base has zapped everyone else—there's not much risk in bringing them with me, but there's *some* risk, and somebody who should know once told me it's all about the risk.

Nugget is furious. Megan seems relieved.

"Who's gonna watch her if you come with me?" I ask him.

"I don't care!"

"Well, one of us does. And that person happens to be in charge."

Through the woods and into the no-man's-land boundary that runs the perimeter of the base, toward the closest entrance and the watchtower beside it. I have no weapon, no means to defend myself. An easy target. No choice, though. I keep walking.

I'm soaked to my bones, and the temperature hovers in the midforties, but I am not cold. I feel great; even my leg doesn't hurt anymore.

CASSIOPEIA

THE GLISTENING GREEN SKIN of the ship fills the window, blotting out the stars. It's all I can see now, and the light from the sun sparks off its featureless surface. How big did they say it was? Twenty-five miles from tip to tip, roughly the size of Manhattan. I'm seeing only a tiny slice of an enormous whole. My heart pounds. My breath shortens, exploding from my mouth in roiling plumes of white. It's freezing in here. I don't remember ever feeling so cold.

With shaking fingers, I reach into my pocket and fish out the capsule. It slips from my grasp and spins like a lure through water toward the top of the pod. I catch it after a couple of tries, closing my fist tightly around it.

Damn, I'm cold. My teeth are chattering. I can't keep my thoughts still. What else? Is there anything else? What have I left undone? There isn't much—I am more than the sum of my own experience now. I've got ten thousand times my fair share.

Because here's the thing: Seeing yourself through another's eyes shifts your center of gravity. It doesn't change the way you look at yourself. It changes the way you look at the world. Not the *you*. The *everything-but-you*.

I don't hate you anymore, I tell the mothership. *And I'm not afraid of you anymore. I don't hate anything. I'm not afraid of anything.*

At the center, right in the middle of my view, a black hole grows, reminding me of a mouth slowly opening. I'm headed right for it.

I slip the capsule between my lips.

No, *the answer is not hate.*

The black hole expands. I'm falling into a lightless pit, a void, the universe before the universe was the universe.

And the answer is not fear.

Somewhere in the mothership's belly, thousands of bombs twenty times the size of the one in my mouth are rolling down chutes into launching bays. I hope they're still in there. I hope they haven't started to fall. I hope I'm in time.

The pod crosses the threshold into the mothership and jerks to a stop. The window's frosted over, but there's light outside; it glimmers in the ice. The hatch behind me hisses. I must wait until it opens. Then I must rise from this chair. Then I must turn and face what waits for me out there.

We're here, and then we're gone, he said to me, *and it's not about the time we're here.*

There's no unraveling us, no place where I end and he begins. There's no unraveling any of it. I am entwined with everything, from mayflies to the farthest star. I have no boundaries, I am limitless, and I open to creation like a flower to the rain.

I'm not cold anymore. The arms of the seven billion enfold me.

I rise.

Now I lay me down to sleep . . .

I draw in deep my final breath.

When in the morning light I wake . . .

I bite down hard. The seal breaks.

Teach me the path of love to take.

I step into the *out there,* and breathe.

ZOMBIE

I'VE REACHED THE GRAVEL PATH that borders the security fence when the sun breaks the horizon—no, not the sun, it can't be, unless the sun's decided to rise in the north and has swapped its gold for green. I whip to my right and see the stars winking out one by one, obliterated by a massive burst of light on the edge of the northern horizon, an explosion in the upper atmosphere that washes over the landscape in a flood of blinding green.

My first thought is for the kids. I don't know what the hell is happening and I haven't connected the projectile hurtling from the base to the enormous northern flare. It doesn't occur to me that for the first time in a very long time, something might have actually gone our way. Honestly, when I saw the light, I thought the bombardment had begun and I was witnessing the first salvo in the destruction of every city on Earth. The idea that the mothership could actually be gone didn't even cross my radar. How could it be gone? That ship's unassailable as the moon.

I hesitate, trying to decide whether to keep going or turn back. But the green light fades, the sky glows rosy again, and no terrified children burst from the woods seeking rescue. I decide to maintain my heading. I've got faith in Nugget. He'll know to stay put till I return.

Ten minutes inside the base and I find the first of many bodies. The place is a tomb. I walk through fields of the dead. They lie in piles, groups of six to ten, their bodies contorted into portraits of silent agony. I stop to examine every gruesome stack, looking for two familiar faces; I'm not going to rush, though a voice screams in my head with each passing minute to *hurry*,

hurry. And in the back of my mind I'm remembering what hap-pened at Camp Haven—how Vosch was willing to sacrifice the village in order to save it.

This might not be Ringer's doing—it may be the result of Vosch exercising the final option.

It takes me hours to reach the last level, the bottom of this death pit.

She barely lifts her head when I open the stairwell door. I may have shouted her name; I don't remember.

I also don't remember stepping over Vosch's body, but I must have: It was in my way. My boot hits the kill switch lying beside her. It skitters across the floor.

"Walker . . . ," she gasps, pointing over my shoulder down the long hallway. "I think he's—"

I shake my head. She's hurt and still imagines I'd worry about him for even one second? I touch her shoulder. Her dark hair brushes the back of my hand. Her eyes shine. Their brightness goes all the way down.

"You found me," she says.

I kneel beside her. I take her hand. "I found you."

"My back is broken," she says. "I can't walk."

I slide my arms beneath her. "I'll carry you."

MARBLE FALLS

BEN

THE LATE-AFTERNOON SUN polishes the dusty windows of the superstore a lustrous gold. Inside, the light has faded to gray. We've got less than an hour to beat the dark back to the house. The day may belong to us, but the night belongs to the coyotes and the packs of wild dogs that roam the banks of the Colorado and wander the outskirts of Marble Falls. I'm well-armed, I've got no love for coyotes, but I hate shooting the dogs. The older ones were somebody's pet once; it feels like giving up all hope of redemption.

And it isn't just dogs and coyotes. A couple of weeks after we crossed the border into Texas, back in late summer, Marika spotted escapees from some zoo drinking a few miles upriver—a lioness and her two cubs. Ever since then, Sam has been itching for a safari. He wants to capture and tame an elephant so he can ride on it like Aladdin. Or catch a monkey to domesticate. He isn't picky.

"Hey, Sam," I call down the aisle. He's wandered off again in search of treasure. Lately it's been LEGOs. Before that it was Lincoln Logs. He's developed a love for building things. He's made a fort, a tree house, and started on an underground bunker in the backyard.

"What?" he shouts back from the toy section.

"It's getting late. We have to make a decision here."

"I told you I don't care! You decide!" Something crashes off a shelf and he curses loudly.

"Hey, wha'd I tell you about that?" I call over to him. "Watch your language."

"Fuckety fuck fuck, shithole."

I sigh. "Come on, Sam, we gotta haul this thing back three friggin' miles, which I'd rather not do in the dark."

"I'm *busy*."

I turn back to the display. Well, the prelits are useless. That leaves either the six, eight, or ten foot. The tens are too tall for the ceiling. Either the six or eight, then. A six would be easier to transport, but it looks like crap. The Texas heat has done a number on it. Needles bent and soft, big bare spots in some places where they fell off. The eights don't look much better, but they're not quite as scrawny. But eight damn feet! Maybe their storeroom has new ones in boxes.

I'm still debating with myself when I hear an all-too-familiar, all-too-sickening sound: a bullet racking into the chamber of a pistol.

"Don't move!" Sam shouts. "Lemme see your hands! *Hands!*"
I draw my own weapon and race down the aisle as fast as my bum leg will allow, slipping on the carpet of rat droppings and hopping over fallen shelving and ripped-open boxes, until I reach the toy section and the kid who's got a downed man at gunpoint.

My age. Wearing fatigues. A 5th Wave eyepiece hangs around his scrawny neck. He's leaning against the back wall beneath the board games, one arm pressing against his gut, the other on top of his head. My heart slows a little. I didn't think it was a Silencer—Marika killed the one assigned to Marble Falls months ago—but you can never be sure.

"Other arm!" Sam shouts at him.

"I'm unarmed . . . ," the guy gasps in a deep Texas drawl.

Sam says to me, "Search him, Zombie."

"Where's your squad?" I ask. I have a vision of being ambushed.

"No squad. Just me."

"You're hurt," I say. I can see the blood, mostly dried but some fresh, on his shirtfront. "What happened?"

He shakes his head and coughs. A rattle in his chest. Pneumonia, maybe. "Sniper," he manages after catching his breath.

"Where? Here in Marble Falls or . . . ?"

The arm pressing against his gut moves. I feel Sam tense beside me and I reach out and put my hand over the barrel of his Beretta. "Wait," I murmur.

"I'm not telling you anything, you infested piece of shit."

"Okay. Then I'll tell you: We aren't infested. Nobody is." I'm wasting my breath. I might as well tell him that he's actually a geranium having a very weird dream. "Hang on a second."

I tug Sam to the opposite end of the aisle and whisper, "This is a problem."

He shakes his head vehemently. "No, it isn't. We have to kill him."

"Nobody's killing anybody, Sam. That's done."

"We can't leave him here, Zombie. What if he's lying about his squad? What if he's faking being hurt? We have to kill *him* before he kills *us*."

His face turned up to me, his eyes shining in the dying light, shining with hate and fear. *Kill him before he kills us.* Sometimes, not often, but sometimes, I wonder what Cassie died for. The tiger's loosed from its cage and there's no capturing it. How do we rebuild what's been lost? In an abandoned convenience store, a terrified girl mows down an innocent man because her trust has been shattered.

There's no other way to be sure, no other option to be safe.

329

You're safe here. Perfectly safe. That phrase still haunts me. Haunts me because it's always been a lie. It was a lie before they came and it's still a lie. You're never perfectly safe. No human being on Earth ever is or ever was. To live is to risk your life, your heart, everything. Otherwise, you're just a walking corpse. You're a zombie.

"He's no different from us, Sam," I tell him. "None of this will end until somebody decides to put down the guns."

I don't reach for the weapon, though. It should be his decision.

"Zombie . . ."

"What did I tell you about that? My name is Ben."

Sam lowers the gun.

In the same moment, at the other end of the aisle, another silent battle is lost. The soldier lied; he was armed, and he used the time he had left to put the gun to his head and pull the trigger.

MARIKA

FIRST I TOLD HIM it was a dumb idea. Then, when he insisted, I told him to wait till tomorrow. It was late afternoon and the store was over three miles away. They didn't have time to get back before dark. He went anyway.

"Tomorrow's Christmas," Ben reminded me. "We missed last Christmas and that's the last Christmas I'm going to miss."

"What's the big deal about Christmas?" I asked him.

"Everything." And he smiled, like *that* had any power over me.

"Don't take Sam."

"Sam's the reason I'm going." He looked over my shoulder at

Megan playing by the fireplace. "And her." Then he added, "And Cassie. Most of all."

He promised they'd be back soon. I watched them from the porch that overlooked the river as they headed for the bridge, Sam pulling the empty wagon, Ben favoring his bad leg, and the sun cast down their shadows, one long and one short, like the hands of a clock.

The crying came with the dark. It always did. I sat in the rocker, holding her in my lap. She had just fed, so I knew she wasn't hungry. I cupped her cheek and gently curled into her, discerning her need. *Ben.* She wanted Ben. "Don't worry," I told her. "He's coming back. He promised."

Why did he have to go all the way to that store? There had to be dozens of houses on this side of the river with Christmas trees in their attics. But no, he wanted a "new" tree and it had to be artificial. Nothing that will die, he insisted.

I drew the blanket tighter around her. The night was cloudy and the wind was cold off the river. The light from the fireplace flowed through the windows behind me and lay gleaming on the boards.

Evan Walker stepped onto the porch and leaned his rifle against the railing. His eyes followed mine into the dark, across the river, scanning the bridge and the buildings on the other side.

"Still not back?" he asked.

"No."

He glanced at me and smiled. "They'll come."

He saw them first, approaching the bridge, pulling the little red wagon with its green cargo behind them. He smiled. "Looks like they hit pay dirt."

He shouldered the weapon and went back inside. The wind

331

shifted. I could smell gunpowder. *Damn it, Ben.* When he came up the walk, grinning from ear to ear like a triumphant hunter dragging the kill back to the cave, I had an urge to slap him upside the head. *Stupid risk for a damn plastic Christmas tree.*

I stood up. He saw the look on my face and stopped. Sam hovered behind him as if he were trying to hide.

"What?" Ben asked.

"Who fired their sidearm and why?"

"Did you hear it or did you smell it?" He sighed. "Sometimes I really hate the 12th System."

"It's not freezing."

"Straight answer, Parish."

"I love it when you call me Parish. Did I ever tell you that? So sexy." He kisses me, then says, "It wasn't us, and the rest is a long story. Let's go inside. It's freezing out here."

"Well, it's cold. Come on, Sullivan, let's get this party started!"

I followed them into the house. Megan jumped up from her dolls and squealed with delight. That plastic tree touched something deep. Walker came out of the kitchen to help set it up. I stood by the door, bouncing the baby on my hip as she bawled. Ben finally noticed and abandoned the tree to take her from my arms.

"What's up, little mayfly, huh? What's the matter?"

She popped her tiny fist against the side of his nose, and Ben laughed. He always laughed when she swatted him or did anything that shouldn't be encouraged, like demanding to be held every waking second. From the moment she was born, she had him wrapped around her inch-long finger.

On the other side of the room, Evan Walker flinched. *Mayfly.* A word that resonated, a word that would never be just a word. Sometimes I wondered if we should have left him in Canada, if returning his memories wasn't a particular cruelty, a kind of psychological torture. The alternatives were unthinkable, though: Kill him, or empty him completely, leaving him a human shell with no memory of her at all. Both of those possibilities were painless; we opted for the pain.

Pain is necessary. Pain is life. Without pain, there can be no joy. Cassie Sullivan taught me that.

The crying went on. Even Ben with all his special Parish powers couldn't calm her down.

"What's wrong?" he asked me, as if I knew.

I took a stab at it anyway. "You left. Broke her routine. She hates that."

So much like her namesake: crying, punching, demanding, *needing*. Maybe there is something to the idea of reincarnation. Restless, never satisfied, quick to anger, stubborn, and ruthlessly curious. Cassie called it. She labeled herself long ago. *I am humanity.*

Sam scampered down the hall to his bedroom. I guessed he couldn't take the wailing anymore. I was wrong. He returned with something behind his back.

"I was going to wait till tomorrow, but . . ." He shrugged.

That bear had seen better days. Missing an ear, fur that had gone from brown to a splotchy gray, patched and repatched and patched again, more sutures than Frankenstein's monster. Messed up, beaten up, but still hanging around. Still here.

Ben took the bear from him and made it dance for Cassie. Stubby bear arms flapped. Uneven bear legs—one was shorter than the other—twisted and twirled. The baby cried for a couple more minutes, clinging to the rage and discomfort until they slipped through her fingers, as insubstantial as the wind. She reached for the toy. *Gimme, gimme, I wanna, I wanna.*

333

"Well, what do you know?" Ben said. He looked over at me, and his smile was so genuine—no calculation, no vanity, desiring nothing but expressing everything—that I couldn't help myself and really didn't want to.

I smiled.

EVAN WALKER

EACH NIGHT from dusk to dawn he kept watch from the porch that overlooked the river. On the half hour, he left the porch to patrol the block. Then back to the porch to watch while the others slept. His sleep was rare, usually an hour or two in the afternoons, and afterward always jerking awake, disoriented, panicky, like a drowning man breaking the surface of the water that would bear him down, the remorseless medium that would kill him.

If he had dreams, he could not remember them.

Alone in the darkness, awake while everyone else slept, he felt the most at peace. He supposed it was in his nature, passed down from his father and his father's father, farmers who tended the land and cared for their livestock. Nurturers, guardians, watchmen for the harvest. That was to be Evan Walker's inheritance. Instead, he became the opposite. The silent hunter in the woods. The deadly assassin stalking human prey. How many did he kill before he found her hiding in the woods that autumn afternoon? He couldn't remember. He felt no absolution in knowing he'd been used, no redemption in understanding he was as much a victim as the people he killed—from a distance, always from a distance.

334

Forgiveness is not born out of innocence or ignorance. Forgiveness is born of love.

At dawn, he left the porch and went inside to his room. The time had come. He'd lingered here too long already. He was stuffing an extra jacket into the duffel bag—the bowling jacket he'd taken from Grace's house that Cassie had hated so much—when Ben appeared in the doorway, shirtless, bleary-eyed, scruffy-chinned.

"You're leaving," he said.

"I'm leaving."

"Marika said you would. I didn't believe her."

"Why not?"

Ben shrugged. "She isn't always right. One half of one percent of the time, she's only half right." He rubbed his eyes and yawned. "And you're not coming back," Ben went on. "Ever. Is she right about that, too?"

Evan nodded. "Yes."

"Well." Ben looked away, scratching his shoulder slowly. "Where are you going?"

"To look for lights in the dark."

"Lights," Ben echoed. "Like, literal lights, or . . . ?"

"I mean bases. Military compounds. The closest one is about a hundred miles away. I'll start there."

"And do what?"

"What I've been gifted to do."

"You're going to blow up every military base in North America?"

"South America, too, if I live that long."

"That's ambitious."

"I don't think I'll be working alone."

Ben took a moment to think. "The Silencers."

"Where else would they go? They know where their enemies are. They know each base has an arsenal of alien ordnance like Camp Haven's. They believe there's no choice now that the mothership's gone but to blow up the 5th Wave bases. Well, I *believe* that's what they believe. It's what I would believe if I still believed. We'll see."

He shouldered the duffel bag and walked to the door. Ben blocked the way. His face was flushed with anger.

"You're talking about murdering thousands of innocent people."

"What do you suggest I do, Ben?"

"Stay here. Help us. We—" He took a deep breath. This was hard for him to say. "We need you."

"For what? You can take the night watch and tend the garden and pick up my slack on the hunts."

"Goddamn it, Walker, what's this about, huh?" Ben exploded in fury. "What's this *really* about? Is it about ending a war or taking revenge? You can blow up half the world and it won't make it right, it won't bring her back."

Evan remained calm. He'd heard all the arguments, many times. He'd fought these battles for months, alone, in the quiet tumult of his heart. "Two will be saved for each one I kill. That's the math. What's the alternative? Stay here until staying here is too dangerous, then move to another place, then another, and another, hiding, running, using the gifts they gave me to keep myself alive—for what? Cassie didn't die so *I* could live. She died for something much bigger than that."

Ben was shaking his head. "Right, so how about I kill you now and save tens of thousands of lives? How's *that* math work for you?"

"You have a point." Evan smiled. "The problem is you're no killer, Ben. You never were."

336

SAM

EVAN WALKER on the bridge crossing the river. Evan Walker with a bag over one shoulder and a rifle over the other, shrinking. "Where is he going?" Megan asked. Sam shook his head; he didn't know.

They watched until they couldn't see him anymore.

"Let's play something," Megan said.

"I have to finish my bunker."

"You dig more than a mole."

"You *are* a mole."

"You gave Captain away."

Sam sighed. This again. "His name isn't Captain. And he wasn't yours. He was mine."

"You didn't even ask." Then she said, "I don't care. Cassie can keep him. He smelled."

"You smell."

He left the front window and went into the kitchen. He was hungry. He grabbed his favorite book to read while he ate. *Where the Sidewalk Ends*. Evan Walker told him it was Cassie's favorite book of all time.

If you are a dreamer, come in . . .

Evan Walker was gone. *Forever*, Zombie said. Sam didn't want to think about that. He didn't want to think about Cassie being gone or Dumbo or Poundcake or anyone from his old squad or his father or his mother or anyone he knew before he came here to the great big house by the river. He was pretty good at not thinking about them most of the time. Sometimes Cassie would come into his dreams, and she would fuss at him about everything. He wasn't clean enough. He wasn't nice enough. He couldn't remember things that she thought were important. In his dreams, her nose was straight and her hair longer and her clothes cleaner. In his dreams, she was the before-Cassie.

Are you being good, Sam? Are you saying your prayers every night?

One night he woke up Zombie—in his head, Sam still called him Zombie—and Zombie took him into the bathroom and washed the tears from his face and told him that he missed her, too, and then he walked Sam outside and he pointed at the sky. *See those stars up there, the ones that kind of look like a sideways W? You know what that is?*

They sat on the back porch and looked at the stars while Zombie told the story of a queen named Cassiopeia who lived forever on a throne in the sky.

"But her throne's tilted down," Sam said, looking at the constellation. "Won't she fall out?"

Zombie cleared his throat. "She won't fall. Her throne is turned that way so she can keep watch over her realm."

"What's a realm?"

Zombie pressed his hand against Sam's chest.

"This is." Zombie's hand to Sam's heart. "Here."